RETRIBU

Books by Venezia Miller:

THE FIND SERIES

THE FIND
EVIL BENEATH THE SKIN
RETRIBUTION

COMING SOON:
THE STORM

RETRIBUTION

Venezia Miller

RETRIBUTION

Copyright © 2022 by Venezia Miller.

All rights reserved. No part of this book may be used or reproduced in any manner whatsoever without written permission except in the case of brief quotations embodied in critical articles or reviews.

This book is a work of fiction. Names, characters, businesses, organizations, places, events, and incidents either are the product of the author's imagination or are used fictitiously. Any resemblance to actual persons, living or dead, events, or locales is entirely coincidental.

For information contact: Venezia.Miller@gmail.com
ISBN: 9798808264762

Book and Cover design by V. Miller, Images taken from www.pixabay.com

First Edition: May 2022

CHAPTER

1

THERE WAS SOMETHING DISTURBING about the silence. His body started to tremble as he felt sweat trickling down his brow. It felt like a knife twisting in his gut. The fear paralyzed him, and he crouched against the wall unable to think straight or even breathe properly. The buzz of the fluorescent lights had been the only soothing noise, but now he heard footsteps again and chairs scraping the floor.

He didn't want to die. Not now. Not ever.

Someone screamed and then there was a loud bang.

Silence again.

He had never been good at telling where sounds were coming from. At the age of thirty-eight, he labeled his hearing impairment a disability and blamed his Italian-born parents. Every conversation, good or bad, always ended with them yelling at each other. And though others might have interpreted this as a depiction of a family on the verge of an all-out implosion, to him their shouts simply evidenced genuine fondness: passion, love, and respect.

Or maybe it was his own fault. He went to far too many parties and nightclubs.

Strange how a man in a situation like this could even think of these pointless things. Shouldn't heroic and philosophical thoughts be going through his head? Wasn't he supposed to watch his life flash by?

Breathing, thinking, everything that seemed so obvious, had never felt so difficult. His muscles were sore, and the reams of copy paper stung his ribs. It felt as if he'd been crammed into the nook between the copier and the silver-colored metal racks for hours. Time stood still. He lived in a void, detached from everything, trapped in five square meters of gray Gyproc where anyone could just storm in. Like a rat in a trap, he could go nowhere.

Run, hide, seek safety!

He couldn't move. He didn't want to move.

Footsteps.

They were close, so close.

The sound of his pulse throbbed in his ears. Holding his breath, he felt the panic well up inside of him. Beads of sweat kept dripping from his forehead down the side of his face, and he felt the water welling in his eyes.

Be quiet! They'll hear you.

Bam!

He jumped up. The shot echoed through the building. Deafening, as if he had been there.

So close.

Moaning. He knew that voice. He had spoken to her half an hour ago. Kim, the management assistant. She had laughed at his stupid jokes.

Now she begged for her life, trying to hold on to that last glimpse of hope.

Bam!

The moaning stopped.

Silence.

And then footsteps again. Those horrible footsteps.

When the shooting had started, he'd been so busy with paperwork he hadn't noticed the first gunshot. He vaguely remembered thinking the noise was coming from outside, from the street, and hadn't given it much thought. It wasn't until the second shot he realized it wasn't going to be a normal Monday.

How many people were in the office? Fifteen, twenty? Were they all dead?

This wasn't the way he imagined he'd react in a crisis. He had never thought himself to be anything less than a hero, that he would jump in, step up, save people, do the right thing. But now, as he stood there shaking like a leaf, he realized that his perception of himself was disappointingly wrong.

Helpless. Useless.

And this wasn't happening. Not in peaceful, quiet, and insignificant Gävle, a place in Sweden that no one would have remembered if one of the most prolific serial killers in Sweden's history hadn't roamed the area. This was an American thing where guns were a commodity, where people were screaming about the Second Amendment, their right to protect themselves while people were dying in meaningless mass shootings and gun accidents.

Bam! Bam!

The shots sounded further away.

"Nick?"

He looked at the cell phone in his hand and froze. When it had started, he had called the only person who could help him: inspector Isa Lindström.

"Nick?"

He raised the phone to his ear.

"Isa," he whispered. The words didn't come out right.

"Nick, what's going on? Tell me something!"

"I ... I don't know."

"Tell me what you see and hear!"

"Shots were fired in the Global Law building," he heard someone say in the background.

"Nick, are you under attack?"

"They're killing people," he blurted. His voice was shaking so much he barely recognized it.

"Where are you?" she said.

He heard her breathing heavily through the microphone. "In the copy room."

The footsteps stopped in front of the door. His heart was racing as if it were about to pop out of his chest. He heard another round of shots and screams in the background.

"They found me," he said.

"Nick, Nick!"

* * *

The phone was on speaker. The call had come in less than ten minutes ago. After those last words Isa sat there, holding her breath, listening to the sounds on the other end of the line that weren't there.

Her eyes drifted to the blank wall of the office. The grayest gray. Depressing and dull, but at that moment it was what she needed. Everything was so vague and chaotic in her head.

The sound of a throat clearing interrupted her thoughts and she turned to the man who had entered the room only moments ago.

"What ...," he said.

She motioned for her boss, superintendent Timo Paikkala, to be silent.

Her voice broke. "They found him."

The silence was unbearable. What if she'd lose him too? Two lovers in six months.

"They're moving on," she heard Nick say.

"Tell him to lock the door, if that's possible," Timo said. "He should lay low. We're coming."

Timo went to the closet and picked up the bulletproof vest.

"I'm going with you," she said.

"No, stay here! Talk to him!"

"But ..."

"Look, Isa, I'll do my best to bring him back, unharmed. I promise, but I need you here. I need someone to coordinate with the Sandviken and Uppsala teams. We need reinforcements."

Without saying another word, he left the room.

"Be ... careful," she yelled, but he didn't hear it.

What was it with men these days? Somehow, they all had to play the hero. It was Timo's job to coordinate the operation, not hers. But she had to admit she also wanted to be where the action was, not be stuck in the office and keep Nick calm. She wasn't the right person for the job. This was too personal. What if she couldn't save Nick?

"Nick?"

"What should I do?"

"Stay where you are, don't move! You'll be fine."

She took a deep breath and tried to keep her cool.

"You have to," she whispered.

* * *

The police car raced through the streets of Gävle, ducking under a bridge and driving along the canal to the large roundabout where at this time of day a long line of cars was lined up. Police officers shouted commands over the radio, but Timo barely understood half of them. He looked at the officer to his left. A young guy in his twenties, about ten years younger than he was. The face said nothing, with a pair of brown eyes staring ahead and a mouth pleated in a meaningless line. It made him nervous. Why? He had done this before. In Stockholm. But he knew people at Global Law. Nick. Anton. He had once told Isa that there was no room for feelings in their line of work. He had lied. Of course, there were feelings, but right now he wished there were an off button for the chaos in his head and the strange mix of emotions and logical reasoning that was constantly tossing him back and forth.

Minutes later they stopped in front of the building. The bulletproof vest jabbed his ribs as he jumped out of the car and yelled into the microphone for the teams to take position. "Evacuate the building!"

A group of armed police officers burst through the glass doors into the six-story building that housed the offices of Global Law, one of the most renowned law firms in Sweden.

The people in the immense hallway, already triggered by the strange noises coming from somewhere in the building, were shocked at the display of violence as the armed officers started running down the hall.

"Lindström, where are the Uppsala teams?" Timo shouted into the shoulder mic.

"Half an hour to go. The Sandviken team will be there in five minutes."

"Damn! We can't wait for Uppsala. We must go in now. People are dying!"

"Agreed. Alpha team is taking position on the roof at the west side as we speak."

"Attackers?"

"None that we can see at this moment," Isa's voice sounded.

"What about Nick?"

"He's safe for now," she said. "But he says it's awfully quiet."

"What are they doing?" Timo said, but before Isa could answer he saw Anton, the husband of Dr. Ingrid Olsson, the police forensic specialist, by the elevators, about to go in, staring at the stream of people passing by.

"What the hell!" Timo shouted. "Anton, get out of here!"

It took a few seconds for Anton to recognize him. "What?"

Timo grabbed the sleeve of Anton's coat, pulled him away from the elevators, and pushed him toward the exit.

"This is a police order, get out," he yelled again, watching Anton finally disappear through the sliding doors.

"The hall is clear," someone shouted.

An officer walked up to him with a map in her hand which she unfolded for him and placed on the reception desk.

"We can't use the elevators. They probably have covered them. There are two entrances that we can reach via the stairs, but the doors are secured with a key card system. There are exits at each side of the building."

"Key card? And the elevators are secured with an electronic keypad. Jesus! This place has more security than the police headquarters."

"They installed the new security system a year ago."

"And we're sure the attackers are on the third floor?" Timo said.

"The other floors have been evacuated. They are only targeting the Global Law offices on the third floor."

Timo looked at the map and sighed. "We have to clear about 700 square meters. That's a lot. And without Uppsala we don't have enough people to cover all exits."

"And the attackers know we're here, and likely they've already prepared an exit strategy. It won't go easy."

"They'll take hostages," Timo said.

"If they aren't dead already," the woman said with a straight face.

He ignored the words that had hit him harder than expected, and asked, pointing to the lines on the map, "This area is all windows?"

"Yes, the floor has windows on all four sides. The elevator shafts are in the center."

"Where are the snipers and spotters?"

"They're located on the north and west sides of the adjacent buildings. We can't place anyone on the east and south. The buildings are not high enough. Moreover, on the east side we have the Tech4You building obscuring most of the view."

"We can place people in the Tech4You building?" he said.

"There are few windows on that side. I doubt we'll have a good view."

"Okay. Do we know how many attackers?"

"From the alpha and delta teams we know at least four."

"In position," someone called through the comms.

For a moment, Timo was in doubt. Was this the right thing to do?

But then he said, "Let's go! This has taken way too long."

As he stood by the door to the stairwell, fiddling with the headset they'd given him, a surge of panic rushed over him. Isa had tried to talk him out of it. She meant well and he had to admit he still didn't know what he was doing there. Was it the need to fulfil a higher moral purpose and save people? That was his job. Or was it just recklessness on his part? His job was to lead the teams, not put himself in the line of fire, but he tended to forget that.

The officer in front gave the signal and with a body full of adrenaline, he ran up the stairs, behind the five police officers, armed with automatic rifles, body armor, and helmets. Two officers jumped through the door.

"Clear!"

Immediately the rest of the team followed, guns ready. It didn't take long before shots were fired.

A man fell to the ground.

"Suspect down!"

The team broke up, and the police officers started sweeping the offices. More shots in the background.

"You two, check the offices on the east side," Timo said and motioned the remaining officers to take another route.

They hesitated. "Sir?"

"We have no idea what's going on there," Timo said. "I'll be fine."

They quickly scanned the area and then moved on.

Timo tried to remember the floor map. Copy room on the north side, near one of the exits.

Suddenly he saw traces of blood on the floor. A soft moan. He aimed the gun. In the corner, under one of the desks, a woman huddled, trembling, tears streaming down her face, supporting her left arm with her right hand.

"Police," he said and approached her.

The woman said nothing but continued to stare straight ahead. Her body rose and fell with the short, heavy sighs she let out.

"Where did you get hit?"

She looked at her arm.

"Okay. Keep pressure on it. You'll be fine, but I want you to stay here. I'll be back."

Before continuing, he pushed the chair in front of the desk, trying to hide her from view. Everything was so quiet as he walked down the hall.

Too quiet.

* * *

Nick hesitated. Everything was so peaceful outside. He'd nestled deeper in the corner during the police raid, shivering, hands to his ears, as if the world were about to end, but when he got up after the commotion had subsided, the silence floating in the air made everything feel so surreal. A strange calm. An alienating feeling that had plagued him since the start of the attack.

"Nick?" Isa's voice sounded through the speaker.

"I hear nothing. Maybe I should go outside?"

"No, stay where you are," Isa said. "Wait until the intervention is over."

Ignoring her advice, he walked to the door, and put his hand on the latch. He'd been hiding long enough and maybe he could still do something for his colleagues. Redemption.

The creaking of the door was louder than he'd expected, and as he stepped outside, he felt his stomach tighten. But he couldn't stop now. He walked a few steps down the hall. On his right, there were four cubicles. All empty. Chairs thrown on the floor, a keyboard hanging mid-air between the edge of the desk and the floor, and the smell of burnt monitors still hanging in the air. On his left, in the corner, where the wall made a sudden turn to the right, he saw a strange pile of clothes on the floor. What was it doing there?

Then he froze. It wasn't a pile of clothes. It was a body squatting against the wall. He didn't recognize her at first. The blood covered most of her face, and only then he saw how the wall was covered with red spatters, in a pattern that strangely looked like a piece of abstract painting. Part of her head was missing, torn apart by the metal bullets that had hit her so mercilessly. But it was Kim. Poor Kim. She had begged for her life. She had screamed and cried. All in vain. She was a mother of three and had worked at Global Law all her life. She didn't even have to be there. As always, she couldn't say no to him, the handsome lawyer who knew perfectly how to use his charm. He had been late with his paperwork and Kim had offered to help him on her day off. The forty-year-old woman, craving for more than the routine of her ordinary life, would have done anything for him.

Her day off. The last day of her life.

And he was responsible. Why hadn't he left his hiding place and tried to save her? He had taken the coward's way out.

Maybe she was still alive. He leaned forward and reached out to touch her face but stopped when he heard the click of a gun cocking behind him. The phone fell and scattered its parts on the floor.

"Nick, Nick!" Isa's voice trailed off as the frame hit the ground.

He straightened and turned around. A few meters away he saw a figure, dressed in a black oversized overall, hair and face hidden under the cap and shapeless white mask.

It was disappointing. Was this the person who would take his life?

There was something familiar about him, but he couldn't put his finger on it.

He looked straight at the barrel. In the next second, a bullet would be fired at more than 2000 km/h. It would pierce tissue, tear organs apart and shatter bones. He would die. And yet his mind didn't seem to realize the gravity of the situation. Where did that indifference come from?

He was exhausted. He didn't want to fight anymore.

Pull the trigger. Finish it!

Then the figure moved the gun away from him and aimed it at something behind him.

"Police, put the gun down!"

The voice sounded familiar, but his mind struggled to process the latest information. The only sound he really heard was his own heartbeat pounding through his head.

The balance of power had changed in those seconds. It was now between the ominous assailant in front of him and the police officer behind him. But he would be collateral. The attacker would never surrender. He was in the line of fire and needed a way out.

And then something strange happened. The cold dark eyes that had pierced him from behind the mask softened. There was doubt. The finger wrapped tightly around the trigger, ready to pull, loosened.

Hesitation.

Why?

Nick turned to the man behind him. Inspector Timo Paikkala held the gun in front of him, his eyes still on the target, not in the least impressed by the attacker's sudden reluctance. Two people almost frozen in time, none of them ready to back down.

"Put the gun down," Timo said calmly, overemphasizing each word as if addressing a child who had done something wrong.

What is this man waiting for?

That sudden change in attitude, was it fear? Fear of being shot, fear of dying. Or was it something else? These attackers were ruthless killers, aggressive, and they would do anything to get away.

And then there was another click. It went so fast. The blast came from the open area, where the cubicles were. It threw Timo against the wall with incredible force, next to Kim's body. Nick saw him gasp, and then the superintendent sank into a dangerous unconsciousness.

* * *

"Nick, Nick," Isa shouted.

She had been circling the same area for minutes. Every second more people came in: police officers, injured and traumatized employees. Some wept, others stared straight ahead. Bodies covered with white sheets. Too many of them. It was chaos in the entrance hall.

She saw a familiar face in the crowd. Dr. Ingrid Olsson walked over to her. "Isa, have you seen Anton?"

Anton! She had completely forgotten about Anton.

"Ingrid," her voice trembled.

"I can't find Anton!" Ingrid shouted. "He's not answering his phone!"

"Calm down. Are you sure he's here? Not with a client?"

Ingrid nodded, tears welling up in her eyes. Isa threw her arms around her and held her tight.

Ingrid sobbed. "Isa ... sorry, I know you're busy and I need to do my job, but ..."

"Ingrid? Honey?"

The women turned. And there he was.

"Oh my God! Anton!" Ingrid broke free from Isa's embrace, put her arms around him and kissed him.

"Are you okay? What happened?" Ingrid asked, holding him as if she wasn't sure he was real. "Why didn't you call me?"

He shrugged. "I left the phone at home, and I wasn't in any real danger."

"That figures," Ingrid said and then kissed him again.

Isa sighed. At least Anton was fine. She started walking down the hall again. The constant buzz, the sound of people running around, she couldn't think clearly. She stared at the policewoman next to her, who tried in vain to talk to a young woman, covered in a gray blanket, trembling, barely able to hold back the tears and say a decent word.

She had to do her job and get this chaos under control.

Be a leader!

But she couldn't. Not before she knew Nick was okay. She cared more about Nicolas Petrini than she wanted to admit. Their relationship had intensified the last months. He wasn't Alex, the man she still considered the greatest love of her life, but Alex was dead, and Nick wasn't.

But where was Nick? Did she have to look under those hideous, clinically impersonal white sheets?

She looked out one of the large windows at the street.

Outside, a crowd had gathered behind the yellow-black taped area. Relatives, colleagues, and disaster tourists.

And then, in the far-right corner, she saw him shriveled up under a blanket. He was alone and looked at his hands with the same numbness she'd seen in so many people around her. He looked unharmed, and she wasn't sure why, but the whole scene frightened her. From now on, there would be a life before and after the shooting.

"Nick," she said and walked over to him.

He looked up and smiled faintly. She knelt, took his head in her hands, and kissed him.

His lower lip trembled as he tried to hold back the tears, but the emotions, now free of all obstacles, flooded his face. He couldn't stop.

"She ..." He could barely find the words. "They are dead."

"Shh," she said, holding his head in her hands.

His skin felt stiff and moist. He looked down and pulled the blanket tighter to hide the urine stain on his pants.

"Are you hurt?" Ingrid put her hand on Isa's shoulder and smiled quickly at her friend before turning to Nick.

He didn't respond.

When Ingrid began the physical examination, Isa stood up and asked, "What happened? The line was cut."

Ingrid frowned as she shone the light into his eyes.

"How did you get out?"

"Isa, I don't think this is the right time," Ingrid said.

"He saved me," Nick said suddenly.

"Who?" Isa asked.

"Your boss."

Ingrid froze and looked straight at him. "Do you mean Timo?"

Nick nodded.

"Shit!" Isa blurted.

"Isa, was Timo part of the intervention team?" Ingrid said.

Isa ran her hands through her hair and tried to suppress the rising panic. Timo was fine. He was trained for this kind of situation, although the man had a nasty habit of getting himself into trouble. In the five months she'd known him, he'd fallen off a cliff, been kidnapped, and held at gunpoint ... twice.

"Isa?" she heard Ingrid say.

But where was he?

She shouldn't have let him go alone.

CHAPTER

2

"**NICK, DO YOU KNOW WHERE TIMO IS?**"

He didn't respond, his eyes still fixed on what seemed to be an invisible point ahead of him, as if he were trapped in a trance.

Isa couldn't shake the feeling something bad had happened when she realized no one had heard from Timo for over an hour. She checked her radio for any sign of his voice but all she got was static. Then she took the phone out of her pocket and dialed Timo's number, reaching voicemail every time.

Why didn't he answer? The raid was over. Where was he?

"And?" Ingrid asked.

"Nothing," Isa sighed and put the phone away.

"Something happened to him." Ingrid tried to sound calm, but her voice quaked.

"He'll probably be at the debriefing," Isa said.

Timo Paikkala was able to handle himself, but this wasn't a normal situation. She should have gone with him.

Then Isa started pacing the hall again, with Ingrid following her lead.

"Have you seen inspector Paikkala?"

Every police officer they encountered denied seeing the superintendent, until Ingrid saw him coming through the stairwell door. He looked drained, and for a while he stood leaning against the doorframe staring at the remains of the many lives that had been cut viciously short just moments before.

A smile appeared on his face when he saw Ingrid looking in his direction, but their moment got interrupted when Isa headed for him.

"Where were you?" Isa said.

"Nine dead, fifteen injured and a dozen more traumatized," he said, ignoring her question.

"Good God," Isa said, "who did this?"

"One of the attackers is dead. The rest have escaped."

"How?" she asked in surprise.

"Stairwell and emergency exit."

"But the exits were covered, weren't they? The teams were in place."

"I don't understand it either and ..."

He stopped suddenly, put his hand on his left side and leaned against the wall, a painful, twisted grimace on his face.

"What's wrong?"

He took a deep breath. The pale complexion, the heavy breathing, something was definitely wrong.

Then he sighed and moaned softly as he touched the left side of his chest. "I got shot."

"What?" Isa said.

"Relax! I was wearing a vest. It's all right."

"Let me see," Ingrid said, interrupting their conversation.

"Ah, Dr. Olsson," he said and turned to her. "Back from holidays I see. How are you?"

"Inspector Paikkala ... uh, I'm okay. Don't change the subject. You're hurt."

"I'm fine," he said. "Besides ... there are more pressing matters."

* * *

Timo turned to Isa. "Nick. Did you get any information from him?"

She sighed and said, "No."

"Can I talk to him?"

"Timo, I don't know ... he's ... look at him." She pointed to the silent figure in the corner, still staring ahead, cup of coffee in his hand.

"I need to know what happened after I was shot."

"Then you talk to him. He barely said a word to me. "

Timo walked over to Nick and knelt beside him.

"How are you?" he said calmly.

Nick shook his head as he continued to stare at the wall across the hall. That had been his focus for the past hour. No one had asked him how he was feeling. Not even Isa. Not really. Timo was the first.

But he still couldn't find the words to describe the horror of the scene coursing through his mind. It wasn't just the sight of the wounds, the people and body parts scattered across the floor, but the thought it could all be over in seconds. Business as usual one minute, dead the next. And what had he been doing all these years? Pointless relationships, endless ambition. For what?

"She died because of me," Nick said.

"No one died because of you. All these people died because of those attackers, not you."

Nick turned to Timo. The inspector maintained his stern attitude, but Nick detected a hint of kindness and compassion in his eyes.

"What happened after I went down? I vaguely remember seeing one of them lean forward and point his gun at me."

"He wanted to shoot you," Nick said.

"Why didn't he?"

"The other intervened, the small one, the one who wanted to kill me."

Timo squeezed his eyes shut as if trying to imagine the attacker. "I remember him. There was something." Then he shook his head. "Never mind. And then?"

"They ran to the emergency exit. When you went down, I thought they were gonna kill me."

"And the others?"

"I didn't see anyone else."

"Let's go back to the beginning," Timo said.

"No, no!"

"I know you don't want to talk about it, but your testimony is crucial. We need as much information as possible."

"I wasn't there ... I was in the copy room ... hiding ..."

Like a coward.

"I know. When did you realize something was wrong?"

He'd been so busy copying and organizing the contracts, in a rush to get everything done. He loved practicing law, but he had never been fond of the paperwork, and his procrastination had put him in a position where he could no longer handle the growing pile of files on his desk. And there were the deadlines. The sound of people running around had lingered in the background for a while, but he hadn't noticed, not really. After more shots were fired, he'd opened the door a crack and seen one of the masked assailants run down the hall.

"I closed the door and hid in the corner."

Like a coward. Like a coward.

Those three words kept running through his mind.

"And then you called Isa?"

He nodded. It became increasingly difficult to control the emotions. He wanted to cry until there was nothing left in him, he wanted to scream at anyone who would listen, and he just wanted to punch a hole through the wall with his bare hands, if only to let out what little energy remained in him.

"Do you know how many attackers?"

"I've seen at least three, but there were more. I could hear them."

"Do you remember anything else?" Timo asked.

He remembered too much; things he didn't want to remember. Thinking objectively about the attack was just impossible, but there was one thing he had to tell inspector Paikkala. "They were looking for someone."

Timo leaned back, with a gush of surprised disbelief in his sharp blue eyes. "Are you sure? Why do you think that?"

"I heard someone shout 'Where is he?'."

"Who do you think they were looking for?"

Nick raised his shoulders. "Don't know. Every lawyer in this building has more enemies than you can count on one hand. It's part of the job, but for people to start killing? That seems ... drastic."

"Was there anything special today? Out of the ordinary?"

"Engersson was there. That was unusual."

"Karst Engersson, the boss?"

"He never comes," Nick said.

"Why now?"

Nick took a deep breath and shrugged.

"Okay, thanks, Nick," Timo said and gave him a pat on the shoulder. "If you need someone to talk to ..."

The kind gesture didn't sink in. Not yet. It just surprised him. How could inspector Paikkala help him? How could this man claim to know what he was going through? He simply couldn't know.

The next moment, he saw the inspector touch the left side of his chest, let out a moan and then reach for his head, before hitting the floor.

* * *

"So, what's this?" Ingrid said.

"What do you mean?" Timo said, rubbing his hands over his face until the haze was gone. The pain was still there. His chest, his head. Everything.

He was lying on the floor in a room he didn't recognize. There was a table and two chairs, a whiteboard that covered more than half the wall, and a small window overlooking the street. White, everything was white. No contrast. A kind of conference room. He wanted to get up, but she pushed him down.

He sighed. "How did I get here?"

"Did you really have to play the hero?" Ingrid said and opened the medical kit she had placed next to him. "You have intervention teams to take care of situations like these. Why did you have to be there yourself?"

He smelled a whiff of her violet perfume as she bent over to let the light shine into his eyes.

"I ... couldn't let Isa go ... with Nick and all. It was better if I took the lead myself and ... Jesus, why am I defending myself?"

"I don't know," she said, took his head and turned it sideways to look at the bruise. "Did you bump your head?"

He scanned her face. Her lip trembled. She was angrier than she wanted to show, as if she were about to explode in rage and scream at him for being so stupidly irresponsible.

"Obviously," he said.

"I mean before you decided to hit the floor in front of Nick."

"I fell against the wall," he said softly. "But I had a helmet on."

"Have you lost consciousness?"

"Yes, I think so. Ingrid, I want ..."

He wanted to apologize, although he wasn't quite sure why. But she didn't give him the chance, forcing the conversation to the sterile, pragmatic questions she'd been taught to ask as a medical doctor.

"Headache?"

"A bit," he said.

"Nausea?"

He sighed and said, "No ... I feel fine. Look, I'm sorry ..."

She frowned. "In the last six months, you fell off a cliff, almost got shot and let's not forget your attempt to chase a suspect through the streets of quiet and peaceful Gävle ... at 180km/h."

"Oh, so you heard about that?" he said. "I crashed the BMW."

"It's not funny." She took a deep breath before continuing, "Don't you think this is a pattern?"

"Of what?"

"Recklessness," she said with a stern face.

He frowned. No one had ever called him reckless.

"Can I go now?" he said, making another attempt to get up.

"No, you need to take off your vest."

Surprised, he turned to her, "Why?"

"You could have sustained serious internal injuries from the impact. I'll have to check that."

"But ...," he stammered.

"It's not up for discussion," Ingrid said.

Removing the bulletproof vest didn't go well. Her eyes softened as she saw him fumble.

"Let me help you," she said, removing the strap and pulling it over his head.

The bullet had penetrated layers of Kevlar and was lodged in the fibers. She put it on the table and turned back to him.

"Your shirt."

"What about it?" he said.

"Can you remove it? I need to examine your chest."

A wave of panic ran through his body.

"Look, I'm fine ... you shouldn't ..."

She gave him another stern look and he obeyed without saying another word. His arm, pressed firmly against the left side of his body, didn't cooperate, and she had to help him again. When she pulled the T-shirt over his head, he let out a cry of pain. The entire act had only lasted a few seconds and it had been painful, but it was the most sensual thing he'd experienced in a long time. Her face so close to his, her soft but cold hands brushing his skin as she pulled the fabric over his arms and torso, it was more than he could bear.

Calm down and concentrate!

There was a centimeters wide bruise around a burn mark, the result of the heat generated during the impact. It ran from the top left side of his chest to the bottom of the rib cage.

"I need to see if your ribs are broken. It can hurt."

He quickly nodded that it was okay, and she began the examination.

"How was France?" he said.

He needed something to distract his mind.

"Great ... relaxing ... the boys loved it," she said as her attention shifted from the left side to the front side of his body.

And she continued, "Oh, and thank you for the suggestion. The kids loved the hotel. The pool was great, and the people were so friendly."

"Good to hear," he said and smiled.

He remembered the cozy family hotel in the south of France where the Paikkala family had spent an unforgettable summer vacation almost twenty years ago. Unforgettable. Sun, sea, great food, culture, everything he had longed for, but also in a negative sense unforgettable, because of the big quarrel between his parents. After that, nothing had been the same. He could still hear his mother screaming. How his father had suffocated her, how she wanted something more in life than to be a showpiece. How pathetic and stupid her husband had been all those years, not knowing that his youngest son hadn't been his. Timo had heard it all and they, his parents, hadn't realized he had witnessed the revelation. It was an eye-opener, the beginning of the estrangement between him and his father. After that, there had been an invisible wall between them. A distance that had grown wider and deeper. He missed his dad and the bond they had shared until then. His parents had stayed together, but the marriage had been reduced to an empty display of ostentatious appearances until his father was killed in that horrific car accident and his mother had barely survived. To this day he still resented his mother for driving a wedge between him and his father.

He had often returned to France, but never stayed in that hotel again. He knew the previous owner had died and his son had taken over the hotel. Sweet and sour memories for him, but he was glad Ingrid had followed his advice.

"Do you have trouble breathing?" she asked.

"No ... it's painful but manageable."

There was a long pause as she continued to examine him.

"And you?" he said suddenly.

She looked up, a flash of surprise on her face.

"It was fun," she said.

Somehow, he didn't believe her. She was only talking about her husband and sons. It was difficult to break the immaculate image of mother and wife she put on, as if it were a shield, an excuse not to reveal anything about herself. Yet, he had to admit he was doing the exact same thing.

Ingrid took a step back. "Okay. Your ribs aren't broken. Bruised, yes, but not broken. And you have a minor concussion. So, you need to rest. The bruises will stay for a while. I can give you some painkillers. That will help you sleep but try to spare the left side of your body as much as you can. I know you like to be where the action is, but this time ..."

"Thanks," he said and took his shirt, "but I can't rest, I have too many things to take care of. This mess here and ... the house."

"Ah, yes, I heard you bought the house on the lake."

"And as you've seen yourself, there is plenty to do. I need to get the rooms painted and sorted out because I'm moving in next week."

"Next week already?"

"Yep."

"Can't someone help you?"

"Nope," he said, sighed and looked at the T-shirt on his lap. She was right. He felt helpless; he couldn't even dress himself.

She grabbed the shirt and slipped the sleeve over his left arm, before pulling it over his head and right arm. As she rolled it over his chest, his eyes stayed on her face. So close. Her breath tickled his cheeks, and the scent of her skin filled his nostrils. She stopped and stared at him.

"I ...," was all he let out.

"I'll help you," she said with the softest voice.

"How?"

"I'm a good painter."

"I don't think that's such a good idea," he said, without taking his eyes off her.

"Hey, what are friends for?" she said with the most innocent smile on her face.

Friends? He hated that word. She'd used it far too often the last months. Friends and colleagues. Why didn't he just take her head in his hands and kiss her? What stopped him? He deserved happiness and it was time to go after the things he wanted, and he wanted her.

29

"Timo?"

He jumped up. "Uh ... Lindström, what is it?"

Isa was leaning against the doorpost. "Can I talk to you?"

He turned to Ingrid. "You were going to give me painkillers?"

"Right," Ingrid said, taking a small box from the medical kit. "One every eight hours but be careful they're strong."

When she handed him the box, their fingers touched, sending chills over his body. Friends? Never. This wasn't how friends were supposed to feel.

He straightened his back, lifted his chin up high, and calmly walked to the door as if he was in total control of his emotions. But his mind was only focused on one thing. The skin that had touched his, and the exhilarating feeling they had shared in those few seconds. It was confusing. He wasn't sure what he was supposed to feel.

Isa looked at him with big green eyes and frowned as if she knew.

"What is it?" he said.

"SÄPO is here."

"SÄPO? The National Intelligence Service? Why?"

"The shooting is considered a terrorist attack. They are taking over the investigation."

CHAPTER

3

"... TWO PEOPLE ARE STILL FIGHTING for their life. The police have made no statement ..."

Twenty-seven-year-old Ilan Bergman had been staring at the TV screen for over an hour, mesmerized by the images of traumatized people, ambulances and stretchers carrying the injured and dead. It felt as if the earth was crumbling beneath his feet. This was his fault. This had been his blackmailer's target all along, and he was an accomplice. He had given the stalker the code and the card to enter. Why hadn't he gone to the police when he had the chance? Why hadn't he told them about the blackmail?

Marie Lång. The woman who had been murdered by a couple of psychopaths after he had hit her with his car and left her badly injured on the road. The charges were dropped as the police had been unable to prove his involvement in the hit-and-run, but it was too late. He had become entangled in a web of lies. His car was stolen, not on the night of Marie's death as the police report said, but on the day Frank Harket, the man he'd paid to get rid of the evidence, was murdered. His stalker had threatened to expose him and kill his wife if he didn't obey.

He should have been in the office, but he had taken a day off. Well, that wasn't quite true. With the ongoing police investigation into his involvement in the Harket case, he had been asked not to show his face too often in the office. But it had been a relaxing day and he hadn't thought of the lingering threat until he had received a very cryptic message from one of his colleagues. "Stay away from the office," he had written. More desperate messages had followed, desperate cries for help. And what had he done? Nothing. Ilan didn't even know if the man had survived. Johan Bengtsson, his cubicle buddy.

He heard the front door open and close again. It was his wife, Eve. How could he face her? He couldn't even deal with his own thoughts.

"Ilan, do you know what's going on at Global Law? The street was closed, and police were everywhere. I had to make a detour."

"Yeah ... I know," he said as she joined him in the living room of the small house in the center of Gävle they had bought a year ago just after their marriage. The house wasn't remarkable, just big enough for the two of them. As his mother frequently reminded him, it was too small if children would come, but at the same time she was honest enough to bluntly tell him she didn't expect the marriage to last. Not because of her daughter-in-law, but her son whom she still considered scum, even if he had tried so hard to turn his life around. He didn't deserve Eve.

He pointed at the TV screen.

As Eve's eyes jumped from here to there with the moving images, the expression on her face gave away nothing. It was stuck in a neutral, almost apathetic gaze.

Then she slowly turned to him, "Ilan, this is terrible. How? What?"

"I ..." He tried to push the words out of his mouth, but they didn't come.

She sat down next to him and took his hand.

"My God, luckily you weren't there," she said.

He nodded but said nothing. He swallowed and swallowed, but he could no longer silence the welling emotions and tears.

She continued. "How bad is it? Do you know who ..."

"Jeez, Eve ... I don't know," he said, pushing her hand away and disappearing into the kitchen, where she couldn't see how he collapsed in front of the sink. He buried his face in his hands, trying to smother the escaping sobs as his body violently moved to the bursts of emotional pain.

"Ilan? Are you okay? Can I do something?"

He took a deep breath and wiped his face with the sleeve of his shirt. "Give me a second."

Minutes passed and then he came back with a glass of cold beer. He placed it on the table and switched the channel as if nothing had happened. But the news of the attack was everywhere. He couldn't escape it.

"... a victim later died in the hospital from the injuries sustained during the attack. This brings the total to ten. The police have ..."

Eve watched him as he kept switching channels.

"Ilan, please turn off the TV," Eve said, running her hand over his back. "It's not good for you."

But the images of wounded people and police officers haunted his mind. He couldn't turn it off. Like an addict, almost like a madman, he stared at the screen.

"... insiders say the police are treating this as a terrorist attack, but they have not released an official statement ..."

Terrorist attack? He was involved in a terrorist attack. The TV image turned into a blur, and his gaze narrowed, like a kaleidoscope. Why was it suddenly so hot? Breathing became harder, as if the surrounding air were deprived of oxygen. He got up, but his legs felt so weak, shaking, as if he were moving on unsteady ground. But the problem wasn't just in his legs: his entire body seemed to fail at once. Something was very wrong. It felt as if a heavy weight was pressing on his chest. Heart attack? The pain grew sharper, and he tried to grab the armrest of the couch, but his muddled vision clouded the focus and he missed it.

His wife's desperate cries were the last thing he heard before he hit the ground and the darkness took over.

* * *

"Kristoffer Solberg."

The tall, blond man with dark glasses and ring beard that seemed a little out of place—a failed attempt to cover his baby face and make him look more serious and awe-inspiring—walked over and held out his hand.

"Inspector Paikkala," Timo said as they shook hands.

"Ah, the Timo Paikkala! Your reputation precedes you."

"I'm afraid to ask: what reputation?" Timo said.

"Don't worry. I've only heard good things about you."

"What's SÄPO doing here?" Timo asked as they walked to the exit.

An eerie silence hung over the building. Only the police officers and the forensics teams remained. The injured had been taken to hospitals, and whenever possible, they had sent the survivors home. The forensics team was meticulously sweeping the rooms, categorizing everything, and collecting as much evidence as possible.

After the hours of bustle, where there was no time to dwell on the dramatic events, a moment had come when the brutality of silence highlighted the futility of the violence so clearly. Too clearly. Timo had seen health workers wipe away tears as they folded the blood-soaked sheets and put them in the plastic bags. Police officers, hardened by years of training, who sat quietly on the bench by the window staring at a shoe, purse, or a piece of blood-stained cloth. He knew what they were thinking, and if he wasn't careful the same thoughts of helplessness and shame, that he hadn't been able to do more, would flood his own mind.

Kristoffer's narrative brought him back to his senses. "In the past two months, we have received information about a potential terrorist attack."

"IS? Al-Qaeda?" Timo asked.

"No. None of those sleeper cells have been activated."

"So, what are we talking about?"

"We don't know yet. But we do know the dead perpetrator is Nils Vollan. Born in Norway, with family ties in Germany. He's been on our radar since he entered Sweden about six months ago."

"Why?"

"Mr. Vollan is a mercenary. He is suspected of being involved in drugs and human trafficking, arms dealing. You name it, he's done it. Europol warned us something was up, and we decided to shadow him, but Vollan disappeared off the grid about four weeks ago. Since then, we've seen an increase in radio traffic and activity from the white supremacist group in Stockholm and several dozen nationalist and ultra-conservative splinter groups."

"I thought they weren't that active anymore?" Timo said.

"Even more than ever. Social and political polarization provides an excellent breeding ground for far-right and far-left groups to fuel their activities. We estimate that the membership of these groups has increased by ten percent in recent years, probably even more. The refugee crisis and the political tension the last years hasn't helped either."

"But why Gävle? Why not Stockholm or Uppsala? And what was the goal?"

"You know as much as we do," Kristoffer answered, opening the door, and stepping outside. The area around the building was demarcated with yellow and black tape, and police cars were still blocking the street on both sides. Dusk had descended on the city, and the streets already bathed in an early mist. The evenings were getting colder.

The lampposts cast a shadow over the police officers on the street. The same strange, ghostly silence that Timo had felt inside the building floated through the air and for a moment the hairs on his arms stood on end.

"A witness claims they were looking for someone in particular. That doesn't sound like a terrorist attack to me."

Kristoffer looked at him as if he had claimed the most ridiculous thing in the world, but then said, "I don't want to speculate, but we'll take it into account. It doesn't exclude a terrorist attack."

"Not one, but at least two witnesses have confirmed that this attack was targeted," Timo added.

"And carefully organized?" sounded the voice of a woman behind him.

Isa and Ingrid joined them.

"Dr. Olsson, inspector Isa Lindström," Timo introduced the women to the chief investigator of the SÄPO team.

An ironic smile played on Kristoffer's mouth as he leaned over to shake Isa's hand. She met his misplaced grin with a frown.

Then Kristoffer said, "Well, I can imagine this attack required a lot of preparation. Carrying out a death raid in broad daylight in an office full of people requires meticulous planning. And they would have needed someone on the inside to provide information."

"They knew the code, and they had a badge to enter the building," Timo said.

Kristoffer sighed. "Probably stolen."

Isa said, "Inspector Paikkala is right. This isn't a typical terrorist attack. I believe they went after Karst Engersson, senior partner, and co-founder. His office is in Stockholm, and it's no coincidence that the attack took place today. He rarely visits the Gävle office, but today was an exception as he was expected to deliver a speech at the Social Democratic Party Convention tomorrow."

"You might be right," Ingrid said. "The attackers first made their way to the central office, injuring people along the way. Injuring, but not killing. After they shot Engersson, his secretary and assistant, they started executing people to leave no witnesses. They used AR-15 assault rifles and handguns, mostly .38 and .44."

"Engersson would step down as CEO," Timo said. "It has long been rumored that he would go into politics."

"Wasn't there something about his son last year?" Ingrid asked. "A scandal."

"Yes, he was involved in some scheme about offshore accounts and tax evasion," Isa answered.

"But I'm still not convinced Engersson was the target," Kristoffer interrupted them. "Why kill all these people if you're only targeting one man? I can think of easier ways to do that."

There was silence. Ten people killed; a dozen injured. Many more traumatized for life. Were they all collateral? Perhaps Solberg was right. It seemed pointless.

"I can't ignore the intel we have received over the past month," Kristoffer continued. "Until I have solid evidence that this is not the case, I must consider this a terrorist attack, and take all necessary steps to ensure the safety of the public."

Inspector Berger Karlsson walked over to them.

"Timo, they found the car," Berger said.

The attackers had escaped through the security door leading to the adjacent Tech4You building. Traffic cameras had shown that they then drove off in a blue van parked in the street on the other side of the building. The police had immediately issued an APB.

"And?"

"Burnt out. It will be difficult to extract evidence."

"And the suspects?" Timo asked.

"No trace. No witnesses."

"Is my team informed about this?" Kristoffer asked.

"Your team?" Berger said surprised and quickly looked at Timo.

Kristoffer gave him a forced smile. "Yes, SÄPO is overseeing this investigation, and I'd appreciate the Gävle team acknowledges that. We'll of course work with you, but this is our case and ultimately, we decide."

"Of course," Timo said calmly, ignoring his team's angry looks.

The friendly tone from a few minutes ago was gone. It was clear who was in control.

* * *

"He'll steer this investigation in the wrong direction," Isa said after Kristoffer Solberg had left them standing in front of the entrance to the Global Law building.

Timo sighed and said, "And as usual you have problems with authority! We need to assume he knows what he's doing. I'm not going to interfere."

"Timo, I don't have such a wow feeling about this. What is your instinct telling you? You were there."

"Lindström, just do as you're told."

She looked at him with furrowed brows. "That's so unlike you."

"I'm tired and in pain," he said in a stern voice, "and not in the mood to discuss this."

"Isa, Timo, we have CCTV," Berger interrupted their conversation.

"At least something," Isa said.

Minutes later they were standing in the observation room with one of the security guards at the control panel trying to find the last recorded footage of the Global Law offices before the attackers destroyed the cameras. Timo had insisted on informing Kristoffer Solberg, and with

Berger and the SÄPO investigator, he stood in the back of the room, that was just large enough for the table that held the equipment and overlooked the screens, and the two chairs in which the guard and Isa sat. The men in the back, all tall in stature and some leaner than others, had hardly any room to move. The split screen was divided into quadrants, showing the images of the elevators and the two exits leading to the stairwell and emergency exit.

The bearded, slightly obese, security guard, sweating profusely and occasionally casting an approving glance at the beautiful woman sitting next to him—naively thinking she might be interested in him—brought up the images taken just moments before the cameras were destroyed.

The black-and-white footage showed men in masks and black overalls, suddenly appearing in the right half of the frame, rifles in hand, as several assailants entered the offices through the emergency exit and stairwell.

"Four, five, six ... in total," Berger remarked.

In the lower images, the men looked straight into the camera before, almost simultaneously pointing their guns at it and firing. A random flicker of white and dark dots remained on the screen.

Timo kept his eyes fixed on the white noise. "They knew the code to get in. There's no doubt about that. And they had a card for the emergency exit. That's why the alarm didn't go off. But how could we have overlooked that the two buildings are connected?"

The guard turned around and said, "They were connected before, but when the owner sold them in 2005, the hallway between the two buildings was sealed off, and the metal doors are permanently locked."

"Who do the buildings belong to?" Timo said.

"This one is owned by the Engersson family. Only the third floor is used for the Global Law offices. The other floors are rented. The building next door is used by Tech4You. I don't know the owners."

The guard, pleased with his contribution to the conversation, gave Isa another glance, but she was fully concentrated on the screen.

"Who knows about the passageway between the two buildings?" Berger asked.

"The previous owner, his family, former employees who worked here," the guard said.

Timo looked at him with his sharp blue eyes and said, "You?"

"Me? No ... uh, obviously I do but ..." The guard took a deep sigh and then continued. "My father worked in the printing house his entire life until he was laid off in 2005."

Berger nodded. "These were the buildings of the newspaper The Gävle Herald. The company went under, and the owner sold the buildings. The printing house was next door. The halls are now used as labs."

"Track down the former employees. Who had access to the passageway? Does anyone else know? Where does the card come from? Find me a clue! Anything!"

Timo heard Berger sigh. Frustration and anger had built up and it was fueled by the bitterness of his own inadequacy. And unfortunately, Berger got the full load.

"That's Vollan," Isa said suddenly, pointing to the man in the back, visible in the top left quadrant.

He was the last to appear, but Timo's attention was drawn to the person in front instructing the other attackers. This was the man who had pointed his gun at him and Nick.

Timo said, "Vollan wasn't the leader. Can you go back?"

The image had changed to white noise, just like the other CCTV images. The guard pressed a few buttons, and the screen showed the same images from the start.

Mesmerized, Timo looked at the man who, with short, strong hand movements, made it clear to the others what he wanted. He was the mastermind, even though Timo could have sworn a frightened little boy had stood before him when Timo had aimed his gun.

"How did they get the code and valid badge to get in?" Isa said but got no answer. "And the key to the passageway?"

"Where is the CCTV footage of the entrance hall?" Timo asked.

"Why?" Berger said.

"They got in the elevator without masks and overalls, entered the code, disguised themselves and went to the third floor without arousing suspicion. So, the cameras in the hall must have picked them up. We should be able to identify them."

The man next to Isa shook his head.

"The cameras have been broken for weeks," he said, "we have no footage of the hall."

"Damn it," Timo yelled. "This is no coincidence! Who knew about the cameras? A law firm that spends so much money on a complex access system and then doesn't have the broken surveillance cameras repaired, this seems odd to me."

"Those cameras are operated by another company."

"What company?" Timo said.

The guard shrugged and turned to the screen. "I'm employed by Global Law."

"And outside?"

"There are a few cameras on the corners, none at the entrance," the guard said.

"We still need the footage from Tech4You, but so far we only picked up the blue van," Isa said.

Berger sighed and said, "So, Vollan is the only lead we have."

Timo took a deep breath before saying, "I want to know everything about this man. Where has he been the past weeks? Who did he speak to? His phone records, his financial situation. His link to Global Law and Engersson. Everything."

"I admire your enthusiasm, but this is a matter for my team," Kristoffer said calmly. "As I said before, we'll take it from here."

Timo saw the angry look on Isa's face. She was right. This didn't feel okay. He remembered the attacker's eyes. There had been a strange mixture of shock and pity. He couldn't get it out of his head.

The frozen image on the screen showed one of the attackers looking straight into the camera before shattering it with the bullet from the gun.

Before leaving the room, Kristoffer suddenly turned. "And inspector Paikkala, there's a press conference in an hour. Be there!"

Timo sighed as Kristoffer disappeared through the door.

A press conference? Timo didn't like it. He knew he'd be there pro forma and probably get the nastiest questions that he didn't know the right answer to anyway. Yet again, they were going to make the Gävle police department look like a bunch of fools.

CHAPTER

4

"I'VE NEVER HEARD ANYONE SAY 'No comment' so many times," Isa said.

Timo ran his hands through his black hair before dropping into the swivel chair at her desk. The chair gained momentum, and the back slammed against the edge of the table.

She watched him closely from behind the desk. How come he always looked so sharp, even at three o'clock in the morning. The day was already more than hours too long. A day full of drama and stress. She hadn't dared to go home, even though Timo and Ingrid had repeatedly told her it was okay to check on Nick. She just didn't know what to say to him, how to behave around him.

She said, "The first press conference is tough. Anders Larsen, your predecessor, used to say, you have to do at least ten of them to get a sense of what you can and cannot say. It's an art like any other."

He turned his head to her and said, "It's not my first press conference as superintendent here."

"Oh ... right," she said suddenly. "Magnus."

She had forgotten about the press conference a few months ago where Timo had reluctantly admitted to the media, with the commissioner by his side, that an officer from their department, Magnus Wieland, her former partner, had been responsible for the death of an innocent civilian. A crime committed out of love for her, not only killing his love rival but covering it up by making evidence disappear.

"Do you understand why I'm careful?" he said, looking her straight in the eye. Sometimes those strange blue eyes of his saw right through her, as if they could penetrate to the depths of a person's soul and mind. And at times they were so gentle and compassionate that she let her mind wander to the most inappropriate feelings about her boss.

"As long as the internal investigation is ongoing, we should keep a low profile," he said.

"The Sandviken case has caused so much damage," she said quietly. And she was largely responsible for it.

"And it's not over yet."

"What are you saying?" she said surprised.

"Have you spoken to Magnus yet?"

"No, and I never want to hear that name again!"

Betrayed by her own partner and ex-lover. The murderer of the greatest love of her life.

He looked at her for a moment, dumbfounded, opened his mouth, then changed his mind.

"Seriously, Timo. We're not going to let the whole Magnus fling silence us. I understand SÄPO should take terrorist attacks seriously, but then let our team look at the other options. I know you agree with me."

He sighed, stood up, straightened his back, and ran his hand across his chest, a painful expression that told her that he had momentarily forgotten the injuries sustained during the intervention.

"Go home. It's going to be long days."

And with those words he turned and disappeared through the door.

* * *

"Look, I know SÄPO oversees the investigation, but you need us. We know Gävle, we know the people, and you need all the help you can get."

Kristoffer Solberg sat in the other chair spinning the pen between his fingers as if signaling boredom. He sighed and looked up at the man who had spent the past half hour desperately trying to convince him of his team's added value.

"With all due respect, Timo, if I may call you Timo," he started, "you may have a solid reputation, but your team doesn't … I know you kinda inherited them."

"Inherited them?"

"In a manner of speaking. People in Stockholm don't like Gävle that much right now. Don't underestimate the damage Magnus Wieland and Isa Lindström have done to this department. People in Stockholm want to see actions from you."

"People in Stockholm? Who might I ask?"

Silence.

Kristoffer turned his attention to the pen again.

As he got no reply, Timo continued, "And what action exactly?"

Then Kristoffer shrugged, gave him a sarcastic grin, and said, "You'll figure it out."

"I'm sure," Timo replied with a frown on his face.

"You were very successful in dodging the bullet, but you may not be so lucky this time. Do you know they're going to reopen the Sandviken investigation? Leif Berg is pushing hard for it."

The news hadn't gone down well with Isa, nor with the families of the girls, serial killer Mats Norman had abducted and killed. In addition to the internal investigation the media had picked up on the story, and the police competence or rather incompetence was again the subject of much debate.

Timo said, "Berg has a lot to gain. Then he doesn't have to explain why he put so much pressure on the police at the time to convict an innocent person for the disappearance and murder of his daughter Anna Berg."

"Can you say with absolute certainty that you arrested the right man, now you know your own senior investigator covered up a murder he, himself, is responsible for? What else is Magnus Wieland hiding?"

"Come on. He can't have killed those girls?" Timo said and threw his hands in the air.

"But maybe those murders weren't related at all," Kristoffer said with an arrogant grin on his face. "Maybe there is no serial killer. Maybe you apprehended an innocent man."

"Are you kidding? The girls lay side by side in the Sandviken forest, and he confessed." Timo got up and walked over to the window.

Rain, nothing but rain these days. He continued without taking his eyes off the window, covered with stripes of dirt and the occasional autumn-colored leaf. "So, we are going to release a serial killer, but nobody even mentions the man who has been in prison for more than twenty years, and is serving a life sentence for the murder of Anna Berg he likely didn't commit? Are we really going to cover this up? I don't understand why the media isn't jumping on this."

"Just saying. Berg is in office now, and he has a lot of influence. Gävle will be chosen as scapegoat."

Timo shook his head. "And nobody stops him?"

"Political suicide," Kristoffer said. "And it gets worse. You know that inspector Magnus Wieland has pleaded not guilty? He claims he was emotionally pressured to kill Alexander Nordin, provoked by Isa's behavior."

"What? They can't honestly believe that. He forged evidence."

"He felt pressured to protect himself and his family. He never wanted to delete those phone records."

"Like he never intended to destroy the footprints," Timo said.

"According to him, that was all the doing of—what's her name—the woman in a coma?"

Timo turned to him. "Nina Kowalczyk. She's recovering."

"Ah, yes, that's true. There are rumors that Wieland tried to get rid of her, but she claims she can't remember what happened. Did Magnus attack her? Was it an accident? Nobody knows."

"He confessed," Timo added.

"Sure, but again, he claims he was under pressure, and the police even used his own daughter."

"Oh, come on, there was no coercion," Timo yelled. "If anything, I should be the one to sue him. He put a gun to my head."

"I know that. You know that, but it's easy to manipulate the public opinion and let the justice system work for you. He's got a damn good lawyer. But the question is, what are the guys in Stockholm going to do?"

Kristoffer got up. He waited for a second and looked at the floor, unsure what to say.

"I'll involve your team but keep an eye on them. Start with Tech4You. We had no time to check that angle."

"Thanks," Timo whispered.

"You really can't afford any more slips or digressions. They're watching you. My advice would be to lay low, very low. Or pack your bags and get out of here as fast as you can. We have a new opening at SÄPO."

"Why do you say that?" Timo stammered.

"I know you're applying for the superintendent position here, but you might want to reconsider."

Timo glanced at him as Kristoffer Solberg disappeared.

He was right. The situation was bad and with every second, he felt the control slipping away. How could he convince the national police commissioner he needed more time to turn things around, that the Gävle team was worth the investment? Maybe he was too naïve?

He needed allies. He had to talk to Finn Heimersson of the Uppsala police. Finn was a friend and he had connections in high places.

* * *

"So, what does Tech4You actually do?" Timo asked, following the chubby slightly balding man, who barely reached his shoulders, and almost seemed to come out of a bad seventies' movie.

Ragnvald Strand was CTO, senior researcher, and business manager all in one. The man struggled to control his nerves when he was presented with a police badge saying the officers wanted to see the labs and offices as part of the Global Law shooting investigation. He looked even completely off balance when he saw the physically fit and almost two-meter-tall police inspectors Timo and Berger who spared nothing to appear intimidating.

"Tech4You is a new start-up in wearables," Ragnvald said, panting as if he had run a marathon, while he led them to the labs on the other side of the building. "We develop clothing that allows to monitor a range of biometric signals, like for example heartrate and oxygen saturation but even EEG and muscle activity. We offer everything from the hardware to the software to analyze the data."

"So, this can be used in hospitals and so," Timo said.

"Even in your own home if you want to monitor your health and send the data to your GP, but also in sport trainings when athletes want to optimize their performance. Why our technology stands out is that we use body heat and the sun energy to charge the electronic components, and we're not talking about a simple watch or glasses here, but sometimes even an entire exoskeleton."

"Impressive," Timo said.

Ragnvald's face turned red as if he didn't know how to handle compliments and he stammered, "It's still in a research phase."

"What are the labs used for?" Berger asked as he passed the desks, covered in wires and what he assumed were electronic components. On some desks were microscopes, computers and impressive equipment, the function of which was completely unclear to the police officer.

"We test the basic components and the final product. The assembly is done elsewhere, in our university lab in Uppsala. For now. The idea is to move the assembly line over here next year."

They stopped at a double steel door, painted in the same green color as the wall and now marked with a police tag.

"This is it," Ragnvald said. His anxiety was getting out of control, with the droplets of sweat on his forehead increasing rapidly in number and size.

"Who knows about this entrance?" Timo said.

"Almost no one ... I think," he said. "I mean ... I know of course, and so does Lage Feldt."

"Lage Feldt, the owner of Tech4You?" Timo said.

"Yes, he's in the US now."

"And who was here yesterday during the shooting?"

Ragnvald pulled a handkerchief from his pocket and wiped the sweat from his face. "Uh, about ten people were here. It was supposed to be a busy day with many experiments and tests to be run, but it turned out differently. I can give you their names, but during the police intervention everyone in this building was evacuated. With our security system, we know who was there and who wasn't."

"But we have no CCTV?" Timo said.

Ragnvald nodded. "It's not optimal yet. We haven't been here for long. We just have a badge system."

"And one you could easily overrule," Timo remarked. "I can simply jump over the electronic gate without needing a badge. For a high-tech company this is disappointing."

Ragnvald's face changed color again and he quickly looked at the floor. Berger felt embarrassed in his place. His boss had shown his most impatient and harsh side again.

"And the offices are upstairs?" Berger said.

"Yes, on the first floor. The second and third floor aren't used yet. There are plans to expand the team next year."

"Coming back to the evacuation," Timo said and let his glance run over the wall. "Everyone left the building and then what?"

Ragnvald sighed. "It was chaos. People were everywhere. They were scared. We didn't know what was going on. And the police had their hands full with keeping passersby away."

"Any unfamiliar faces, people you noticed who shouldn't have been there?" Berger asked.

The man took a few seconds to think about the question and then shook his head.

"And who wasn't there?" Timo said.

Ragnvald frowned and then said, "What do you mean? Everyone who entered the building in the morning, left during the evacuation. I checked the logs myself."

"Could someone in the lab have unlocked this door?"

"What are you saying? That one of our employees is an accomplice? They don't know, and no one has a key, except maybe Feldt."

"Yet, this door was open yesterday and the attackers used it to escape. They got help. Either someone opened the door for them, or they knew. I want a list of all your employees. If someone is involved, be sure I'll find him."

And with those words, inspector Paikkala walked back to the entrance where they came from.

* * *

"How are you feeling?" Ingrid asked.

Timo shrugged. "Okay, I guess."

He didn't want to bother her with his problems, but he was pissed. Ragnvald Strand had tested his patience and the memory of his injury was enough to make him feel the uncomfortable pain on the left side of his body. The night had been difficult—a constant struggle to find the right sleeping position—and in the morning, it felt like a truck had run over him. Tired and pain all over his body. Coffee was his thing. He was a caffeine addict, but today he'd drank enough to put him in a state of continuous agitation, dragging himself through the day, with cycles of deep fatigue, followed by heart rate increasing unrest, induced by the overload of caffeine.

"You haven't taken your medicine," Ingrid said, giving him an angry look.

"I need a clear mind and with that ..."

"A clear mind means you need to sleep. That's why I gave you the painkillers. You look awful."

"Oh, thanks," he answered with an ironic grin on his lips.

She turned and looked at the table behind her. The pale, half-covered naked man with a typical Y-shaped incision in the chest, a remnant from the autopsy, a yellow hospital bracelet on his wrist, and a paper toe tag, was waiting for them. The room was spacious with five tables and felt clinical and cold. Against the wall, there were steel cabinets and a countertop, where the medical tools were displayed on a cloth. The slanted, aluminum autopsy table was sprayed clean and besides Timo and Ingrid, a few dieners and doctors were present, preparing for the next autopsy.

"Nils Vollan, twenty-seven, Norwegian," she started, "shot three times, with the last bullet, entering the heart, which was fatal."

"He was killed by a police bullet."

"Indeed," she said. "The autopsy also revealed he had many fractures: ribs, skull, femur."

"Well, he was a mercenary, a fighter."

"Some are several years old. Other than that, the body doesn't tell us much, except that he was a drug addict."

"Drugs?"

"Puncture marks on the arms suggest he was probably on heroin, but the toxicology report of the blood and hair should tell us more."

"What about the search of his apartment?"

"You have to ask Lars," she said and let out a sigh.

"What's wrong?"

The expression on her face had changed from happy to gloomy in a matter of seconds. He didn't like to see her so defeated.

"The cases are piling up on my desk," she said.

"You need help?"

"Mila needs help," she said.

"Mila? Who's Mila?"

"My new assistant," Ingrid said, looking at the young woman who, as soon as she heard her name, had turned her head and was now walking toward them.

She had a kind and cheerful, but childish face, and she was no more than twenty-five. She was petite and slender, and Timo almost didn't dare to shake her hand, thinking the frail woman would break any moment.

"Mila Hillborg," she said and took his hand, full of enthusiasm and vigor, which took him by surprise.

"Inspector Timo Paikkala. Nice to meet you and welcome to the team," he said and then frowned. "Sorry, but have we met before? You look so familiar."

"I don't think so," Mila said with a smile on her face. "But I wish I had."

Surprised by what she'd said, he gave her one of his brightest smiles, while Ingrid looked at them with pursed lips and furrowed brows. A flash of irritation crossed her face.

"We've got a really bad case," Ingrid said, leading him away from Mila to the refrigerator where the older bodies were kept. She unlocked the metal door and rolled out one of the body trays. Beneath the white sheet lay a charred corpse, frozen in a twisted, unsettling position, limbs partly missing, incinerated by the heat, with garments melted into the remaining flesh.

"The body was found weeks ago on the beach near Brädviken," Ingrid said.

"I remember seeing the report. Brädviken. That's a very crowded area during summer."

"Yes, but the victim wasn't killed there."

"No identification yet?" Timo said.

"Berger ... uh, inspector Karlsson is looking into it," Mila intervened.

Ingrid threw her another angry look.

"And does he have a lead?" Timo asked.

"Not yet. We have sent dental records and DNA from the long bones to the NFC, the national forensic center, but so far, no identification of the victim. The DNA may not be useable due to the extreme heat. So, inspector Karlsson is reviewing the missing persons reports to see if any of them can be matched to the body, but it's not easy to get an idea of the body features."

"Thanks, Mila," Ingrid said, "can you take care of Vollan's body?"

The young woman nodded and left them.

"Berger may be busy for a while with the Global Law case," Timo said and turned to Ingrid, "but I'll see what I can do."

She smiled. "Thank you."

There was another unguarded flaming moment between them as she looked in his eyes. He wanted to hold it as long as possible.

"Timo, I meant what I said about helping you," she said softly.

"I'm okay and that wouldn't be appropriate. I'm your boss. We should ..."

"Technically, you're not my boss. I only help the police. And we're friends. Friends can help each other, right?"

"It's just ..."

"Okay, if it makes you feel more comfortable, I'll ask Anton. You saved him. We owe you something. And you need help."

"No, you don't owe me anything. I was just doing my job, and Anton wasn't really in any danger."

"I'll ask him," she said.

"But ...," he started, but couldn't finish his sentence when he saw her walk away.

* * *

Svante Engersson felt lost. He had brought his lawyer with him, but he hadn't spoken to him or even given him so much as a glance. It may have been overkill but his dad had always told him to be prepared for any situation and a good lawyer by your side should always be part of the plan.

Svante sighed as his eyes filled with tears. It was impossible for him to focus on anything else after the police had told him his father was among the victims of the Global Law shooting. He'd been in a state of complete apathy ever since.

"Why am I here?" he stammered.

"Our condolences on the passing of your father," Isa said.

"My father," he mused.

He couldn't even get a decent sentence out of his mouth. He shook his head and then stared at his hands.

"The investigation is still ongoing, and several routes are being explored, but we have reason to believe that your father was targeted specifically. He wasn't just collateral damage."

"Really?"

"You had a good relationship with your father?"

Svante nodded. "He was demanding. He had unattainable standards, but yes, we had a good relationship. We respected each other."

"Really?" Isa said, and after Lars handed her the file, she started flipping through the pages. "There were rumors he wanted to go into politics, but he didn't. Was it because of your legal problems? The sacrifices a father must make. Did it lead to friction?"

"No, of course not. Besides ... he had lost the support of the Social Democrats."

"Why?"

Svante shrugged. "I don't know. He never told me, but I happened to overhear a few ... difficult phone calls between my father and representatives of the party. I don't know the details, but he was agitated."

"When was this?"

"A few months ago. He never said anything about it. I guess his speech at the Convention and his meeting with Leif Berg were supposed to put him back on the favorites list with the party."

"What about Global Law? His work as a lawyer. Any enemies?"

Svante shrugged and then said, "He had plenty. That was the nature of his job. He defended criminals, sometimes the worst."

"Global Law changed the entrance procedure about a year ago for all their offices. Badges, entry codes that change every month. Increased security. Why?"

"There were a few unrelated incidents."

"What happened?" Isa asked.

"Some crazy guy attacked one of the secretaries," he sniffed. "It was a brutal attack outside the building in Stockholm and then threatening letters were sent to several lawyers."

"What were the threats about?"

"Death threats. Some were very specific, others were vague."

"Did your father get any?"

"Yes. At that time, he was working on the Breiner case. Most of them were."

"You mean the police officer who was murdered in Stockholm?"

Svante nodded. "There was talk that the victim was in fact on the payroll of the mafia. Witnesses were also intimidated."

"What was your father's role?"

"He was Rune Breiner's lawyer. He was with the guy when Breiner was shot that evening when they came out of the Global Law building in Stockholm."

"So, your father witnessed the murder?"

"Yes. It had a huge impact on him. And then he started to receive the threatening letters and emails, just like the other members of Breiner's defense team."

"Did he go to the police?"

"Yes," Svante said, "but there was nothing they could do: no prints, no sender, not even the IP address to trace the emails."

"Do you think Breiner's murder, and the threats could have anything to do with the shooting?" Isa said.

"Are you asking me?"

"What do you think?" Isa said.

"Maybe ... "

"And where were you during the shooting incident?" Isa said.

He jumped up and shouted, "Are you kidding me?"

His lawyer put his hand on his arm to calm him down and then said: "Is my client a suspect?"

"No, he's not. It's a standard question."

"Really? It indicates the direction you are thinking, and you have no proof. What reason would my client have for killing his father? Besides, it's hard to believe that only my client's father was targeted. This was clearly a terrorist attack, and as you can see, my client has no ties with extremist groups. I don't think ..."

"Let us be the judge of that," Isa said, and gave the man at the opposite side a sharp glance. The man sighed and then leaned back.

"So, where was your client?" Isa said.

"I was home, alone," Svante said. "I have no family, no wife, no kids. I have been suspended pending the verdict in the trial. The decision was taken at the general meeting of shareholders a few months ago."

"So, you're out of a job," Isa said with an almost sarcastic grin on her face. "And no alibi for the shooting."

"Why on earth would I kill my father?" Svante yelled. "I needed him."

Then he looked at his hands and continued, "He was going to fix everything."

Isa sighed. "Was there anything suspicious in the past weeks before the shooting? Something unusual your father might have mentioned?"

Svante shook his head, but he couldn't think of anything. They had talked little. His soon-to-be-conviction was starting to strain the relationship with his father. As always, he had asked his dad for help, but it wasn't another bailout after a night of drugs and women where it was easy to make the charges disappear. This time, he didn't even know if his father could help him. Why had he done such a stupid thing? He had his life on track. He had started an IT company that was doing well, but he had screwed up again. It was all just another version of the same story, just one more example of how good things always end up going sour for him.

Should he tell them about the letter? The strange one-word letter he'd found in his mailbox over a month ago. A white envelope with a single white sheet and the word 'YOU'. It probably had nothing to do with his father's death. Just a prank. Maybe he wasn't even the intended recipient.

"Nothing?" Lars asked.

"No, nothing," Svante said softly.

His father's death had left him orphaned and distraught. Their relationship had been more difficult than he'd made it out to be, but deep in his heart he understood his father had wanted to give him every chance in life to succeed. And he had screwed up repeatedly. Messed up big time. There were things he had never been held accountable for.

His mom. He had to be there for his mom. His mother hadn't said a word since she'd learned of her husband's death. She just sat in the living room of the enormous villa, staring outside, into nothingness.

There were so many reasons why someone would want his father dead. Clients he hadn't been able to keep out of prison, angry clients and their families, competitors, colleagues, politicians.

The Breiner case? Maybe. In every layer of society, his father had enemies. But would they have gone so far as to kill him? It was hard to imagine. His lawyer was right. This was a terrorist attack, and his father was the wrong man at the wrong place and the wrong time.

He had to believe that.

CHAPTER

5

NICK TURNED THE CEREAL BOX upside down and let the multi-colored rings fall into the bowl and onto the kitchen table. Making no attempt to clean it up, he sat down and poured milk over it. Isa watched the entire scene in silence. Like the day before, he was mesmerized by the stirring of the spoon, creating a small whirlpool in the center of the bowl. The rattling sound of the metal hitting the rim of the bowl echoed across the room.

Just days ago, he had been energetic and full of joy, bubbling over with ideas. He knew she missed seeing that side of him. She missed the boisterous, overly excited Nick who had always something to talk about. The way his voice filled the air around him, sometimes so loud she was glad to get in her car and drive to work to get some rest. He could imagine she missed the seductive Nick who, with a few glances and sexy whispers, could get her undressed in no time. But he couldn't be that man anymore.

"Are you alright?"

She'd asked this question so many times over the past days. And as before, he said nothing and bowed his head to look at the floating cornflakes. By now, most of them were so soaked with milk it had become a sticky, filthy mixture. He put the spoon down and sighed.

No, he wasn't okay. He wasn't okay at all. He felt lonely because he didn't know how to talk about the emptiness. The words failed him, and he'd never had a problem with words before. For the past days, he'd been sitting on the couch, in Isa's living room, undressed, unshaven, letting the images on the TV flash by without really grasping what they meant. The only image that stayed with him all the time, day and night, was Kim's damaged body lying in the hallway of Global Law. It was the first thing he saw when he woke up in the morning; it was the last thing he saw when he fell asleep, after hours of tossing and turning, exhausted from the constant rumination and the nightmares that woke him up in the middle of the night, trembling and with a pounding heartbeat.

"I'll be off then," Isa said.

She picked up the phone from the table, put on her jacket and walked over to him.

"Nick," she said, took his head in both hands and kissed him, "you need to talk to someone."

"What's the point?"

He knew she was worried and afraid the man she loved would be gone forever. And he didn't have the strength to fight the dark thoughts, the flashbacks, and the panic attacks, and return to the man he'd been before. But did he want to be the carefree and selfish person he had been for the last thirty years?

His head was foggy. It didn't work properly. Thoughts were going nowhere. Perhaps it was a natural defense mechanism to numb the pain that occasionally peeked through. Most of the time, Kim's image was met with a certain distant abstraction, as if he were watching a show on TV. He wasn't there, but in his dreams and those unexpected moments the walls of protection were broken down and every feeling, every detail of the horror was so overwhelmingly real. It wasn't just Kim; it was the gun pointed at him; it was watching Timo get shot and his body crashing into the wall; it was that one moment when he really thought he was going to die.

"You're not well and obviously I can't help you," she said.

He turned his head away from her, avoiding eye contact. The tears welled up in his eyes. He didn't know what they were for. The people who were killed or for himself?

"They have professionals like Dr. Wikholm. He's good."

"They don't know," he said, "they don't understand."

"How can you say that? Nick, please try!"

He shook his head, left the bowl on the table, and shuffled like an old man to the living room.

"Nick, you have to eat," she said.

"I'm not hungry."

Everything fell silent again. An eerie, uncomfortable silence.

"Okay then," she said.

By the time she joined him, he had switched on the TV and was watching the daytime commercials. She stared at him for a moment and then left.

Behind the wheel, Isa took a moment to reflect on their relationship. Nick was the rebound after Alex and Magnus. She was annoyed it was no longer about her and at the same time shocked that she was ready to give up on him so easily. People were right, she was too shallow and impulsive to hold any decent relationship. Neither with the men in her life, nor with her own children.

Her children. The letter lay on the passenger seat next to her, the official letter from Viktor's lawyer telling her a court hearing on the adoption was scheduled. She hadn't seen her children in years. She had to decide and end it. Viktor, her ex-husband, was a good father, and his new wife would be the mother she could never be. But why hadn't she done it yet?

Magnus. Even now it was hard not to label him as the murderer of her greatest love, but she recalled he had been very clear in his opinion about the situation with her kids. Children needed a mother, and she was their mother.

Alex, sweet Alex, understood why having a mother wasn't always the best thing. Sometimes it was better not to have parents at all.

Nick had no opinion. He didn't want to take a stand. In all the conversations they'd had, he was the one who provided the new insights. When she said A, he said B. After a while, she realized he just wanted her to come to a conclusion she felt comfortable with. She didn't need anyone else to tell her what to do. She had to be convinced herself. Like Timo, he had a weird way of taking people through their emotional rollercoasters.

She tossed the letter back on the seat, put the key in the ignition and drove off.

Inside, Nick was still watching TV. Isa was gone, and only then he realized he hadn't even said goodbye to her. What if it was the last time, he would see her? What if she had an accident and died? What if there was a shooting, and she was killed? Just like Kim. Had Kim's husband said goodbye to her that morning? Had she hugged her children? Had she told them she loved them and would never leave them? Did she know it would be her last day?

As these thoughts flashed by, his heart soared, with every beat fueling the anxiety. Where was his phone? He had to call Isa. He had to say goodbye to her. His hands trembled uncontrollably.

Pow, pow.

He didn't know where the sound was coming from, but the next moment he saw every detail again, every sound, every smell. He felt everything, as if he were back in that Global Law office, hidden in the copy room behind the racks, hearing the attackers shoot his colleagues one by one.

They are coming. Pow. Pow. I'm going to die.

He rocked back and forth. Oh, God! He couldn't stop. The tears gushed down like waterfalls, his entire body trembling. Breathing was difficult, and dizziness came. With his chest bouncing vigorously up and down, gasping for air, he laid his head on the floor. When the sobbing finally stopped, he tumbled back in a soothing state of emptiness and numbness where the fog clouded his mind, where all responsibility was carried away by his mind's inability to process the information.

He dozed off, but suddenly woke up with a jolt.

Those eyes.

It was important, but now it was gone.

* * *

"How do you feel today?"

Isa had put her hands in her lap. She never knew how to behave around Dr. Wikholm, as if he monitored every body movement, every facial expression, as if he knew every thought before she knew it. The man leaned back in the black leather chair on the other side of the desk. She estimated him to be fifty, but she wasn't sure. He had told her all about his young wife and the new baby that kept him up at night.

The sessions had started a month ago. She had come to him asking how she could get her life back on track, and why she couldn't understand her own behavior. Maybe Magnus' confession had been the trigger, but after a few conversations, she began to wonder if she was there to talk about herself, but rather to learn more about Alex, her dead lover, Nick's predecessor, and the cause of all the drama in her life for the past year. Wikholm had been Alex's psychiatrist, and she knew the man in front of her wouldn't be able to talk about his former client, but, even more than before, she felt the need to talk about Alex, to keep the memory of him alive.

It was all about Magnus and Mats Norman these days and it seemed like the victims of the whole affair had just disappeared.

She had to do penance. Because of her, Magnus had become a murderer. She'd told Nick she needed professional help to deal with the guilt and the what-ifs that were haunting her mind.

"So how do you feel?" Dr. Wikholm repeated the question when the answer didn't come.

"I'm not sure how to answer that," she said.

"Try."

"Irritated."

"Why?"

She looked at her hands again. "I should probably feel something else, but I can't."

"How should you feel then?"

She dropped her shoulders. Answering questions with questions. It made her so tired. It reminded her of the conversations with Timo. Why was she sitting here if she had to answer her own questions?

"Worried, supportive. It irritates me I can't help Nick and that he even doesn't want to help himself. I don't understand."

"Tell me about Nick."

"What is there to tell?"

"How did you meet?"

She gave him a mocking grin and then said, "We had sex in the restroom of a nightclub, and then I took him home with me."

"Do you do that often? Pick up men and take them home with you."

"Jesus! I'm not here to talk about that. I'm ..."

"So, why are you here?"

"I ..."

"Hear someone say it wasn't your fault? That it's okay to continue living your life as you've done so far, without accountability, avoiding problems. Is that it?"

He had said it with an icy calm, without straining a muscle, without even taking his eyes off her. He'd said what everyone thought. The rare group of people who had dared to confront her with it, she had either banished from her life or silenced by turning the conversation to something else, like a consummate denier. Ingrid, Viktor, Magnus, they had all tried.

"I think I should be somewhere else," she said.

He lowered his eyes and sighed. "Okay then. Short session today. But I hope you think about what I said."

* * *

Timo looked at the empty cupboard behind the desk, and then ran his eyes over the dark walnut bookcase lining the entire right-hand wall. Anders Larsen, the previous superintendent, had exhibited his medals and pictures with high-ranking officials, just like most of his superiors did. When one had reached a certain level in the police organization, it was expected to impress the audience sitting on the other side of the desk with memorials of key moments in the career of the person whose office they had stepped into. How disappointing the sight of his office was. He could see it on the face of the newcomers who entered.

The office was small, but with almost nothing in it, it seemed bigger than it was. After almost six months, he still hadn't dared to give it a personal touch. Everything was uncertain. An interim position he didn't know whether he could keep, or even wanted to hold on to.

He dropped onto the chair and looked outside. That was the only interesting thing about the room. The office faced the street, often reminding him that there was more to life than the horrific cases they dealt with day in and day out. Daily life rippled on. Perhaps he had made a mistake and should have gone back to Stockholm. It wasn't too late. His assignment was to end at the end of this year. By then they should have a replacement. But why had he run for the position? No one would blame him if he went back. No one?

"Timo, the Breiner case," Isa said as she burst into the room.

"Knocking is apparently difficult for you."

She ignored his comment and sat down in the chair on the other side of the table. "You were involved in that case."

He straightened his back and said calmly, "Just for a short while, a few months. I wasn't the only one. There were others."

"Maybe you can give me more info. I can't access the files."

"I know. The case is confidential, very sensitive."

"Then tell me what you can," she said.

"Why?" he said and frowned.

"Svante Engersson mentioned him. It could be a lead. Or maybe not."

"There isn't much to say," Timo said.

"Just tell me what you know."

He sighed. "Okay then. Rune Breiner was a cop with the Stockholm police for over twenty years, but for years there were rumors that he was paid by gangs, criminals to make evidence disappear, to leak information about interventions. Organized crime. In particular for Ormar, a notorious gang of hardened criminals that operate out of Stockholm. They are difficult to stop. They use teenagers, boys as young as ten years old, as drug dealers and couriers. But they are basically into anything. Also, murder. There was never any evidence of Breiner's involvement, and he was considered harmless."

"Harmless? I wouldn't call that harmless."

"Let's say he wasn't high on the priority list, and they made sure he couldn't do a lot of harm and restricted his access to sensitive information."

"Was there nothing they could do?"

Timo shrugged. "Five years ago, on a night out in a pub, he was drunk and started bragging to some of his colleagues that he wasn't alone and that he was part of a larger network of dirty cops. At the same time, a major drug operation went horribly wrong. Fifteen officers were injured, two killed and the perpetrators disappeared with hundreds of kilos of drugs, worth millions. Internal affairs decided to start an undercover operation targeting Breiner with the ultimate goal of infiltrating the network. Breiner was eventually arrested, but no one else. The night of his death, he made a deal with the prosecutor in exchange for a reduced sentence. When he left the Global Law building together with his lawyer, he was shot, and died a few hours later in the hospital."

"I remember they claimed that Ormar was responsible," Isa said.

He sighed and shook his head, "That's what the commissioner wanted everyone to believe. In fact, we believe that not the mafia, but police officers are responsible for his death."

"Good God. People inside the police?" Isa asked.

"That's why it's so sensitive. After Breiner's death many of us were removed from the case. Nobody knows what's going on. We don't know if there are any suspects. Nothing."

Isa said, "Karst Engersson saw who shot Breiner, and that's why he needed to die."

"But why now? Why not a year ago when Breiner was murdered?"

"I don't know, Timo, but we have to find out. This is a valid lead. We may not have access to the files, but Solberg has. You need to talk to him."

"Lindström, we need to convince him first. Get me solid evidence. Links to Engersson, Breiner or anyone else I can use. And what do you think of Svante Engersson?"

"Well, it's one of those guys who despises their family's money but when the going gets tough, they run back to daddy for help."

He raised an eyebrow and said, "Oh, one of those."

She looked at him surprised, not realizing he was referring to himself, and then continued, "I don't think he's involved, not directly, but I can't rule out that his lifestyle may have been the trigger. They could have killed the father to send a message to the son."

Timo pushed the chair back and straightened. "What if this has nothing to do with Engersson at all?"

"But then what?"

He shrugged. "We have to be careful. There's too much at stake. The police are already under fire. We need to be thorough."

"Okay, I'll start with Vollan. SÄPO has released his record, but I think there's more they aren't telling us."

* * *

Ilan hadn't worn the suit in years. The last time was at his grandfather's funeral, and since then he'd put on weight, thereby straining the buttons of his jacket. The rain was pouring down, and he pulled his wife closer under the black umbrella, feeling the splash of cold water on his face and the sides of his arms. Eve had dragged him to another funeral he didn't want to go to. She had said in a harsh voice that it was his duty to pay respect to the colleagues who had died in the shooting.

Johan Bengtsson, thirty-three years old, lawyer, had been killed in the Global Law shooting. They had shared a cubicle together. He remembered how Johan had opened the red backpack every morning and had taken out the lunchbox and thermos. A scene that reminded him of the time when his father went to work. As Johan had started his computer to go through his emails, he had talked about his wife and children. Ilan had never heard anyone speak of his family in such a loving way and with so much respect. Johan had been special in his own quirky way. He hadn't cared if others found him old-fashioned or boring. He had met the sneers with a joke or a laugh.

His wife, two young children, just toddlers, were standing only a few meters away from him. He couldn't bear to look at them. If only they knew he was the man responsible for Johan's death.

Eventually, the police would figure it out. As these thoughts raced through his mind, he felt a surge of anxiety take over.

Not now. He couldn't have another panic attack. Not in front of these people. His hand, wrapped around Eve's, tightened. She gave him a scowl, and then pulled her hand from the painful grip.

He looked around. Who were all these people? He didn't recognize half of them. Some he had seen at Christmas' and New Year's parties, but many were strangers to him. He was sure more than half of them didn't even know Johan.

Half an hour ago, they had flocked together to exchange the horror stories. How Johan, hiding in the office next to the CEO's, had pleaded for his life when the attackers had invaded the place, and how they had shot the man in cold blood in front of Engersson's management assistant. She had survived, barely.

Now Ilan stood there, the cold seeping through his clothes, his feet slowly sinking into the mud. What was he doing here?

"Sorry, I have to …," he said, handed the umbrella to his wife and turned.

"Ilan?"

He walked to the exit. The icy rain came down so hard it felt like tiny needles. His head, his face, his hands, everywhere. He deserved it. He deserved it all. He had to be punished for what he had done. He should have gone to the police after Marie's accident. He should have told them about Frank's murder, about the threatening phone calls, about the voice. He turned to look at the group of people in the distance, mourning their loved ones, wondering why this had happened.

He sighed. His ears felt like they were about to fall off. His hands were cramped, and his legs were so sore he could barely move. But he deserved it. He deserved it all.

* * *

"Inspector Karlsson," Mila turned when she saw the inspector enter the lab.

Berger wasn't sure, but he saw a sparkle of cheerfulness in her eyes as he approached. A few weeks ago, he'd met Dr. Olsson's new assistant, Mila, and that same week he had stopped by more times than he should have. There was something about her. A certain joy and positivity that almost seemed out of place in a setting where people had to deal with death every day. She was petite, a head shorter than him, and he was afraid she would fall apart if he touched her. But her attitude demanded respect. She was an ambitious woman. He appreciated that. Like him, she felt a constant urge to prove herself, to show she was better than the rest.

He was ambitious too. He would show the Isa Lindströms of this world he had potential. Isa had always questioned his abilities. But who was she to judge? She had made so many mistakes herself.

Magnus Wieland. Did he really kill Alexander Nordin? Had Isa been involved? It was all swept under the carpet. No one on the team had said anything, but everyone thought it. Everyone questioned her integrity. So why did Timo keep her on the team? Why was she even his right hand?

She had repeatedly shown she couldn't be trusted to do her job with integrity and professionalism. Why hadn't Timo asked him to take over? He was senior enough. And now he got landed with this irrelevant case. What had he done wrong? The only good thing about it was that he could spend more time with Mila.

"Inspector Paikkala told me you needed my help?" he said.

"Yes. The burnt body. Any progress in identifying the victim?"

"No, not really," he admitted, "with the shooting, I've had little time to look into this, but I've checked the missing persons reports."

"The shooting? Everyone is busy with the shooting. There are other cases that need attention. This could be your chance to solve a case on your own."

She gave him a friendly smile.

"I doubt it. The shooting is high-profile and SÄPO is finally willing to work with us, so I can't spend all my time ...," he answered.

"Oh, Mr. Karlsson is only interested in high-profile cases," she said.

"No, but ..."

"It's fine. What have you discovered so far?"

Her medium-length, straight hair fluttered over her shoulders and neck, and for a moment it caught his eye. Even irritated, she was so beautiful.

"There are a few people from the missing persons reports who might qualify," he replied, handing her the file.

"Okay, let's see," she said.

She pushed the table with a corpse aside and sat down at the desk next to it. As she flipped through the document, he kept looking at the other tables, some empty, others covered with a white sheet that no doubt contained a dead body. He only wished she'd chosen a place other than the morgue to discuss the case.

One of the dieners, spraying the metal dissection table with water, gave him a quick, indifferent look and then moved on to the next task: inspection of the medical tools on the side table.

Mila said, "The weight of the man is about eighty kilos and estimated height is 1.80m, and he's probably not older than thirty. So, we can already rule out these."

She put the papers aside and flipped through the other documents.

"These six remain. We have DNA and dental records, but we need to compare them to something. So, we should ask relatives if they want to provide DNA samples."

"Anything else?"

"We have pieces of the clothing that were embedded in the flesh. Jeans, a blue shirt, and white sneakers. Maybe that helps to identify him."

"Okay, I'm on it. You can help me if you want."

"Uh, I'd rather not. I'm better with dead bodies than with people."

"No problem. I'll keep you posted on the progress. Anything else I can help you with?"

"Yes," she said, got up and signaled him to come closer.

"I had a really great time the other day," she whispered, trying to keep her voice low.

"I was wondering ...," she continued.

"If we could do it again," he said and smiled.

"Yes," she said and took his hand.

"I'd love to."

They had gone on a first date a few days earlier. It had been a pleasant, uncomplicated evening. After all the commotion at work, the stressful situation with SÄPO, the overtime, Timo's constant pressure on the team to get results, the night out was a welcome distraction. A beautiful woman in front of him, a tasty pizza in a cozy restaurant in the middle of the city. What more could he want?

There was a click. They had both felt it. His last relationship was two years ago. A nasty breakup involving one of his best friends. And there had been casual flings, nothing worthwhile. He longed for a stable relationship with the right woman. And Mila could be the one.

"Friday night, 8:00 p.m.?"

"Absolutely," he said, gave her a wink and walked away.

* * *

"Why did you run away?"

Eve put the coat on the rack and joined her husband in the living room. He had left a trail of dirty footprints in the hallway and living room. She heaved a sigh of frustration when she found him on the couch, soaked, still trembling, pale and exhausted. All he could give her was an indifferent shrug.

"These are your colleagues. You know ... you knew them. You've worked with them, talked to them, shared laughs, and personal talks. It's difficult, I know. It's only natural that ..."

"I don't know them," Ilan said in a shaky voice.

"Ilan ..."

She sat down next to him and took his hand. "Jesus! You're all wet. Why are you still sitting here? Change your clothes."

"Eve ..."

"What's wrong?"

For a brief, almost indefinable moment, he wanted to tell her everything, but he couldn't. He stared at her with a weird expression on his face, unable to explain why he'd run away, why he'd been so distant and cold these days. Unable to voice his thoughts and feelings.

"What's wrong with you? These last few months you've been ... different. Is it the accident? And now, the shooting?"

"Probably," he said.

"Would you like to talk to a professional if you can't talk to me?"

"I'll figure it out," he said and walked to the hallway, while saying, "I'll take a shower."

He put the wet clothes in the basket next to the washing machine and ran up the stairs.

The hot shower thawed his frozen limbs. He let the warm water run down his chest to his legs. So comforting.

"Ilan, I'm going to the store. I'll be back in thirty minutes. You need something?"

When he didn't answer, he heard the front door open and close again. As the water hit his face, he thought about his relationship. Eve felt left out, helpless, dealing with a husband who was falling apart before her eyes. But he was disappointed. When they first got married, she never passed up an opportunity to join him in the shower, and he so needed her arms around him. Now she just ran away. It had been ages since they had made love. He couldn't remember the last time. But maybe it was him. He wasn't great company these days. And it wasn't just the accident. It had started long before that. Months before. He didn't dare to confront her, but he knew she was having an affair. With glamor boy, Nick Petrini, his colleague. He had followed her once and seen her check into a hotel with Nick. He should have confronted her, but he couldn't. Maybe he didn't want to. What was wrong with him? What husband wouldn't want to fight for his wife? But he could never match Nick's good looks and success, and probably she was better off with her lover.

The water grew cold, and he turned the tap wide open. It was too hot now. The heat of the water took his breath away. It was about to burn his skin.

He deserved it; he deserved it.

Those three words were still haunting him.

The ringing of his phone, lying on the bathroom sink, startled him. He let it ring. It stopped but started again after a few seconds. Who could it be? Then a beep he had received a text message. What was so urgent?

He turned off the water and stepped out of the shower, almost slipping on the pool of water.

He froze as he read the message on the display.

"Pick up the phone! Don't play games!"

His blackmailer hadn't contacted him in weeks. Now he knew why. Global Law had been the target.

The phone nearly fell to the floor as the ringing resumed and with his finger hovering over the accept button, he couldn't decide to answer the call or let it go.

He let it go.

A second beep. The message contained a link. When he opened it, he saw a photo of Eve's car in front of their house. Another text message said, "I can get to her anywhere, anytime."

"Shit," he said, and his hand started trembling again.

The phone rang a fourth time. This time he answered.

The metallic voice, twisted by the changer, made his hair stand on end. After all this time, he still wasn't used to hearing it. "You're hard to reach, but I see I've got your attention."

"What do you want?" Ilan said.

"Well, let's not get ahead of ourselves here. What do you think of my masterpiece?"

"Masterpiece? The shooting? Ten people were killed!"

"Ilan, Ilan, don't put it so dramatically. But you're right. It's my best work to date."

"You've done this before? But why?"

"Because I can. And you helped me. I couldn't have done it without you."

Tears welled up in his eyes. The deep sadness he had left in the shower took hold of him again. He didn't understand. If it had been a noble act, if there had been a reason, money, power, love, he might have made sense of it. Even then, it was hard to understand, but now it seemed so meaningless.

"No, no ... I didn't!"

"Oh, come on, Ilan. You were instrumental to the success of this project. I congratulate you."

"No, no, no!"

"How does it feel? Knowing that ten people died because of you. Exhilarating, isn't it?"

Ilan threw the phone against the wall. His body trembled uncontrollably as he stared at the pieces of a life that was slipping through his fingers. He had never felt such a coldness before.

Nobody could help him. No one.

* * *

The connection dropped. The figure, dressed in black, face partially covered by the hood of the sweater, placed the phone on the passenger seat.

Ilan Bergman wouldn't last much longer. A sadistic grin played on the lips. The plan had been set in motion, and it went well.

What came next would take courage. Everything was planned so carefully. Down to the smallest detail. The first time, there was hesitation, doubt. This time it was different, something to look forward to. Energizing. It brought back the anger and the need to hurt.

To hurt. To kill. To torture.

The figure turned to the open window of the terraced house. A woman was feeding her children. She laughed and motioned them to sit down as she fetched the steaming cooking pot and put it on the table. Her husband gave them the cutlery.

She led an ordinary life, and she was content.

But the happiness was fleeting she would soon learn. Little did she know that in the car parked across the street, hidden in the darkness of the evening, horror lurked. In the safety of her own neighborhood where nothing ever happened, a killer was watching her.

CHAPTER

6

"**MAYBE WE SHOULD TAKE A BREAK?**", Ingrid said. Her right shoulder was already hurting. She wasn't a tall woman, and it was a chore to reach the upper parts of the wall, even with the roller. The handle felt heavy and was difficult to use. The muscles of her body would pay the price tomorrow. Why had she bragged she was a professional?

They had been working for the past two hours. The smell of the paint had triggered a headache. Fresh air wouldn't be bad. She took a step back and examined the result. Somehow, it didn't seem right.

"Do you think this is a suitable color? Looks a bit pink."

And pink wasn't Timo's color.

Then she looked at the wall on the other side Timo was painting, and she was disappointed. How could he be further than her, with the bruises and contused ribs? Fair enough, it was his left side. His right arm worked fine. He turned and burst out laughing.

"What?" Ingrid said, surprised.

"Olsson, the idea is to paint the wall, not your face," Timo said.

He pointed to his own forehead and cheek to show her where the problem areas were. Then she ran the back of her hand across her forehead, spreading it even more, and the wet paint ended up in her hair and eyebrows.

His smile deepened as he watched the entire scene. Her hands were trembling as she moved them across her face.

She sighed and said, "I made it worse, didn't I?"

He nodded and kept the smile on his face. She had never seen him so relaxed and cheerful. Timo Paikkala was the most serious and gloomy man she knew. He had a dark sense of humor, which he typically used to make a point, correct people, make them feel small, but at times, he was the guy you'd tell your most embarrassing secret to, and he listened without judgment. It was refreshing to see another part of him he usually kept hidden from everyone.

"Wait, let me help you," he said, turned and picked up a cloth from the floor.

"It's clean," he said, moving closer and taking her face in his hands. She was amazed at how soft his hands were as his fingers ran over the skin of her face. Goosebumps. Disturbing little signs of euphoria.

He moved the cloth over her forehead and then went to her right cheek, without looking at her, fully concentrated on the job.

"It's not too bad, I removed most of it," he whispered. "The bathroom is downstairs. I'll get us a drink while you freshen up."

"Okay," she let out.

These tantalizing moments confused her. It made her even angry. Why did he let it happen and then cut it off so abruptly?

Maybe he was the sensible one. Or maybe he didn't know what to do with those feelings either? She had told him months ago they could only be friends and colleagues, and he'd accepted it without too much fuss. Secretly she had expected drama, his confession of love. That he couldn't live without her. Silly aspirations. She wasn't a love-struck teenager. She was better than that. Grown-up, responsible.

"Watch out. I use the bathroom for storage. Don't trip over any boxes," she heard him yell as he descended the stairs.

She took a few breaths. Why had she come? She had promised to send Anton. But that Saturday afternoon she had stood at the front door of Timo's ramshackle house and told him Anton had been too distraught to help. It had been a lie. The funerals of the last days had demanded a lot from her husband, but not to the extent he would have been reluctant to do some physical work that distracted him from the drama. She had never asked Anton.

She walked down the wooden stairs to the bathroom. Timo was right. The bathroom looked like a mess with dozens of randomly placed boxes, in the bathtub, shower, on the toilet lid, as if he had thrown them in the room. If he had stacked them a little better, it could have been more efficient, and he could have stored more stuff.

She could barely reach the sink. The mirror had a large crack on the left side that ran through her field of vision. She tried to remove the residues from her face. The box at her feet was annoying, almost making her trip. As she bent over to pick up the half-opened box, she saw a framed picture lying on top. She took it out. Through the thin layer of dust, she saw the features of a young woman, long brown curly hair, amazing green eyes. The woman looked a bit like her, but she was slimmer, more beautiful, and had a look full of ambition and determination. She couldn't take her eyes off it.

"Are you ..." Timo was standing in the doorway, and she jumped up, the photograph still in her hand. "... okay?"

He stared at it for a moment.

"I'm sorry ... I shouldn't have," she stammered.

He said nothing. She couldn't fathom what he was thinking. The expression was neutral, not happy, not sad, or angry. He reached out, took the photo from her hand, and brushed the dust from the glass frame.

"It's her, isn't it?"

"Caijsa," he mumbled and returned to the living room.

She stepped over the box and followed him.

"She's beautiful," she said, and looked at him. "Have you been together for a long time?"

"I knew her since high school, but we became a couple only years later. She was a few years older. She gave my brother and me extra language lessons after hours when our family returned to Sweden. We became friends and then ..."

"You must have loved her very much."

"She was my first love," he whispered.

"How did she die?"

His voice broke. "Ingrid, I can't ... not yet."

"I'm sorry, I shouldn't have," she said, took the photo from his hands, went to the bathroom, and put it back in the box.

So stupid. Why did she have to pick up that picture? It was none of her business. The relaxed vibe was gone, and she had to fix it. Quickly.

"What's this?" she said.

She came back with two more unframed photos. They were in the same box under Caijsa's picture.

"What?" he said and took the pictures she gave him.

A smile appeared on his face. The first photo showed Timo, dressed in a race driver's outfit, leaning against a shiny red car.

"Mmm ... some of my old digressions," he laughed.

"You raced? Seriously?"

"I did. This was taken five years ago. We came in second. The only time we won anything."

"We?"

"George and I. George is one of my best friends, actually one of my father's old friends. He took care of me when ... well, when Caijsa died. George lost his son in a car accident years earlier. He knows what it's like to lose someone you love. These days I see him a lot less, but whenever I need him, he's there."

"And this one?"

"The Kilimanjaro in Tanzania," he said, smiling at the admiring glances she gave him.

"It's nothing special, it took me seven days to get up there," he laughed.

"It would take me forever, I guess," she said. "Are you still racing?"

"No, but I'm still climbing. Mostly indoors. In the summer, I occasionally go climbing around Stockholm and Vastervik. But no big excursions anymore. Maybe one day."

She put the photos on the counter.

"And what do you do?" he asked.

"What do you mean?" she said, surprised.

"What do you do if you're not a doctor, a forensic specialist, a mom, and a wife? What are your hobbies?"

"Hobbies? I don't have any. The boys take up so much of my time and at work ... well, the boss is demanding," she said.

"I'm not your boss, remember."

"But you are demanding."

"I'll take you climbing."

She frowned and said, "I'm not sure that's for me."

"Why not? You'll like it."

"Sports and I, we don't go well together," she added.

"So, what did you do when you were younger?"

She looked down, ashamed of what she was about to say.

"Ballet, I did ballet until I was twelve."

"Why did you stop?"

There was not the slightest sign of contempt or disregard on his face.

"Well, look at me, I couldn't compete with those skinny, graceful girls. They were more elegant and beautiful than me."

"But were they better?"

"I ... I don't know," she said.

"Are you still interested?"

"What do you mean? Yes, I like ballet performances. I like art in general. Musicals, plays, opera, but I haven't been to many shows in recent years."

"Why not?"

So many questions. She had forgotten how tiring he could be.

"Well, the boys and Anton. He's not really into ballet. It's not that he refuses to go, but when I drag him along, I see he's bored, uninterested, constantly watching his phone. Once, halfway through the performance, he fell asleep. I had to wake him up when he started snoring. I love that he's making the effort, but I feel guilty most of the time and it shouldn't be that way."

"Okay, let's agree on the following: I'm going climbing with you, and you can take me to a ballet or opera, and I promise I won't snore."

She laughed. "Are you sure?"

"Yes, I am. Oh, damn, the coffee!"

He ran to the kitchen, at least what was supposed to be the kitchen, and returned with two cups and put one on the counter in front of her.

"I stopped drinking coffee a long time ago," she said and smiled.

"Really? Why?"

They'd had this conversation before and no matter what arguments she brought it was impossible for him to understand why people wouldn't drink coffee.

"Because I don't want to end up being an addict," she said with a straight face.

"Do you want something else?"

"Water would be nice, unless you can bring yourself to making tea."

He smiled. "Water it is, and two cups of coffee for me."

"Timo, you shouldn't drink so much coffee." She watched him drink both cups, one after the other, without a pause.

"I've gotten used to it by now," he said.

He waited a few seconds and then asked again, "So, yes or no, will you go climbing with me?"

"Okay, okay, just let me know when," Ingrid said.

"Perfect. Now, let's paint some more."

They went up the stairs. He stopped at the entrance of the bedroom.

"You're right, this is too pink," he said.

* * *

Isa wandered around the room. The apartment was small and old, built in the seventies, simple, uninventive, downright ugly. Grand architecture and the seventies rarely went together. There wasn't much furniture, and what was there looked about to fall apart. In the living room, a frayed sofa against the wall, a wooden coffee table with dried food stains in front of it, and in the kitchen, she noticed a gray metal table and chair. With her gloved hands, she picked up the papers as she passed by the only desk in the room and put them back. Nothing special. SÄPO had already swept the apartment.

She sighed. "Why didn't SÄPO take all this stuff with them?"

Lars shrugged. "Probably not that important."

"And what exactly are we looking for?" she said.

Lars glanced over the books on the shelf, turned and said, "I don't know, but Timo said we should be thorough."

"I think our boss feels a bit threatened by the SÄPO colleagues," she grinned.

"Colleagues? Those idiots think they know best. They so-called want to work with us. Really?! They don't let us in on anything. Timo is right. We should do our own research. I don't think theirs is going in the right direction."

"Oh, does Timo think that?" she said. If she hadn't insisted on widening the investigation, Timo would never have considered anything other than a terrorist attack. Or maybe not? She had often underestimated her boss.

"Right. And that's why we are checking Vollan's apartment again?"

"Yes, grumpy," Lars said and turned his head away from her.

From the moment she had stepped through the door that Monday morning, she had complained and questioned everything to the extent Timo had grown tired of her whining, and he had sent her to Nils Vollan's apartment with Lars.

"So, what do you think about Berger and Mila?" she said casually.

"What about them?"

"I saw them last Friday at the Indian restaurant in Bomhus. They were having a good time ... really good time."

"What were you doing there?"

She frowned. "None of your business. So, Berger and Mila, what do you think?" she said, pushing the couch a few centimeters from the wall.

Lars shrugged. "Why don't you ask him?"

"Berger and I, bonding? Don't think so." She threw another glance at the living room and then sighed.

"SÄPO didn't find much and neither did we," she said, and headed to the bedroom.

The room was so small she could barely walk around the bed. There was no closet, just a wooden bed, covered with a thin white sheet.

"That's kind of the problem," Lars said, standing in the doorway. "They found no laptop, no phone. Hell, not a single sheet of paper with anything useful! Only one empty USB stick in the kitchen bin."

"He hid it."

"Probably."

"Do we know who he's been in contact with over the past weeks?" Isa said and knelt, wriggling herself between the wall and the edge of the bed to look underneath.

"Don't bother. SÄPO likely has already checked that."

She got up and walked back to the door where Lars was standing.

"I don't think we'll find anything," he said.

"It's all too neat, too clean, too staged," she said. "He knew he wasn't coming back."

"Or someone else cleaned up," Lars said.

She went back to the living room, partly kitchen. The trash can, standing on the ground next to the sink, was still full.

"Really? Why didn't SÄPO check the trash?"

"You like going through garbage?" Lars asked. "They did. That's where they found the USB stick."

"Yes, a USB stick and I guess that was the focus of their attention, but they overlooked a few things," she said, pulling out some receipts. "Like why Vollan went to the same store several times a day to buy the same thing: milk. He must have loved milk."

"Let me see." Lars took the scraps of paper from her hand and studied them.

"It's just around the corner," he remarked.

"Let's buy some milk then," Isa said and smiled.

* * *

A few minutes later, they were standing in front of a shabby-looking store, wedged between two modern, and recently renovated taller buildings that looked almost mockingly down on the little shop. The sign above the store had faded and there was a thick layer of dust and dirt on the window. It was closed, but through the glass Isa saw the dim light from the refrigerators in the back. The counter was barely visible through the stack of boxes and bins pushed against the window. The shop looked like it hadn't been used for ages. Yet Nils Vollan had been here a few weeks ago.

"It's closed," Lars said, shuffling back and forth in front of the store.

"Are you sure?" Isa said with a mischievous smile.

"Isa, don't do anything rash," Lars yelled. "If you screw up this investigation, you're done."

"Really?"

"Let our good friends take the lead," he said.

"And then we'll have to explain to them why we were in Vollan's apartment," she added.

"Okay, fine," he sighed and pushed against the door.

The door fell open.

"One problem less," Isa smiled, took the gun from the holster, and stepped inside. The hallway was narrow with a door on the left that led to the shop and a flight of stairs to the floor above.

"Anybody home? Police!" Lars yelled and followed her up the stairs.

With the gun pointed in front of her, she slammed the door at the top open.

They were now standing in an open space. Rays of sunlight streamed through the street-facing windows, partially covered with shutters. In the center of the room was a large metal table with remnants of electric wires, a solder bolt, and printed circuit boards.

"What were they doing here?" Lars whispered.

"Something other than preparing for a mass shooting," Isa said.

"Jesus ... SÄPO is right. It's a terrorist attack."

Isa said nothing as she walked around and scanned the rest of the room. In a bin, on the floor next to the table, she found the burnt remains of a laptop.

"We need to call it in," Lars said, looking at her for confirmation.

"I guess so," she said.

* * *

"We found traces of explosives in the room," Kristoffer said, and threw the file on the ultra-clean desk in Timo's office.

"Fingerprints?"

"Few. Mostly Vollan's."

"And the laptop?" Isa asked.

Kristoffer gave her a snobbish look and said, "It will be sent to our lab in Stockholm. Our IT guys will handle it. We have the best experts."

"I'm sure," she let out.

Timo frowned and signaled her to calm down.

"Why were you there anyway?" Kristoffer snapped.

"At my request," Timo interrupted and as Kristoffer turned his attention to the man on the other side of the table, inspector Paikkala continued, "in the end, it wasn't a bad idea, you got more information, didn't you?"

"I'm still in charge of this investigation. I just tolerate you and your team, but I don't necessarily need you. From now on, you discuss this with me first."

Kristoffer got up, a look of annoyance on his face, and on his way toward the door gave Isa, still leaning against the wall, another belittling grin and slammed the door shut as he walked out.

"Idiot," Isa whispered.

"You should have called SÄPO when you discovered the store and let them handle it."

"Timo, you asked us to go there," Isa raised her voice.

"I know, but we have to be careful … you have to be careful," he admitted. He didn't dare to look at her. She was already in a foul mood, and this would spark another surge of anger and resentment, but oddly enough she stayed calm and asked, "He's going after me?"

"Well, he's not your friend," Timo said, sat down and pulled the papers, Kristoffer had left on the desk, toward him.

"Are you?"

"What?" he looked up and stared at her in disbelief. "I could have suspended you a trillion times, but I didn't."

"A trillion times," she laughed, and then her face turned serious as she looked at him. "Solberg knew we would go to the apartment."

"Why do you think that?"

"They took the USB from the trash but left the receipts. Come on. I have no high opinion about SÄPO, but this is amateurish. They knew we would find them."

"But why would they do this?"

"To make us believe it's a terrorist attack, to derail us, to discredit us. He doesn't want us on this case."

"I don't think this was staged," Timo said. "This is real, Lindström. NTC raised the terror threat level yesterday to level four. The probability of a terrorist attack is high. We need to help them, not obstruct the investigation."

She looked at the floor.

"What's wrong?" he said. "There is more. Get it off your chest."

She shrugged. Her expression became murky. "Do you know anything about Sandviken?"

"No," he said quietly, "just that they are going to reopen the case."

She shook her head gently, as if she had to convince herself.

"But Isa, there is something else."

"What more can there be?"

"Magnus ..."

"Don't mention that name," she said in a stern voice. "I told you before, I'm not ready to deal with him."

"You'll have to," he said, "he claims you put him up to it."

Without saying a word, she got up and ran out of the office, leaving a surprised Timo behind.

Magnus. He had ripped out all those memories, those great memories of them together. Now she could no longer see him as something good that had happened in her life. He evoked a feeling of repulsion that turned her stomach and she wanted to throw up every part that had ever longed for that man. It was unfair to Alex. Betrayal and bitterness. After the dramatic confession in Timo's office, where Magnus had held a gun to her boss' head and had threatened to kill him because in Magnus' delusional mind, she and Timo had been a couple, she had burnt every piece of clothing he had ever touched, every reminder of their time together, every photograph, every letter, every recording. He no longer existed; he had never existed. But now he wanted to wrench his way back into her life. Because that was what it was. A cry for attention. Her attention.

***

Pauli Nyström looked at the paper. One word. 'YOU' was printed at the top of the page. Months ago, the envelope had been shoved under the door of his apartment. Assuming it was yet another reminder to pay the rent and electricity, the envelope had been sitting on the kitchen counter for most of the day, until in the evening, after a long day of doing nothing useful besides drinking and hanging out with his friends, it had caught his attention again. Now, for the same inexplicable reason, he had taken it out of the drawer. Was it because of the Global Law murders? Was it because his brother was missing after receiving the letter? Or was it ... He looked at the newspaper, lying on the desk next to the letter, and picked it up. In bold capital letters it read, "Death and despair in Gävle."

He knew people at Global Law, and he knew family of friends at Global Law. Old friends. People he wanted to forget, people who weren't worthy of his grief and concern. But it wasn't Global Law he was thinking about. The photo showed the entrance hall of the building where paramedics with stretchers carried the injured to the ambulances, bodies covered with sheets, and police officers. He'd been staring at one man in the article. It couldn't be. He stared at the photo again. It was him. How was this all connected? He didn't see it. But he knew it couldn't be a coincidence.

YOU. Was this a warning? Someone knew, but how? And was it him? He had to disappear.

On the display, he saw at least ten messages from his father, left throughout the day. His dad. An old, senile man who loved money more than his sons. His dad had probably gotten hold of his phone again. He loved nothing more than to terrorize his eldest son with endless calls. Until the people in the nursing home would find out and take the phone away. Did his father even realize what he was doing?

The last months Pauli had seen him more than what was good for him. After his brother's disappearance, his father had looked at him with increasing suspicion. His brother was an average guy who lived an unremarkable life, unlike him, the black sheep of the family. The dropout, the good-for-nothing. His father was quick to conclude that Pauli had something to do with his brother's disappearance, but he hadn't.

He folded the letter and put it back in the envelope.

He had to disappear, even if it was for a short while until everything calmed down.

CHAPTER

7

WHERE AM I? *What is this smell?*

She could barely keep her eyes open. Everything was blurry. Why couldn't she focus? It was so dark, and breathing was hard. Her neck hurt. Was she on the floor? No, it was a chair. She closed her eyes again, finding it difficult to keep them open. It made her dizzy, and her head fell to her chest.

How did she get here? She tried to remember what she had done before. What was the last thing she recalled? The children had left for school, and Gert ... No, Gert was on a business trip. He wouldn't return until today. What day was it anyway? Was it evening already? Night? The scent. The area smelled of something old, oily, musty. A garage? An old warehouse? A factory hall?

There was something in her mouth. A gag. Now she knew why she had such a difficulty breathing and why she felt like she was about to throw up.

Her hands. They were tied behind her back with some sort of tape. She tried to free them but couldn't. If she'd push it too far, her arm would pop out of the socket.

Her legs were free, but useless. She was stuck to the chair, unable to move the upper part of her body.

And then the panic came.

Oh, God, what is happening? This isn't good.

She could only hear her frantic moans. But she wasn't alone. She could feel his presence. She just didn't know where he was.

Her eyes were now accustomed to the darkness. But it wasn't completely dark. There was a dim light casting a shadow on the wall in front of her. It was her, in the chair, desperately trying to break free. She turned her head, but the position she was in didn't give her enough wiggle room to explore the entire space. He had made sure of that. It was a game now. A game she wouldn't survive.

Oh, my God!

On the wall the outline of a slender figure was drawn, the head covered with a hood. For a moment, the figure stood still, making sure she understood the situation and was aware of what was coming.

No, please! Please!

"Let's get started," the voice said.

And before she had recovered from the shock of hearing the voice, she felt the rope being thrown around her neck and starting to scratch the skin of her throat.

* * *

"Have you heard anything about the laptop?" Isa asked as she passed by Lars' desk.

He jumped up. She had taken him by surprise as he was playing with his pen, occasionally staring at the screen of his computer, caught in a daydream. She pushed aside a stack of papers, which lay dangerously close to the edge of the desk, and sat down, facing him.

"Uh, well, it was too damaged to get anything useful out of it," he said, "at least that's what SÄPO told us."

"Their so-called great experts would fix it," she let out a sigh of sharp sarcasm. "Kristoffer Solberg and his bunch of arrogant helpers."

"Or maybe they've known all along what was on that laptop," Lars said.

"Why do you say that?"

"SÄPO conducted a neighborhood survey after the raid on Vollan's flat and several witnesses told them Vollan frequented the store, which is why the place was high on their priority list to investigate."

"But they didn't do a search?" Isa asked.

"No, we were too fast. The search warrant was still pending."

"I thought SÄPO has carte blanche, especially in times of terrorist threat?"

Lars shrugged and said, "So to come back to the laptop: maybe we should have a look at it anyway?"

"I agree, and I know just the right person to do this," she said with an arrogant smile on her face.

"Are you thinking of Sivert from IT?"

"Good God, no! The guy is good but not brilliant ... and arrogant on top of that. I wouldn't be surprised if they'd fire him one of these days for sexual harassment."

He frowned. "So, what are you up to then?"

Usually this meant she had something in mind he'd better not know.

"Nothing illegal or against the rules," she said, "but I need the laptop."

"But ..."

"Again, don't worry, I'll do everything nicely by the book, as the boss wants."

"I am not too worried about Timo," he started, "but have you read the newspapers recently?"

He took a piece of scrap paper from the bin and held it in front of her. She looked at him a little surprised. He was conservative for a guy in his late twenties, and many a colleague had wondered at times if he was a digital illiterate. Who still read newspapers these days? But he thought nothing could replace the smell of the print and the cheap ink on his fingers next to a cup of steamy black coffee in the morning.

Scent and memory. It reminded him of his dad when he had still been this vibrant man, not the shell of the man he was right now, fading away in a nursing home as one of the youngest Alzheimer patients on the ward. It reminded him of the time his dad had bought him a typesetting kit for his birthday, and he had used it to print the monthly family newsletter. Scent and sweet memories.

"I've seen the articles," she said with a straight face.

"And?"

"What am I supposed to say? Why do I have to answer for it? This is all Magnus' doing, not mine. I don't take any responsibility for what he's done."

"I'm just saying, please don't do anything to make it worse."

"As if I haven't heard this from, well, let's say dozens of people over the past days," she said angrily and stood up. "I'm fed up with it!"

"Maybe there's a reason people give you this advice," he said.

Without a word, she turned and stepped away from the desk. Direction didn't matter. As always, she wanted to make a dramatic exit. Sometimes she could sulk like a little child, he thought.

Then he sighed and ran after her.

"Isa, stop," he said when he caught up with her, "I didn't mean it."

She turned, bowed her head, and looked at her feet.

Yes, a little sulking child.

She said, "It's okay, but with everything that's happened: the shooting, Nick, Magnus ... it's sometimes too much."

"So, we're good?" he said.

She nodded and turned to leave him, but he took her arm.

"Isa?"

"Yes, something else?"

"You were right about Berger and Mila. What do you think of her?"

"Mila?"

He nodded.

"Well, nothing special," she said surprised. "She seems nice. Why?"

He raised his shoulders.

"Oh, did she let you down?" she laughed.

"Just leave it."

It was his turn to feel offended.

But yes, Mila had let him down. They had gone out a few times. Both dates had been fun, but the fact she hadn't called since that last rendezvous didn't bother him, nor the fact he hadn't felt a click, no attraction. But what had been on his mind for the past week was why she had suddenly shown up in the forensics lab. She'd never told him she was a forensic anthropologist or that she was applying for a job in the lab. He realized how much he had told her and how little he knew about her.

He couldn't put a finger on it, but she was pushy, overly interested, and clingy. And now, Berger. He had seen them together a few times, flirting. She seemed so innocent, kind, but in the back of his mind there was a lingering feeling something was wrong. Was he paranoid? Was he the only one who felt it?

Berger didn't know Mila was the woman he'd been talking about months ago. And Mila obviously hadn't told Berger. There was nothing to talk about anyway. Maybe he should just tell his friend. But how could he tell him about the vague suspicions, totally unsupported by any tangible evidence, without sounding like a jealous ex-boyfriend?

This was all in his head. There was nothing to worry about.

"Lars, Lindström," Timo's voice sounded through the open door of the office they had passed.

"Yes, boss," Isa said and trudged into his office where also Lars joined her.

"Ilan Bergman," Timo said. "We need to pay the man another visit."

"Why?"

Timo put the file on the desk in front of them. "His name has popped up in the Global Law shooting."

* * *

Mrs. Bergman didn't quite know how to behave. In the ten minutes that Isa and Lars had been there, she had asked twice if the inspectors wanted a cup of coffee. And each time they had politely declined.

Her husband Ilan was nervous and shuffled back and forth on the kitchen chair at the black metal table that seemed to take up a proportionally large amount of space in the small room.

"Look, if this is about the Harket case, I'd rather have my lawyer present," he said immediately.

Ignoring his comment, Isa said, "You work at Global Law?"

"Yes." He looked her straight in the eye and in that one second, she saw fear, so much fear.

"You weren't there when the shooting took place. On holiday? That was very convenient and lucky for you."

"As I'm still a suspect in the Harket case, I have been advised not to show up in the office for a while until the case is cleared up. Unpaid leave."

His wife Eve took his hand when she saw how difficult it was for him to get the words out.

"I have nothing to do with that case," he continued.

"Which case? Harket or the Global Law shooting?"

"Shooting? No, of course not. Why? Am I a suspect there too?"

"The attackers had the code to get into the offices. And the badge for the stairwell and emergency exits."

"And?"

"The badge that was used was modified," Lars said, "but it was a deactivated badge that you reported lost."

Ilan jumped up. "So? It was lost. I don't know when or where I lost it. Anyone could have taken it and used it."

Isa never let her eyes slip from his face as he said it. Fear. So much fear. This man knew more than he was saying.

"Where were you during the shooting?"

"Oh, come on. Here at home. Why would I take a card that I've used and put the suspicion on myself?"

"This is a card with a lot more access privileges than most employees are entitled to. Why do you have this card anyway? Only a limited number of people have the privilege to enter the building via these alternative routes. We learned they are not only used for the emergency exits but they open the secured doors to the other buildings of the business center, and the Tech4You building."

"I have never been in the Tech4You building, but I've used the emergency exits a lot. Occasionally I must escort certain ... high-profile clients into the building. Clients who prefer not to be seen."

"Clients like Rune Breiner?"

99

"I don't know who that is," Ilan said and looked at his hands on the table. His fingers gripped Eve's hand so tightly he thought he would crush it.

"Strange. It was you who received him over a year ago when he was here to consult his lawyer Karst Engersson and the team you were part of. And it was you who set up the fatal meeting in Stockholm where Breiner got shot."

"I was part of the team, but what does this have to do with the shooting?"

"Do you know a Nils Vollan?"

Ilan shook his head. "No, who is that?"

"One of the attackers," Lars said and showed a picture of the man's head.

"I don't know him," Ilan said.

"Okay, Mr. Bergman, that's all for now, but I won't make any travel plans if I were you. We'll be back."

Isa stood up, followed by Lars, leaving Ilan Bergman at the kitchen table with his head down.

For a moment, Isa felt a sense of pity and sadness come over her as she saw the man looking up at her, as if he was stuck, caught in a bad dream. He wanted to get out but couldn't, almost pleading for help.

As they walked through the hallway to the front door, Isa suddenly heard hasty footsteps behind her.

"Inspector," she heard a soft voice say.

When she turned, she saw Mrs. Bergman looking at her. For a moment, she reminded her of Mila Hillborg. Small, thin, but with a pretty face with big dark eyes, almost like those porcelain dolls, flawless. She didn't even look twenty.

"What is it?"

"Can I talk to you privately for a moment?" Eve said and gave Lars a quick glance he understood, and he stepped outside.

"So, how can I help you, Mrs. Bergman?"

"How's ... Nick?" she said and quickly looked at the kitchen door.

Isa frowned. "Nick? Nick Petrini?"

"I knew him ... a while back."

She vaguely remembered Nick talking about his affair with Eve Bergman, but she hadn't realized it had been anything serious. At least not in Nick's mind, but Eve seemed genuinely concerned.

"He's okay. Shocked of course, and it'll take some time to process the trauma, but luckily, he survived."

"Yes," Eve said. "It must be terrible to realize it could all have been over in a few seconds. He called a few days ago."

"He called? Why?"

"He just wanted to know if Ilan was okay. I had some time to talk to him, but not a lot. He sounded okay, but you never know, of course."

"I suppose," Isa said.

Then the young woman smiled and said, "Anyway, send him my regards and good recovery."

"I ... will," Isa said, somewhat puzzled by the strange conversation that had unfolded, and opened the door to go outside.

* * *

Isa stood at the top, near one of the exits, trying to dodge the stream of students leaving the lecture hall. It brought back long forgotten memories of her university days. The smell. It was a scent of authenticity, of knowledge, of importance. The red tip-up seats, the green-colored chalkboards, the white projection screen on the right, the wooden lectern in the front. Every time she came to the Uppsala campus, it felt like it was a place where important things were discussed, where people still had the freedom to unleash their creativity before life and routine caught up with them. Good old times! But when she saw the young men and women pass by, she felt old. They looked so young. She could have been their mother.

Up front, on the raised podium, she saw the man she was looking for. He put the phone and papers in the black briefcase standing on the desk. Robin Gilmore. He looked more mature and distinguished than the last time they had met at Alex's funeral. She wasn't sure if he would recognize her, remember who she was, but when he looked up, finished with the task and about to leave, he stopped. He froze.

"Your Swedish is quite good," she said.

"Have you been there long?"

"Long enough."

"Well, it was my last lecture," he said.

"Your last lecture?"

"I'm going back to the US by the end of the month."

"Why?"

"There's nothing here for me to stay. I mean the PhD is done and uh ..."

He glanced at his shoes. "Sweden has been good to me. I came here for an internship of a few months and see ... it turned out to be years."

He gave her a faint smile before continuing, "But now it's time to go back. I have a postdoc position at MIT. I start next month. I only wish ..."

"How have you been?" she said, interrupting the difficult monologue.

"Okay, I guess."

He waited a moment before continuing, "I've read about Magnus and ... the Sandviken case. Are they seriously going to let Mats Norman go?"

"I can't say much about it, but it seems so."

Her partner had killed his best friend. She couldn't blame him if there was resentment. He seemed happy to see her, but people didn't always show what they really felt or thought.

"I'm here on business," she said.

"That's what I thought. So, how can I help you?"

She walked to the wooden table, put her bag on it and took out the burnt laptop, covered in a plastic bag, sealed with a tag.

"Can you do something with it?"

"Wow, what happened?" he said and tried to take the bag to have a closer look, but Isa stopped him.

"This is evidence."

"So, what do you want me to do?"

"Do you think you can retrieve data from the hard drive?"

"Depends on how badly damaged the laptop is, but in principle, yes. Haven't your guys been able to do anything?"

"No, but maybe you can? How long would it take?"

"Maybe a few days, maybe a week. Hard to say."

"That's great," Isa said, "tell me what you need."

"What do you mean?"

"You'll work as a consultant in the forensics lab. You'll get reimbursed."

"No need. I'm happy to help."

"I have to do this by the book," she said.

"Okay, I understand," he nodded, "I can start as soon as the paperwork is done then."

"Thank you," she whispered and put the laptop back in the bag.

"Why me?" he said.

"Even if I don't really know you, I know Alex trusted you and thought highly of you, and that means a lot. One evening, we had this conversation in a bar in Uppsala. It started as an interview but turned out to be one of the most pleasant conversations I've had in years. I guess that was the moment I fell in love with him, although I didn't realize it until much later. Anyway, he told me about you, that you were his only friend. He kept talking about how great you were and how smart ..."

She stopped when she saw the tears in his eyes. And with his tears, her tears came. How disappointing! Not because she was so emotional, but because she suddenly grasped how much she had boxed the memory of Alex over the past months. It had all been about her, about Magnus, about the serial killer, about Nick, but Alex, how could she have forgotten him. It had been barely six months since he died. In that ambulance, with herself sitting next to him, unable to save him. And in no time, she had replaced him with Nick. This couldn't be. This couldn't be right. And it wasn't. The pain vibrated through every fiber of her body. It was shocking how much grief there still was.

"You know, this was supposed to be his lecture. He would have done it a lot better than me," Robin said.

They were two people connected in sorrow. Silent tears ran down her cheeks. She just couldn't respond, not without letting out the pain.

"Well, I don't know about that," she stammered, "you ... were..."

She had to take a deep breath.

He took her hand and held it for a moment.

"Let me know when I can start," he said in a low voice, "you've got my number."

He picked up the briefcase, walked up the stairs and left the auditorium.

* * *

"I think I've found the identity of our burn victim." Berger burst into the office. Timo looked up from behind his computer, deep in thought.

"Oh, sorry, you were busy?"

Timo sighed. He had forgotten to close the door. By now, everyone knew the boss could be disturbed when the door of his office was open, but he should never be disturbed when the door was closed. Berger had interrupted him. Annoyed by his own mistake, Timo signaled him to stay and close the door.

"Daniel Nyström," Berger said, putting the file on the desk in front of Timo.

"He's the one?"

"Missing since June, before the summer. He worked in a local grocery store in the center of Gävle. So far, no trace of him. But he matches the physical traits of our victim. I can have a chat with the family and people who knew him?"

"Who reported him missing?"

"Colleagues."

"Not the family?"

"He seems to be a bit of a loner. Not married, just an on-off relationship with a girl at work, no children. His father is still alive, and he has a brother we haven't been able to reach yet."

"Go ahead and check if we can match the DNA. Something else?"

"No, no, I just ... are you okay?"

Timo sighed and looked at him.

"Yes, no ... this interview ... well, it's just ... never mind."

"The interview?"

"For superintendent," Timo clarified.

"I thought it was just a formality?"

"Apparently not. There are more candidates."

"But you've been here for what, six months now?"

"Almost. It doesn't matter anyway, nothing for you to worry about," Timo said and turned back to his computer screen.

"But you are worried?"

Without looking up, Timo continued, "Magnus Wieland. That case doesn't particularly help."

"If there's anything I can do …"

"Thanks, Berger. You just concentrate on figuring out what happened to this man."

Berger turned around and then stopped.

"Look, Timo, I need to apologize."

"Why?"

"When you came here, we were all so cautious after what happened to Anders, we never really made you feel welcome."

"That's okay, Berger, don't worry about that."

"No, you should know we …," Berger said and then sighed. He wasn't a gifted speaker like Isa or Lars. He usually struggled to express the simplest idea. And emotions, well, that was a disaster. He wondered why Mila hadn't run away yet.

"I know," Timo said and smiled.

Berger nodded and left the room.

Timo put the laptop aside, leaned back in the chair and closed his eyes. He had been so confident he would get the job, but now that he had learned who the other candidates were and who was on the committee, he wasn't so sure anymore. Magnus Wieland was a thorn in his side, and he hadn't managed to tidy up the department the way he had wanted to. Isa was a loose cannon and still needed continuous supervision. They still didn't work as a real team. It needed time, time he didn't have, and he knew how the people on the committee thought. He needed solid arguments to defend his leadership. Maybe he wasn't good enough. He knew people were disappointed. They had sent him here with a certain goal in mind, and he had done his own thing. That was not the way to make friends in a politically loaded environment. What would he do if he didn't get the job? He didn't want to leave.

The beep from his phone indicated he had a new text message.

It was Ingrid.

He really had to stay away from her, but she was an addiction. He thrived on the attraction and the sexual tension that hung between them.

"Anton and I can be there around eight. See you then."

And now they were using her husband as a cover, as a deception to show that nothing was going on. How immoral was that? But he couldn't wait. He couldn't wait to throw her glances, long enough to grab her attention and short enough to make her long for more, to be so close to her the air between them sparked with electricity, without even touching her.

"Okay, thanks," he typed and then put the phone down. Tomorrow he would move into the new house. He'd better make sure he got the job. Otherwise, it was another vacation home his family had plenty of.

CHAPTER

8

A **WIDE-SHOULDERED MAN,** thick gray hair, fashionable ring-shaped beard, bright blue eyes with a mischievous twinkle, casual white shirt with the top buttons open exposing part of his still muscular chest, opened the door. For a moment Ingrid thought she was standing in front of the wrong house. She stared at him open-mouthed. He seemed as surprised as she was. Then a big smile appeared on his face.

"You must be Ingrid and Anton. My name is George. Friend of the family."

He extended his hand to welcome them and opened the door further to let them in.

"Please go right through. The truck will be there in half an hour or so. Again, thanks for helping. It won't take long. Timo doesn't have a lot of stuff, anyway."

With such calm and ease—as if George lived there himself— he walked down the hall and led them into the empty living room.

Ingrid was surprised. A week earlier, the room had been filled with boxes scattered across the floor, now there wasn't a swirl of dust or box in sight. The walls were decorated with light-colored wallpaper with a fine gray texture, stylish in its simplicity. It made the room look bigger than it was, bright and open. Less was more. Ingrid let a faint smile appear on her face. The other day, she had teased him that the interior lacked elegance and a woman's touch, but she had underestimated him.

She recognized the cadence of Timo's footsteps, walking around upstairs, and then glanced at her husband. Anton walked aimlessly around the room, now and then looking out the large window that opened onto a patio. She could already imagine what it must be like to watch the sunrise over the lake early in the morning, of course, sitting on the patio with a hot cup of coffee in Timo's case. When she told Anton about the house, he didn't understand why someone like inspector Paikkala, having a substantial family fortune, would buy such a hovel, and neither did she, but seeing what Timo had achieved in such a short time, she too fell for the charm of the house.

The moving van arrived twenty minutes later and, as George had said, the unloading didn't take long. The furniture was a mix of old and new. While the men took care of the heavier stuff, Ingrid helped with the smaller boxes. As she watched the two men fix the small wooden table in the living room, her heart suddenly jumped with joy. The quick glances she threw weren't really meant for her husband. She couldn't take her eyes off Timo. Her glances were met with the same secret little, almost unnoticeable expressions of interest. Could she finally admit she was in love with him?

* * *

Ingrid and Anton left in the early afternoon. Timo pushed the coffee mug across the counter to his mentor while George was staring at the living room. A small white table with six chairs in the center of the room, slightly elevated above the area leading to the kitchen and the sitting area. He turned his head and looked at the light-gray sofa at the end. It was simple, but stylish and so Timo-like.

"Where are the cars?" George said, taking a sip of the steamy hot coffee. It wasn't just hot; it was way too strong for his taste, but it was exactly how Timo liked it. After all this time, he had forgotten what a caffeine addict the youngest Paikkala really was.

"I trashed one of them and sold the other."

"Why? Those cars belonged to your father."

"I don't need them," Timo said calmly and took a chair. He was proud of the kitchen island that also served as a table. "They were too ... flashy. And it's time to move on, not dwell on the past."

George frowned, then said in a slight sarcastic tone, "Right, not dwell on the past."

"I can ride a bike," Timo teased, "very ecological and practical."

"Really?"

"No, relax. I'll buy another one. Small, toned-down car. Until then, one of my inspectors can drive me around in her old polluting Volkswagen. We can't be too eco-friendly. Although her driving style may cost me a few years of my life."

"Mmm, a female inspector. Interesting."

"Again, relax. There is nothing going on in that area."

"I can see that," George remarked.

Timo put the cup of coffee down and stared at him. "What do you mean?"

"Timo, a married woman? Be careful. That never works out."

For a moment, Timo didn't know what to say, and George waited for a response that never came.

"I can see why you're fond of her," George said. "She looks like Caijsa."

"She's nothing like Caijsa," Timo said.

"You talk about living in the past but isn't it time to move on? It's been eight years. Ingrid is not the answer. Plus, married women usually think they need something more, something different, more exciting, better, sexier, but in the end, they don't, and they end up breaking your heart," George continued.

It all made sense now. Why would Timo want to stay here, in this forsaken place? He had nothing against Gävle, but it wasn't exactly the most exciting place in the world. The Paikkala family, having traveled the world, having been invited to the most fascinating and privileged places, would aspire to something more than that. George, like his former best friend Yrjo Paikkala, was accustomed to a certain level of luxury that the youngest member of the family had discarded years ago. George had his own opinion about the choices Timo had made, but regardless, he had always supported him.

This was new, and it surprised him. It didn't fit the uncompromising and righteous nature of the man he'd seen growing up. But love was complicated and sometimes impossible to understand. There was no logic, and rules—if there were any—were usually broken. He too had learned it the hard way.

"Like you and my mother," Timo said.

George heaved a deep sigh and put the cup of coffee down in front of him. This was a conversation they've had so many times.

"Timo, there is nothing going on between your mother and me, never has, never will be. I'm not your biological father and it saddens me you let this come between you and your mom. She is a good and decent woman. She loved your father, and she doesn't deserve to be treated like this. Maybe it's time you let this go and talk to her."

"I know what I heard," Timo said.

George sighed and shook his head. "Your mother can be ... how shall I put it, overly dramatic at times."

"I know that, but not about such a thing. What would she gain by telling dad I wasn't his son?"

"I don't know, Timo. The only thing I know is that she and Yrjo stayed together until your dad died, and he loved her with all his heart."

Timo looked him straight in the eye. Icy blue eyes. George had never seen such intense sharp light-blue eyes before. Maybe in one person, but he couldn't just throw his suspicions out there. He had promised Timo's mother never to talk about it.

Then Timo said, "I know genetics, George. How can I have blood type B when both my parents are O?"

"Timo, just stop with these accusations! She misses you. Call her!"

"So, you've seen her recently?"

"She's in Helsinki. We visited her a month ago while we were there."

"We?"

"I have a new girlfriend," George said.

Suddenly he felt his cheeks glow as if he were a boy talking about his first crush.

The hard expression on Timo's face softened and he said, "Good for you."

The new girlfriend was a shot of happiness in his life. Maybe he would finally be happy. He had been divorced for years. His marriage hadn't survived the death of his son more than fifteen years ago. And there had only been one serious relationship, but that had ended in a brutal way. After that, there had been no one and he had been content to live alone, travel the world, and devote most of his time to his many hobbies. Besides climbing and racing, he was an avid painter and sculptor, not exhibition material, but good enough to hang on the walls of his mansion in Helsinki or to display in his New York apartment.

"But Timo, I'm really worried about you."

"There's nothing going on between Ingrid and me," Timo sighed, "we're colleagues and friends."

"But you want it to be more. I can see it in your eyes. There's only one thing standing in the way of sleeping with her."

"And that is?" Timo frowned.

"Your own moral standards," George turned his head as if he wanted to monitor his friend's reaction, "but love is difficult and complicated, and sometimes everything gets thrown overboard, how hard you try."

"Thanks for the advice, but ..."

"Love can be brutal. I know you think you love her. But is it love for her?"

The look on Timo's face was even more one of confusion.

"Look, Caijsa's death was horrible, and it almost destroyed you," George said. "I don't think you'll survive another heartbreak. Talk to your mom, really talk to her, and she'll tell you how painful it was for her to see you like that. Think about this carefully before diving in."

Timo got up and gave his friend a pat on the shoulder as he passed by on his way to the bathroom.

"Thank you," Timo whispered.

* * *

It was a lovely day. The last weeks it had gotten colder, but it was dry and sunny. A perfect day for a walk. The kinship with nature was so reinvigorating, yet it put a certain calm to the restlessness in his mind. He took the leaf-covered path through the forest to the open field. It was a surprising feature in this part of the woods. No one knew that beyond the darkness, sealing off the blue sky, filtering the sunlight and confining the environment to a world of its own, with its flora and fauna so different from the world of men, there was a clearing where his soul seemed to breathe even more.

He was panting. His physique was no longer what it had been. Now that he was in his fifties, it was a lot harder to keep his muscles trained. He continued his way. The soles of his boots were thin, and he felt every unevenness of the rocks and branches. The mud gave the ground a slippery smoothness that took even more energy to move forward. A bird on a branch caught his eye. It wasn't particularly beautiful, but the way the animal moved its head from side to side, like clockwork, was intriguing. He stopped and stared at it for a while. What went through that tiny skull under the brown plumage? Was it a conscious act or was it a reflex, triggered by an ancient process written in DNA? And then it flew away, as if the job—whatever it was—had been done, and the bird was now called to serve another task.

In a few meters he would leave the cover of the entangled branches and go into the open field where he could see the glowing hills of green grass, with patches of darkness left by the shadows of passing clouds, now and then turning the sky dark when a big cloud moved in front of the sun. He closed his eyes and took a deep breath. The color palette of gold and scarlet overwhelmed him. There were no words to describe it.

Luckily, he didn't have the dog with him. Otherwise, he wouldn't get a chance to take in all the beauty that lay before him. The dog would run around restlessly, sniff every rock, bark at anything and anyone, wagging its tail and making so much noise that it scared off most animals. The dog wouldn't know when to stop, and before he knew it, he'd be running after the animal, instead of the dog following him. Probably running toward that strange-looking crooked pole he saw in the distance, a little downhill from where he was standing. He couldn't remember seeing it before.

What exactly was it? A dead tree, a stone or metal pole? He was too far away to make out the details, but his curiosity was aroused, and he strolled toward it. As he approached, the blurry shape turned into something recognizable. A jacket, a hat. Was it a scarecrow? Why was it there? How odd. There were no crops in the area.

As he approached, there was a distinct stench, not strong, but coming from the weird-looking figure standing in the middle of the grass field. He kept his eyes on the blackish coat and the red sweater, sticking out from underneath. He didn't recognize the smell, but it wasn't pleasant. The straw hat hung over the bag that served as the head. There was something wrong with the entire scene, but he couldn't put his finger on it.

Then he saw the hands. These weren't just gloves. There was something in it. So many flies were sitting on it. Now he knew what it was: the smell of rotting flesh. He stepped back in horror. It wasn't just the hands. At the bottom of the wooden stake, there were a pair of shoes with feet still in them, severed just above the ankle, bones clearly visible. The flesh was full of maggots and flies, with nibbled edges as if rodents had gotten their way with it. He had trouble breathing. The horror of it! He turned his head away and threw up next to the scarecrow before he took the phone out of his pocket and called the police.

* * *

"It's Daniel Nyström," Mila said.

The cheerful smile on her face and the message she delivered were hard to reconcile.

"So, the DNA matches?" Berger asked.

"Yes, and as an extra check, also the dental records match. This is our man."

"We can assume he was murdered."

"It seems so unless he set fire to himself."

"He was burnt alive?"

"Yes, it's horrible," Mila replied.

"But it wasn't a suicide or an accident?"

"Absolutely not. Someone moved him. There were no signs of a fire on the beach where he was found, neither in the neighborhood. And the autopsy confirmed he had likely been restrained during the burning. The ligature marks were still visible."

"Like being burnt at the stake?"

"Yes, something like that. Were you able to talk to the family?"

"Not yet. I have an appointment with the father. He lives in a nursing home. And I'm still trying to reach his brother, but no luck so far. The brother has a criminal record. He did time for drugs and arms dealing and was released from prison about a year ago. Since then, he has stayed under the radar."

"What about neighbors or colleagues?"

"I still have to talk to them," Berger said and smiled.

"What?" she said.

"You look cute when you try to be a detective," he said and walked over to her.

There was no one else in the room. He took her head in his hands and kissed her. A long kiss, gentle but at the same time full of hunger for more. The kiss of a young lover, beyond the hesitation of a fool struck by a crush, with the confidence of a man who had taken the relationship to the next level. He hadn't felt that way in a long time.

"It was nice yesterday," she whispered, still recovering from the kiss, "very nice."

"You were gone when I got up," he said.

"Sorry, I had to leave early, but I'll make it up to you tonight. I'm cooking this time."

She kissed him as she ran her hands down his back. Her voice, her touch, everything about her aroused him and his entire body longed for more. He could hardly hide it.

"I'm looking forward to it," he said and smiled.

She nodded and sighed.

"What's wrong?" he said.

"Oh, nothing serious. But it will probably be the last time I can invite you to the flat. By the end of the month, I should have found something else. It's difficult. There are not that many decent homes that are affordable. It's really disappointing."

He suddenly took her hands in his.

"Look, Mila, I was wondering ... maybe this is all going too fast, but when I know, I know, and I know I really like you. I ... love you, and maybe we should ... what I'm trying to say ..."

He took a few deep breaths. Why was this so difficult? "I think you should move in with me."

She took his hands in hers and looked at him for a few seconds. Her face was so serious and for a moment he regretted asking her, but then she gave him a radiant smile and said, "Are you sure?"

He nodded.

"Yes, I'd loved to," she said.

And they kissed again.

* * *

"Vollan's financial records show he regularly received payments. Large sums of about 50 000 kronor per month in the past six months. But he didn't keep it. The money was transferred to a bank in Germany."

"Family?" Kristoffer said.

"Likely," Isa said. "But also, Russia."

Kristoffer was pacing the room for the past thirty minutes. It made her nervous, but she said nothing and continued, "But he really kept himself under the radar the past month. The owner of the apartment said Vollan paid the rent in cash and there is, besides the payments to his family and the Russian account, which we have yet to verify, no activity of any sort registered to his account."

"Yes, we've noticed," he replied quickly.

"How did he get the supplies? We know he didn't work alone. But who?"

"We're completely in the dark there," he said, "the owners of the shop, a Russian couple, disappeared. Their identities unknown, the names were false, and no one can even give a decent description."

Isa sighed. "So, it's valid to assume they were in this too. But were they the clients? Did they order this massacre?"

"We don't know who his companions and his clients were. We have nothing!"

"Kristoffer," she started, but couldn't finish the sentence when he interrupted her.

"Where's Paikkala?"

"Timo has taken the day off. Personal reasons."

"What the hell! In the midst of a crisis, he's taking a day off! This should be his priority. He'd better be at the press conference this evening. I knew he couldn't be trusted and he's just as incompetent as the rest of his team!"

"What are you saying?"

She had been accommodating in every way. She had kept her mouth shut when he had made subtle insults in the conversations between the SÄPO and the Gävle teams, but now that he so openly questioned the competence of her colleagues, she had to stand up and counter him. This arrogance was intolerable.

"You know exactly what I mean," he came closer and stood there, shoulders back, chest out, towering over her. His entire posture just screamed intimidation.

"No, enlighten me," she said calmly.

"Your incompetence, your reckless behavior, your unethical conduct, that's why we're in this mess. Not only does it affect this ... this bunch of morons in this God-forsaken town, but it reflects on all of us, decent cops who are just doing their job. You made us lose our credibility with the public, and I don't understand why they haven't kicked you out yet. But if it were up to me, and maybe it could be in the future, you wouldn't work here for a second longer than necessary."

"It's finally out in the open," she said, tilted her head, while she kept staring at him, and she stepped closer. She was a lot shorter than him, but she wasn't impressed by his macho behavior. Before he had thrown the insults, she had wanted to tell him Robin had finally managed to get something off the burnt hard drive. Not much, but it was a start. That she had a first lead to a man frequently seen with Nils Vollan, and that she even had a name. But now she didn't see the point. Whatever she told him, he would either use it against her or take the credit himself.

"So, if we're all just idiots and we're a disgrace to the police force, why are you still here? I'm sure you can find better ways to spend your time."

"Timo. He convinced me to give you a chance. But like the rest of this team, he is a big disappointment. His reputation is worthless."

Timo. How could she have ever doubted him? He was on her side, on their side. He was finally one of them. The more she thought about it, the more she respected him.

She spoke. "So, feel free to go. You obviously don't need us."

"I understand why Magnus Wieland fell for you and I keep wondering if you manipulated him to kill Alexander Nordin. I see you have that power over men."

He leaned forward to bring his head closer to hers. She felt his breath blow across her face. It sent a chill down her spine. She could only feel disgust.

His lip quivered slightly as he curled it up in a sarcastic grin, and said, "Oh, and by the way, if I were you, I'd ask your boss about his relationship with Rune Breiner. There's more than what he wants us to believe."

"What ... what do you mean?" Isa stammered.

"Ask him," Kristoffer said and disappeared, leaving her with a seed of doubt in her mind.

CHAPTER

9

"WHERE IS EVERYONE?"
When Isa couldn't find Lars or Berger, she turned to the young police officer at the front desk. The woman in her early thirties looked up from the computer screen and gave her a faint smile.

"Body parts in an open field," the woman said.

"Really? Where?"

"Near Södra Bomhus."

"Since the guys are gone, can you help me find an address? My computer is down. Blue screen and I can't restart it."

"You should have requested a new one ages ago. Why are you so attached to old stuff?"

"Yeah, yeah, I know," Isa said.

"Maybe your new IT guy can have a look at it. He's cute, by the way."

"Robin? Is he?"

"He is. So, what's the name?"

"What are you doing?" A deep voice thundered through the air and made her turn in surprise.

"Ah, boss! Well, uh, ... I thought you were going to take the entire day off."

Was he checking up on her?

Timo sighed and motioned for her to accompany him to his office.

He closed the door saying, "What have you been up to? Should I be worried again?"

She felt like a child being tapped on the fingers by one of her parents.

"Nothing. I just want to check up on a lead."

"A lead? Which one?"

"The neighbors of the store haven't given us much information. I think they were scared, probably threatened. However, I found someone living across the street who gave me a description of a man regularly seen with Nils Vollan. No name. But he had a distinct neck tattoo in the shape of a snake. I checked with the owner of a pub nearby and he recognized the description. He identified him as Sören Kempe."

"And you were going to check this on your own? Are you crazy? Why didn't you tell Kristoffer?"

"Well, inspector Solberg was too busy insulting me ... and the entire team for that matter. He accuses me of having manipulated Magnus to kill Alex!"

"That's what Magnus claims as well ... maybe not in so many words."

"Jesus! Has the entire world gone mad?" she cried. "I have nothing to do with this. I'm the victim, not him."

"Small correction: Alexander Nordin is the victim. Anyway, have you talked to him?"

She frowned. "Who? Magnus? No. I want to forget about that man."

"At some point, you'll have to face him, Isa."

"Not now," she hissed. "By the way, coming back to the conversation with Solberg, he did make an interesting comment ... about you."

He folded his arms across his chest, and for a moment she was distracted by the tense muscles of his upper arm emerging from beneath the black T-shirt. "What then?"

"Uh, he said you knew Rune Breiner better than you led us to believe. I also thought you weren't comfortable talking about Breiner when I asked about the case. Why?"

She looked at him expectantly, but the answer was disappointing.

"It has nothing to do with this case. Let me put it this way: Breiner and I were indeed not the best of friends."

"Why did they take you off the case?"

"At my own request," he said without flinching. "It got too personal, and everyone deserves a fair investigation. That's all you need to know. I'm sure Solberg can tell you the entire story and more, but I ask you to trust me."

A long inhale and then a long silence. Trust him? There was no question about that, but why did it have to be steeped in mystery? Couldn't he just say what needed to be said? How bad could it be?

But he was the boss.

She said, "Okay then."

"And let's see where mister Kempe lives and pay him a visit," Timo said, and took the jacket from the peg. "You drive."

* * *

Isa parked the car in front of the apartment complex. They hadn't said a word since leaving the police office. Timo was deep in thought, and she hadn't dared to initiate the conversation. Solberg's comment kept running through her mind. Timo could sometimes get on her nerves, and it seemed as if he was deliberately trying to leave that mysterious haze around him. And the frustration of having him meddle in her activities had reached a peak just before stepping in the car and driving to the building. He had wanted to lecture her about the dangers of not informing him about the details of the investigation and the dangers of going off alone. The procedures had been carefully quoted and laid out for her again. She knew he was right, and she knew he was doing it to protect her, but the hormonal chaos in her body had been on the rise since that morning after another attempt to get through to Nick, after Kristoffer's threat and the thought of having to deal with Magnus, eventually. Timo was just the wrong man in the wrong place, at the wrong time. Everything that came out of his mouth had sounded so patronizing. But he was right.

She took the key out of the ignition and looked at the building through the raindrop-covered windshield. Vollan's flat was only a few blocks away, but this neighborhood made a very different impression. A shabby apartment building in a run-down part of town. Every apartment looked the same: gray, old-fashioned, seventies-style large aluminum windows and frames, plain, with no animation or brightness, and on the balcony of almost every floor people hung over the railing with a cigarette between the fingers and an almost indifferent glance on the face looking at the passersby.

She turned to Timo who was taking deep breaths as he stepped out of the car.

"Lindström, don't argue with me, but I'll drive back," he said, slamming the door shut.

She frowned. What was the problem?

A group of youngsters huddled at the entrance of the building, disinterested, unmotivated, scanning everyone who passed by, envious of everything and everyone, and blaming everyone but themselves for their so-called misfortune. The group parted hesitantly as the inspectors approached. Isa and Timo walked on, ignoring them. The door to the hallway was open. The lock must have been broken a long time ago, and the light didn't work. Food wrappers, plastic bags, and toilet paper littered the hallway that smelled of urine. And that was the more harmless-looking rubble. Isa heard the metal needles of used syringes snap under her feet.

"Jesus," she cried.

The last thing she wanted was for an HIV-infected specimen to find its way into the flesh of her feet.

The walls were covered in the ugliest graffiti Isa had ever seen, and she preferred not to know the origin of the big stains scattered on the wall. Some looked like dried blood, as if someone had been thrown against the wall, leaving a trace of the sustained injury. How could people live like this? How could this place even exist in Gävle? It was like walking around in a cliché crime movie.

Timo grabbed a flashlight and let the beam illuminate the narrow hallway. The boss was prepared, and that was more than she could say. Perhaps it hadn't been such a bad idea for him to come along.

They found flat number twelve all the way in the back, hidden behind the corner. Timo took a deep breath and looked at Isa. They had to be ready for whoever was inside. He knocked. A soft sound came from behind the door. It would have gone unnoticed by any unwary bystander, but not by the two inspectors.

"Mr. Kempe, police, open up, we need to talk to you!" Isa yelled.

More stumbling behind the door. Mister Kempe was at home, but he wasn't eager to welcome them and was trying to find a way out.

"He's escaping," Isa said.

Almost at the same time, they pulled their guns from the holster. Timo put his foot on the door and kicked it hard. The wooden door was so thin it flew open without a hitch. The first thing she saw was the sheet-covered sofa and the big plastic bags on the floor. The window was open, and the curtains swayed back and forth with the wind that was heaving through the room.

"You take the front," Timo yelled, and ran to the window before sliding through in a fluent motion.

Isa turned and ran for the entrance. She was already panting. In what a terrible shape she was! The youngsters, deemed harmless a few minutes before, were now blocking her way. Before she knew it, they had surrounded her and were getting closer. She held the gun in front of her and kept moving it around from one side to the other, but they didn't seem impressed.

"Police! Stop!"

Meanwhile, Timo had almost caught up with the man in front of him. The open area around the apartment buildings wasn't ideal for hiding.

The man, dressed in a dirty blue T-shirt sticking out from under a black hoodie, army boots, greasy hair, and a stubble, struggled to keep his distance. He was no match for the well-trained inspector who was following him.

"Police, stop," Timo yelled several times during the pursuit, but the man didn't comply. Now the distance between them was reduced to only a few meters, and in a last-ditch effort to take the suspect down, Timo pushed off and jumped. The full weight of his body landed on the man's back, pulling him down. After that there was hardly a struggle, and as Timo handcuffed the man, he read him his rights.

"I didn't do anything!"

"Then why did you run away?" Timo said, taking the man's arm to lead him back to the building.

"Intimidation," Sören Kempe wailed, "pure intimidation."

"Well, feel free to consult your lawyer and file a complaint," inspector Paikkala said calmly.

But where had Isa gone? She should have caught up with them by now. He turned his head and scanned the area. Brick walls, graffiti, the endless repetition of the same bleak buildings and the unkempt gardens full of rubble and mud.

He felt his stomach drop.

Where was she?

"You're worried about that bitch of yours," Kempe said and turned his lips in a nasty grin.

Timo pushed him forward. "Come on!"

"Get back," Isa yelled.

The tall, skinny young man, who looked like the leader, had made a few sudden movements, forcing her backward, and her back was almost literally against the wall. He was laughing. They all were.

"Oh, oh, the little lady is angry!" the man on the left said.

"I think she wants some of this," the leader said and touched his crotch. "I'll show her what a real man is."

She moved the gun from one target to another. Five men against one police officer. Even if she'd shoot one, the group could overpower her in no time. She had no control over the situation. The man on the left lashed out, but she stepped back in time to avoid him hitting her.

And then a gunshot echoed through the air. They turned around. Timo put his arm down. He had fired one bullet in the air and now aimed his gun straight at the leader. Isa grabbed the gun tighter and did the same.

The look in the man's eyes was flushed with anger.

"If I were you, I'd think really hard about what you're going to do next," Timo started, "you'll be on the ground before you can even take one step and then I'll shoot him, and him ..." He aimed the gun at each of them, while holding Sören Kempe with his right hand, who had been watching the entire scene in amazement.

"I think our good friend here persuaded you to do this," Timo said and quickly looked at Kempe. "I'll give you five seconds to get out of my sight, or I'll arrest each one of you for assaulting a police officer."

They didn't have to think twice, and in no time the group dissolved and moved away from the entrance.

"Are you okay?" Timo asked as Isa walked toward him.

She nodded her head. She was fine, but she hadn't handled the situation well. How would this have ended if Timo hadn't intervened?

"Let's take mister Kempe here to an interrogation room," he said.

* * *

"Do you know who this man is?"

Nils Vollan's photo was placed on the table.

"I don't know him," Sören said, twitched his nose, and ran his hands through his greasy, blond hair.

Timo pushed the picture further toward the man. "Are you sure? Maybe you should have a closer look?"

Isa, next to him, had been staring at Sören's trembling hands from the moment he'd sat down at the table in the interrogation room. This wasn't fear. These were the tremors of Adderall withdrawal.

"What do you want?" Sören said in a low, hoarse voice, the result of heavy smoking since he was barely ten years old. "You can't keep me here. What are you accusing me of?"

"Based on the Terrorism Act, I can keep you up to two weeks without charge," Timo said.

"Terrorism?" Sören said, surprised, and turned to his pro bono lawyer who, with fear in his eyes, jumped up.

"Is he charged with acts of terrorism?" the lawyer asked.

"We haven't charged him yet, but he'd better have a good explanation why he was seen with a man suspected of terrorism."

"I don't really know him." Sören shook his head. The snake tattoo on his neck moved with the rhythm and his bony body looked as if he could fall apart at any moment

"For a man who didn't know him, you spent a lot of time with him," Timo said.

Kempe looked at his hands and said nothing.

"Nils Vollan was killed in the mass shooting at Global Law. He has been identified as one of the attackers. We believe you were involved too."

"What?" Sören jumped up. "No, no, I've told you before I have nothing to do with him."

"You are Ormar," Isa said, and pointed at the tattoo. Ormar, a gang that had been very efficient in recruiting a network of teenagers dealing drugs and stealing. In Gävle they usually hung around the train station. Almost every week, one of their guys was sitting in this interrogation room, but they could never hold them for long. Stockholm was their playground, and she still couldn't get her head around the fact that this criminal group might stage something as big as a terrorist attack. For them it was better to stay low.

"So what?"

"Do you know a man called Rune Breiner?" Timo said.

"No," Sören said.

"Rune Breiner was a dirty cop, suspected of working for Ormar, but he was killed a year ago and now his lawyer has been killed as well. Maybe you were just the messenger, maybe not, but I believe Ormar hired Vollan to kill Karst Engersson."

He said reluctantly, "Vollan paid me, not the other way around."

"To do what?"

"To run errands," he laughed.

Timo turned to the lawyer: "I would advise your client to cooperate with the police. He's in a lot of trouble."

The lawyer replied, "Where is the evidence?"

"And what if we took a closer look at all the fingerprints and DNA in Vollan's apartment? Would we find a match with our mister Kempe?'

"Okay, okay," Kempe shouted in exasperation, "he asked me to help him with weapons and supplies."

"Supplies for what?" Isa asked.

"Chemicals, explosives."

The door was pushed open, and Kristoffer Solberg entered the room.

"Inspector Paikkala, inspector Lindström, thank you for your help, but we'll take it from here," he said.

"But ...," Isa started, but Timo kicked her under the table.

"Sure," Timo said and got up to allow his SÄPO colleague to take a seat. Isa looked at him confused. He motioned her to leave, while Kristoffer looked at them in surprise.

In the hallway, Isa rushed up to Timo, "Why did you let him do that?"

"Take it easy! There's nothing we can do right now. Let him have this victory. Let him have Kempe."

"This was our witness, Timo. This is our investigation."

"Come on." And he pulled her into the observation room. From behind the glass, they followed the rest of the interview.

"Where did you meet Vollan?"

"In the Night Bar, a pub a few blocks away from where he lived. I was sitting there one night, and he started talking to me. He knew who I was. I think I was a target."

"Why are you so important?"

"I can arrange things. And it's no secret I'm with Ormar."

"And what have you done for Vollan?"

"As I told the other inspectors, he needed weapons for a first big operation. And all sorts of stuff for something else he was planning."

"We found drugs, weapons, hand grenades and explosives in your apartment. Care to explain?"

He shrugged and gave them a disinterested look.

"Did you give him what he wanted?" Kristoffer said.

He sighed and looked down. "No, I didn't."

"Come on, Sören. Don't insult me!"

"No, really. He found another supplier."

"Who?"

"I don't know. But overnight he stopped contacting me and I didn't see him again until I learned he was involved in that shooting."

"Where did you meet?'

"In his apartment. Sometimes in the store."

"Have you ever seen anyone else?"

"No. Except for the couple who owned the shop, and they barely spoke to me. Bloody Russians. But he got regular phone calls."

"What calls?"

"I don't know what it was about, but it stressed him out. It was important. After each call, he usually threw me out of his apartment."

"Someone else is involved," Isa whispered.

Timo sighed. "We all know Vollan didn't plan this. But we are no closer to finding who ordered this attack, and to finding his accomplices."

"We need to get access to that laptop."

"What if there is nothing on it?" Timo said.

"There must be. Why else would they have tried to destroy it?"

"But the money also left traces. That's the other route."

Isa sighed and looked through the one-way glass at the man at the table. Karst Engersson and Rune Breiner. Was this the connection? Were they on the right track? It somehow didn't feel right.

* * *

Inspector Karlsson had been warned Mr. Nyström was no longer so lucid, and that he sometimes forgot things or switched them around. In his better days, he could still carry an intelligent conversation. In his worst days, like today, the old man sat in a chair by the window of the nursing home, and he didn't look up when Berger introduced himself. He stared at the trees, the grass, the raindrops on the window, as if nothing really rippled through.

"I'm investigating the death of your son," Berger tried. "My condolences."

The old man didn't respond, and Berger took a seat next to him. The nurse looked at him and shook her head.

"When was the last time you saw your son?"

"That bastard," the old man said suddenly.

Berger looked at him in surprise.

"Sometimes he gets his boys mixed up," the nurse said and turned to the old man.

"The inspector wants to talk about Daniel," she said and knelt next to him.

The old man mumbled, "Daniel? Yes, he was here. Such a nice boy."

"When was he here?" Berger asked.

"He wasn't," the nurse said. "Pauli came to see him a few weeks ago. They had an argument. Mr. Nyström always gets upset when his oldest son comes to visit him. Then he started harassing Pauli. Little did we know Mr. Nystrom had obtained a phone from one of the guards and had been calling his son constantly. We confiscated it after Pauli reported it."

"They don't get along?"

"No, they don't, and that is putting it mildly."

"Such a nice boy," the old man mused.

"And Daniel?"

Berger had given up getting information from the old man. And the nurse had been very willing to help. Neela Johansson loved the distraction. She wasn't bored, but now and then she missed having an intelligent conversation with someone, and a police inspector who came to visit didn't happen every day.

She said, "Daniel is his favorite. It's hard to imagine anyone wanting to kill him. He was always so friendly."

"How was the relationship between the brothers?"

"Good, I guess."

"Why did Pauli come to see his father a few weeks ago?"

"I don't know."

He gave her a smile. Mrs. Johansson knew all too well what was going on in the nursing home. She didn't want to eavesdrop, but it was sometimes difficult to ignore the conversations between the residents and their families.

"But you might have picked up a few things while he was here," Berger tried.

She stared at the floor, then got up and looked at him. "Yes, it was about money. Pauli wanted to know where his father hid the money."

"Money?"

The old man hadn't moved, frozen in a mind that was trapped in another time.

"I was surprised myself. The way Pauli talked about it makes me believe it was a lot of money, but I didn't think Mr. Nyström had any. Daniel was the one who financially supported their father, and his brother. With Daniel gone, I don't know what will happen to Mr. Nyström."

She sighed and continued, "Mr. Nyström was quite lucid that day. He just laughed at the threats his son was making and blamed him for Daniel's disappearance."

"Really! Why?"

"Again, I don't know the details, but I know they started yelling at each other and I had to call one of my colleagues to remove Pauli from the premises."

Berger turned to Mr. Nyström, but it was no use. The old man was in his own world.

Then Berger thanked the nurse and went out.

The brother. That was an interesting lead, unless Daniel Nyström wasn't the ideal son. Where did he get the money to support his family? He had been a simple guy, working in a grocery.

Mila was right. This case was more interesting than he had expected.

CHAPTER

10

"**WHAT'S GOING ON?**"
His whole body was shaking out of control. As her hand searched the darkness for his naked body, Isa felt how much he had sweated, leaving a wet spot in the mattress and blanket.

"She's coming for me, she's coming for me," Nick stammered.

"Nick, who?"

"She's coming," he cried.

Isa sat up and wanted to throw her arms around him, but she felt the shock ripple through his body and pulled back.

"It's just a nightmare," she said softly. "This isn't real."

The moonlight streaming in through the window gave his face an almost ghostly look, but it was those dark, large eyes that stared straight ahead in terror that scared her.

"You're in the bedroom of your apartment," she said.

She took his hand. His flesh felt cold. "You can feel my fingers on your skin. You're with me, your girlfriend, Isa. It was just a nightmare. Kim isn't here. She can't hurt you. It's not your fault."

Tiny beads of sweat glistened in the moonlight and ran from his forehead down his face. When the drops reached his nose and mouth, and he made no attempt to remove them, she waited for him to voice his thoughts, but there was silence on his part.

"Nick?"

He turned his face away from her and put his head on the pillow.

"Nick, talk to me," she said and let her hand ran over his arm.

"Kim? Yes, yes, Kim ... she isn't here," he stammered.

She sighed, gave him another glance, and then pulled the blanket over her.

"Her eyes, her eyes," he whispered.

How could she help him? It had gotten worse. Nothing she said or done had lifted him out of that zombie-like state into which he had retreated for the last weeks. The nightmares had increased. Almost every night, he was screaming about Kim. The helplessness had subsided, giving way to frustration and irritation.

"Tell me about Nick," Dr. Wikholm had asked her again.

Talk about Nick? For the first time, she felt there was nothing to talk about. They were alike, the same hollow, immature people, who only valued outward beauty, and sex. Nick didn't complement her. He was her. This wasn't love. She felt down and alone. After all this time, why hadn't she learnt? Viktor, Magnus, Alex, Nick. She was so naïve.

But even more than in her other relationships, she felt trapped. How could she leave a traumatized man, a man in need of help? She had to get her act together. She couldn't continue shipping people off the moment it got difficult. Like her children. But she didn't know how to fix it, not even where to start. Why was her life such a mess?

* * *

What lay on the table was more disturbing than any disfigured, beaten, and sliced open corpse Isa had ever seen lying there. Two severed feet and two severed hands.

"The same victim?"

"Yes. Female. They were attached to the arms and legs of the scarecrow with nails and staples. A hiker found them in the open fields near Södra Bomhus."

"And the rest of the body?"

"That hasn't been found," Ingrid said, putting on the latex gloves. She pulled the metal dissection table closer. The assistant was waiting for her to ask for the medical instruments, but she ignored him and took the forceps as she leaned over the body parts to take a closer look.

She continued, "Based on the shape of the wound and the presence of blood, I would say the victim was not alive when the hands and feet were removed."

"Fortunately," Isa cried out.

"A chainsaw was used to cut the limbs, but it wasn't entirely successful. It must have taken a while to cut the bone and it took several attempts as you can see here and here."

Ingrid bent down and pointed with the forceps to the spots near the bone in the center of the foot.

"Why are the edges so irregular?"

"Rats. They nibbled at the flesh."

"Who does such a thing?"

"Someone really disturbed," Ingrid added.

"How long has she been dead?"

"From the flies and the maggots found in the wounds and given the weather conditions, I'd say at least three days."

"No idea yet about her identity?"

"Lars is going through the missing persons reports. If we can select a few possibilities, we can try to match the DNA. Maybe the scarecrow's clothes can help. We found no other DNA on them except for the shoes. These are men's shoes, two sizes too big. They were wiped clean except for one spot in the interior near the toes."

"If we're lucky we find a match," Isa said.

It was hard to wrap her head around it. She had never witnessed such an atrocity. This was anger; this was hatred.

The plastic of latex gloves snapped as Ingrid removed them. She tossed them in the bin, and then turned to her friend. It was a concerned look.

"How are you?" Ingrid asked. "We haven't talked since the shooting."

"I'm fine," Isa said.

"And Nick?"

Isa looked at her feet and shook her head. She didn't really want to talk about it.

"Bad. I don't know how to help him. He won't talk to me; he won't leave the house. He just sits there all day staring at the TV."

"Is he talking to a psychologist? PTSD is not something that just blows over. He needs professional help."

"No, he refuses to talk to anyone. Even his parents and sister have tried."

"I'll give you the number of a friend of mine. He specializes in these things."

Ingrid walked down the hall to her office, with Isa following her. In the small room, she opened the desk drawer, took out the business card she was looking for, and handed it to Isa.

"Thanks," Isa said. "How's Anton?"

"Anton," Ingrid said and let out a sigh. "Anton is fine ... Anton is always fine."

"Are you okay?"

"He wasn't really in any danger. There are the funerals, the fact that he needs to work from home now, but everything is always fine in Anton's world. I just wished he ..."

Isa walked up to her friend. "What's really wrong?"

"That for once it wasn't just about him, but about us. Even now, when he's at home, I'm left with all the decisions, organizing everything, the work, the kids. He takes it for granted and when he does get involved, everything needs to be done his way."

She had to let it all out, in an almost unstoppable stream of words, none of which seemed to go to the core of the problem.

"And then there is ...," Ingrid said and then stopped.

"Timo," Isa said.

Ingrid sighed. "We're friends."

Isa looked at her. "You've been saying that a lot lately, but I've seen you two together. You are different with him, and he's different around you. I know when there is attraction between a man and a woman."

"I'm not denying that," Ingrid said and threw herself in the chair as she tried to tuck the strands of hair back in her bun. "But you know I will never give into that. It's me ... Ingrid."

Isa took the other chair and moved it closer to the desk. This was a conversation they should have had months ago, and not here, in the four walls of the forensics lab. "I know you'll never leave Anton and the boys. I know you. You couldn't live with the shame and the guilt, but ..."

"But?"

"He makes you feel ... something. Perhaps you should ask yourself why?"

"Are you now telling me I should give into those feelings?"

Isa smiled. "No, maybe you should examine why you're interested in him. Maybe it's not him, but Anton or you? Of course, this is advice from a woman who has had so many men I can hardly count on two hands anymore. Maybe it's worth nothing."

Ingrid leaned forward and took her hand. "I missed this. I missed us."

"Me too ... I ... my life is a mess, Ingrid. Nick, the kids ... Magnus."

"Magnus," Ingrid sighed.

"Everyone tells me I should talk to him, but I can't. I think I'd put my gun to his head and pull the trigger, as I've imagined so many times."

"I went to see him," Ingrid blurted.

Isa looked up in surprise. "Why?"

"He is ... was my friend too," Ingrid said calmly. "I needed to understand how he could do such a thing."

"And? Did he give you any insight as to why?"

Isa had said it with a flash of sarcasm.

"I'm not going to tell you what he said, but no, I still don't understand. Maybe he doesn't either and it's best you don't see him right now. But, Isa, they are taking his accusations about you seriously."

"Timo told me, but I'm not worried. Let them come up with proof!"

But she was worried. Not about the impact on her career. Her career was in the doldrums anyway. But how could anyone think she had orchestrated the death of the man she had loved so much that just mentioning his name felt like ripping out her entire being? The love of her life. As she walked down the hallway, away from Ingrid's office, she thought of Alex. For the second time in a short period, she burst into tears over the man she had lost. She just knew she would never meet anyone like him. She just knew. No Viktor, Magnus or Nick could ever match him. She missed him so much. She had played too much with the feelings of the men in her life. Even Alex. She stopped and leaned against the wall.

Then she wiped the tears and took the phone from the pocket of her jacket.

"Nick," she said when his voice sounded on the other end of the line.

"Why are you calling?"

"No reason. I just wanted to hear your voice."

It was quiet on the other side.

"Nick?"

"I'm still here."

"I just need to talk to you."

"About what?"

"Magnus."

She heard a deep sigh. Was he bored? How could he react like that?

"Nick?"

"I have no time right now. We can talk about it tonight."

No time? What was so important he couldn't even talk to her? All he did these days was sit in front of the TV and watch the same silly commercials and mind-numbing soaps over and over again. Was it too much to ask to listen to her? Couldn't he muster that energy?

She heard him say goodbye.

Phone in her hand, she kept staring at the gray, bare walls, until the ringing of the same phone startled her, and she almost dropped it. It was Robin Gilmore.

"Hey, Robin, what's up?" she said.

"I have something for you," he said.

"What?"

"I have retrieved more files from the hard drive."

"That's great, I'll be right there."

* * *

When she entered with Timo, Robin was sitting at the small desk by the window looking at the laptop. It was an old storage room. She hadn't been able to negotiate more than that for him, being an interim IT specialist, but he hadn't complained.

"So, what have you got for us?" Isa said.

Robin turned and said, "Inspector Lindström and ..."

"This is inspector Paikkala, the boss," she said and smiled, knowing very well Timo hated it when people called him boss.

"Lindström here says you're a genius," Timo said.

"Uh, genius? I don't know," Robin stammered.

"But you managed to do what SÄPO experts were unable to do," Timo said in a stern voice and then fixed his eyes on the young man who was still staring at him in confusion.

"Okay, just show us what you found," Isa intervened. The boss could be intimidating at times and Robin was clearly browbeaten.

Robin gave the chair a twist, so the momentum pushed him across the room to the corner where on a second table an old desktop stood. The burnt remains of the laptop were lying next to it.

While he opened the files on the desktop, he said, "I was able to retrieve five files. There are more, but I'm still working on them. These files were accessed a few days before the attack on Global Law."

"What's on them?" Timo said.

"See for yourself," he said and clicked on the first file.

"A map? Of what? What language is this? I can't read it." Isa narrowed her eyes, trying to focus and read the symbols. She'd needed glasses for years, but vanity and the idea that they didn't really suit her had pushed the care for her eyesight to the bottom of her priority list.

The cursor moved to the top left of the image and zoomed in.

"It's Russian," Timo said.

She frowned and turned to Timo. "How ...?"

He said, "Mom."

"Ah, yes, your mother is Russian. By the way, I recently saw a movie of hers."

Timo raised his brow and said, "So, you like B-movies?"

"B-movies aren't necessarily bad," Isa said and then continued, "Valesca Ignatova in 'Murder by the lake'. She's beautiful by the way. The movie wasn't that bad. A bit of overacting and too much drama here and there, but for the rest ..."

Timo crossed his arms, sighed, and looked at Robin. "This is the map of reactor one of Forsmark."

Isa stopped and looked at him with big eyes. "Wait! What? The nuclear power plant? Then it's a terrorist attack after all."

All this time they had been wrong in thinking this was something else. This was SÄPO's business. How could Timo stay so calm?

"And the other files?" Timo asked.

"Same. I think these are the plans of the three units," Robin said and closed the file. "The picture is a copy, or rather a scan."

"It's taken by someone from the inside," Timo said. "Thanks, Robin. Can you send me the files? This needs to go to SÄPO."

Robin said, "And there is more ..."

"What do you mean?" she said.

"I've traced Vollan's whereabouts since he arrived in Sweden. The airport surveillance camera showed that he arrived on 16 March. He spent two days in a youth hostel near the train station. A few days later, he showed up at the Gävle Central Station, carrying a black backpack. He moved into his apartment that same day. He met with Sören Kempe and with the Russian couple a few days later."

"The Russians gave him the maps, files, everything," Timo said.

Isa turned to Robin, "But how do you know all of this?"

"All the information is there, in your database."

He took a book from the small backpack that sat on the floor next to the desk and showed it to her.

"Facial Recognition Using AI," she read aloud.

"Not particularly new, but it allowed me to search through thousands—probably even more than that—hours of CCTV and surveillance data, in only a few hours."

"Wow, but we didn't give you access to the police database."

He smiled and then said, "Remember, I'm a hacker, just like Alex."

Timo raised a brow. "Well, there goes the fantastic safety of our computer system. What else have you discovered?"

"Uh, he was picked up by a traffic camera, driving a dark-blue Peugeot. I checked the license plate, and that car was reported stolen, months ago."

"When was this?"

"25 April, around 7:00 p.m."

"Where?"

"Near Järvsta."

"And the car is registered to?" Timo said.

"To ...," Robin said and threw a quick glance at the paper in front of him, "to Ilan Bergman."

Isa gasped for air. "Ilan Bergman? That car was used in the hit-and-run of Marie Lång, but we've never been able to prove it. The car was never found. What does Nils Vollan have to do with this? I don't understand it."

"The car drove south for a while, but then I lost track."

"You said Järvsta?" Isa said.

Robin nodded.

Then she turned to Timo. "Frank Harket's workshop is in Järvsta."

"Who's Frank Harket?"

Isa said, "A garage owner, found murdered last April, could be 25 April. I need to check that. Ilan Bergman was a suspect in the murder, but we had no evidence. I can check Vollan's fingerprints and DNA and compare it to what was found at the crime scene. But it still doesn't explain what this has to do with the Global Law shooting."

"Robin, it's really impressive what you've done," Timo said, "so what more can you do?"

"What do you want?"

"We have three unsolved cases. The shooting, the body on the beach, the hands and feet that were found near Södra Bomhus. Can you identify the most likely suspects?"

Robin sighed. "Are you asking me if these algorithms can be used to solve your cases?"

Timo crossed his arms and said without hesitation, "Yep."

"Well, no. This goes way beyond doing predictive policing, pattern identification, crime prevention or anything like that. It's like playing a game of Cluedo, only the people are not known, the murder weapons and places neither."

"Exactly. Fun, no?"

"Fun? You want machines to do your job?"

"No, but I want help," Timo said.

Robin nodded and stared at the screen. "I don't know. Maybe Alex's research could help, but it was still in its infancy, and he couldn't finish it. I have less than a month, and I need time to adapt the algorithms."

"I'm not looking for names. Just see what you can find out about the victims. Maybe that gives us an idea."

"Okay, fair enough," Robin said, "but I'll need access to your database."

Timo said, "Looks like you already have access to it, no?"

CHAPTER

11

KIRSTEN JEPPESEN, THIRTY-SIX, married, mother of two young children, ages five and seven. Her husband Gert sat across from them, in the living room of the house he and his wife had bought five years ago, when the youngest was still a baby. Five years ago. If he had known they would only have five more years together, he would have made different choices. It was a nightmare. He felt like a zombie. Twenty minutes ago, the two inspectors had told him that his wife was probably dead, and that pieces of her had been found in an open field on the other side of Gävle. After that, his mind had gone blank and the words difficult to find. The woman had started to say they felt sorry for his loss, but somehow the words didn't get through, and like an idiot he was staring at the cushions on the couch.

"You reported your wife missing last Thursday?" Isa said.

He nodded.

"Can you tell us what happened?"

"I was in Stockholm on business. I left on Wednesday. I planned to stay the weekend and come back the following Monday."

"So, the weekend as well?"

"Yes, it was a sales conference and the company I work for had organized a team building activity that weekend."

"That is Semi International?" Berger asked.

"Yes, but I got a phone call that Thursday. Kirsten hadn't picked up the children. That was unusual because she had the afternoon off. I tried to call home, but no one picked up the phone. I tried her cell phone. Nothing. That's when I got worried, and I called my mom and asked if she could go to our house and check what was going on."

"And what did your mother find?" Isa asked.

Mr. Jeppesen took a deep breath.

"She found the front door open and immediately called the police."

"And the police didn't find anything out of the ordinary?"

"No. Her phone and purse were still there, on the table in the living room. There was nothing out of the ordinary. No sign of a struggle or attack, as if she had disappeared off the face of the earth."

"What do you think could have happened?" Berger asked.

He shrugged. What could he say? She was just gone. Of course, he knew he would be the first suspect.

"I don't know. We're just normal people. We have no enemies."

"No problems at work?"

"No, nothing like that. She works ... worked as a teacher. Her students loved her, and she had a great relationship with her colleagues."

"Mr. Jeppesen, I have to ask, but how is your marriage?" Isa asked.

"My marriage is fine," he said.

There it was. He was the cheating husband who wanted his wife dead. The marriage had been good. Of course, there had been frustrations and when the children were born the romance had been put on a lower level, but they respected and loved each other. She had been his childhood friend and, later, in college, his first and only girlfriend.

He was lost. How could he go on without her? He wasn't Mr. Jeppesen without his Kirsten. And the children? What was he going to tell them? They were so young. They just wouldn't understand. The little one cried for his mummy all the time. The eldest sensed something was wrong, but he was afraid to ask. At school, children were talking, parents were talking, and teachers were talking.

His hands were shaking, as if they weren't really his. This wasn't his body. He wasn't there, and his wife wasn't dead.

"You do that a lot, staying away for the weekend?"

"What do you mean?" he raised his voice. "Are you implying I have a mistress or something?"

"You tell me," Berger said.

"No," Mr. Jeppesen shook his head wildly, "just ask my colleagues, anyone from the company, there was an event planned."

"That doesn't mean you're not having an affair; or maybe your wife did, and that's why you killed her," Berger continued.

"Prove it then," Gert shouted.

"Okay, okay," Isa intervened, "anything else that comes to mind, Mr. Jeppesen?"

"Such as?"

"Have you seen anything suspicious in the past weeks or days before your wife disappeared?"

He concentrated on his hands, then looked up at the inspectors.

"No, nothing that I can think of. We're just simple people. I never expected that something like this could happen to us. Maybe to my brother-in-law, but not to us."

"Why your brother-in-law?"

"My wife's brother is involved in criminal activities. A lot. Kirsten and he were very close, but I warned her again and again to stay away from him. He manipulated her. She couldn't refuse him anything. She protected him. I'm not sure why, but I think it had to do with the fact their mother died at a young age and Kirsten has always taken care of her younger brother. I understood that, but he abused her generosity. He stole money from us, and one time, about a year ago, I found out he had brought drugs into our home, and I threw him out."

"So, you think your brother-in-law is behind it?"

"Not him per se. His so-called friends. Drug dealers and users, thieves."

"Okay, we'll check that. What's his name?"

"Hilko Ingberg."

"And that's all?"

He raised his shoulders. He felt exhausted. Why couldn't they just leave him alone? The boys were with his mother. He just wanted to crawl into his bed and filter the world around him. And why didn't they give him more information?

"And what are the police doing?" he started. "You guys, have no leads, nothing. Instead of focusing on me, you should be looking for whoever did this!"

"Mr. Jeppesen, I understand your frustration, but we're not just looking at you. I wish I could tell you more, but at this moment we don't have much to go on."

"When I told the police about my wife's disappearance, they didn't believe me and lost time. Precious time. And now, you still don't believe me. I think this conversation is over. I want to be alone now."

* * *

"What do you think?" Isa asked as they walked through the quiet street lined with cozy family homes, with small gardens where children played in the summer, where nothing ever happened. A sleeping neighborhood, bathed in perhaps a naïve and false sense of security, thinking they had excluded the big bad world where children could get hurt and wives could disappear.

"I hate to say it, but I believe him."

Isa nodded. Exactly what she thought. Mr. Jeppesen might not have burst into tears, thrown himself to the floor or collapsed in front of them, but his behavior had been real. This was a man whose life was frozen in time, who had lost the love of his life.

"But what happened? It can't be that nobody saw anything."

Isa stopped and looked around. In this neighborhood, anything out of the ordinary must have been spotted. It was just a matter of finding the right witness.

"Have the police checked with the neighbors?" she asked.

"Yes, they did. But so far, nothing useful."

"He must have watched her," Isa said as they strolled down the street to the parking lot where she'd left the old Volkswagen.

"Just like Daniel Nyström," Berger said.

"Daniel Nyström?"

"The burn victim."

"Oh, right. What did you find out about him?"

"Practically nothing. Ordinary guy. Disappeared suddenly. We don't even know when. Reported missing by his colleagues, probably days later. I went to see his father."

"And?"

"The guy is a plant. I didn't get anything from that man, but the nurse was chatty enough. She told me Daniel's brother Pauli also has a criminal past."

"Like Kirsten Jeppesen's brother."

"Yes, and like Kirsten Jeppesen, when the police went to Daniel's house, the front door was unlocked. Daniel was gone, but nothing was stolen."

"Mmm, this looks very similar," Isa said.

She opened the door on the passenger side and then walked to the other side.

"Serial killer," Berger asked as he got in.

"Not again. Every time someone disappears here, it's a serial killer! But I have to admit there are some striking similarities in the cases. Were neighbors questioned about Daniel's disappearance?"

"Yes, but nothing. No one saw anything suspicious."

Isa took a quick glance at her cell phone and then said, "Timo wants to see us."

* * *

"Where are we?" Timo asked.

Isa, Berger, and Lars had gathered in Timo's office.

Lars took the stage. "SÄPO confirms the blueprints are from Forsmark, but they also found files related to the Karlskrona naval base, the Vattenfall power station in Uppsala, and the Riksdag in Stockholm."

"Jesus," Timo called out.

"They've increased the security on all those sites," Berger added.

"Has it been confirmed that Vollan was driving Ilan Bergman's car?"

"Yes, boss," Lars said, "traffic cameras picked up Vollan in Ilan Bergman's car weeks after the accident with Marie Lång."

"So, he stole the car?"

"Yes, but we don't know when," Isa said. "The car was reported stolen the evening of Marie's death, but I doubt that's true."

Timo frowned. "There is an Uppsala police report about the theft, hours before Marie died. How did Bergman manage to do that?"

"I don't know," Isa said.

Timo wanted to reply but then changed his mind. The thought that was flying through his head, was better not to be said. It was easy to forge a declaration ... if you were a police officer.

She continued, "Frank Harket had a criminal record; he was convicted several years ago for his involvement in two armed robberies. So he probably knew Vollan."

Timo needed to get it clear in his head. "Vollan goes to Frank Harket in Bergman's car that evening in April to discuss the shooting. They have an argument, and he kills Frank. Is that what it is?"

"Vollan is seen driving away in the car, but he was never seen arriving with it," Lars said.

"So, the car was in Harket's garage, and he stole it that evening."

Isa was standing in the doorway, back against the doorpost, observing her colleagues. Timo thought she looked too relaxed. Usually that meant she had been doing something behind his back that wasn't too kosher.

"Ilan Bergman is the connection to Global Law," she said.

"Everything points to that man," Lars interrupted. "I had a closer look at the account from which Vollan received the money. It wasn't hard. The owner of the account is Ilan Bergman. He opened it about a year ago."

"So, we have the car, the card and the account," Timo said. "Is he our man?"

"And Bergman's name popped up on a list of members of a far-right group," Lars added.

"I don't know," Isa said. "This looks too obvious. Where did he get the money to finance all of this?"

"It's probably not just him," Timo said. "There is an entire organization behind it. We need to get him to talk."

"We bring him in?" Berger asked.

"Yes. And I want to know everything about Bergman. Financials, phone records, everything," Timo said.

"I can put my IT guy on it," Isa said and smiled.

"No, Sivert should be able to do this. We should keep Gilmore on the other cases. He did a great job recovering the files and tracing Vollan's whereabouts. We only have a few weeks left. No way Gilmore could stay longer?"

"I can ask him, but he seems determined to leave," Isa replied.

"But are we absolutely sure Vollan stole the car?"

"We'll see. Forensics are still comparing Vollan's fingerprints and DNA with the evidence found in Frank Harket's garage."

Timo sighed. "Let's bring in Ilan Bergman for questioning. Let's also get a search warrant for his house." Then he turned to Lars and said, "What about Tech4You?"

"Everyone who works there seems to be clean. Nothing suspicious. I don't think any of the Tech4You employees helped them. The only strange thing is Lage Feldt, the founder of Tech4You. He's a very private person. Few people have seen or talked to him. Besides a few articles, you can't find anything on social media about him. No pictures, no Twitter, Facebook or Linkedin accounts. Four years ago, no one had even heard of him and then he suddenly rises to fame with a technology that was essentially developed by Ragnvald Strand and his friends at the University of Uppsala. I'll look into it more, but right now it can't find anything that links Tech4You to the shooting besides being in the building next to Global Law."

"And former employees of the Gävle Herald?" Isa asked.

"Man, that is a mess. We're talking about hundreds of people, and no one can give me a complete list of employees. The owner of the newspaper died years ago, and his widow's memory is failing. She gave me a few names I could contact. I'm doing the best I can, but I think it's a dead end."

Timo couldn't hide the disappointment in his eyes. "These guys were prepared. They knew about the passage. I need to know who gave him the information. Ask Gilmore to help you."

"Timo, Robin is already overloaded," Isa said, "you can't dump everything on him!"

He quickly turned to her and snapped, "Then I'll pay him overtime."

A wave of shock washed over the faces in the room. Maybe he was too harsh, too demanding, but they needed to feel that this was no joke.

"Another thing ... Daniel Nyström," Timo said and pulled the file lying in the corner of his desk toward him and opened it, "looks like we didn't get very far."

Daniel Nyström. Timo looked at the photo of the young man. What was it about this case? Average face, brown hair, already noticeably thinning—although he was barely into his twenties—and a big nose that took up a proportionally large part of his face. The man looked familiar, but he didn't know where and when he had seen him before.

"Mr. Nyström's neighbors couldn't tell us much," Berger said, and let out a sigh of relief when his statement wasn't met with another lash-out or frown.

"Neighbors are usually great sources of information," Timo remarked.

"A woman claims she saw a dark-blue car on the street, days before the disappearance. It stayed there for a few hours and then the driver took off."

"Did she see the driver? License plate?"

"No, but she reported it to the police," Lars said. "Unfortunately, with the lack of resources these days, we never looked into it."

"What about his family?"

Berger said, "The father is still alive, but I couldn't get anything useful from him. Dementia. Mother and stepfather died in a car accident six years ago. The brother, Pauli Nyström ..."

Timo no longer heard the rest of Berger's words. He saw his mouth move, but everything had suddenly slowed down. He was taken back to a time and place where he didn't want to be. Pauli Nyström. He knew the man; he had seen him before. And Daniel was his brother. He bore a remarkable resemblance to him. But he couldn't let the memories surface. Not now. How did this all come together? It could only be a coincidence. Nothing more.

"... he also has a juvenile record, domestic violence against his stepfather, theft, drugs. It wasn't too surprising. They had an abusive stepfather who regularly beat the mother and the boys. The stepfather was in and out of prison until he died in 2012."

"What about Daniel?"

Should he say anything? No. This had nothing to do with Daniel's murder. It couldn't be. That case was closed. The culprit found and locked away. But then there was Breiner. Another coincidence?

"No criminal record. He was the youngest brother, but we should talk to Pauli Nyström," Berger said.

"A good idea, go ahead," Timo said.

He took a deep breath and got up. Pauli Nyström. He should tell them. They'd find out. Although he could still hide behind the blissful ignorance he hadn't recognized him. It wasn't as if he had hindered the investigation. He just needed oxygen, to clear his mind.

"Berger, you can talk to Pauli Nyström; I'll take the Jeppesen case," Lars said.

Isa said, "Timo, are you okay?"

"Uhm, I just feel a bit under the water. Sorry, I need some air."

As he stumbled outside, the other inspectors looked at him, surprised by the sudden exit of the superintendent.

"What's wrong with him?" Berger asked.

"I don't know," Isa said.

* * *

"I have nothing to do with this," Ilan yelled, hiding his face in his hands.

His whole body went up and down with the sobbing. That morning Berger, Lars, and a team of police officers stood at his front door with a search warrant in hand. Thereafter, Mr. Bergman was kindly requested to accompany them to the police station, where he, assisted by one of his fellow lawyers, was confronted with the account in his name from which regular deposits were made to Nils Vollan's account.

"Where does the money come from, Ilan?" Berger said and showed him the list of deposits that were made into the account since the start. Several ten thousand Swedish crowns per month.

"I ... I have to tell you something," Ilan stammered. "I'm being blackmailed."

"Blackmail? Who?"

"I don't know, but it started with Marie Lång," Ilan said and quickly looked at his lawyer, who didn't know how to react.

"Tell us," Lars said.

"I admit I hit Marie with my car and left her on the road, but when I drove away that night, she was still alive."

"We know that by now."

"But someone saw me," Ilan said.

"Who?"

"I don't know, but this is the person who has been stalking and threatening me for months. Not just myself, but my wife as well."

"How?"

"It started with pictures of the hit-end-run. Then my car was stolen in Harket's garage. He wanted to frame me for that murder. Then the Global Law card and code. Oh, God, I have given him what he wanted, but I didn't know he would do this."

"How did you manage to get your car reported stolen, before it was even stolen?" Lars asked.

"I don't know, but it's all his doing. He is more powerful than you can imagine. You have to help me."

Ilan ran his hand through his hair.

"So, Nils Vollan ..."

"Forget about Vollan! I don't know him," Ilan cried out. "Vollan is dead. Whoever's stalking me is still very much alive. He has everything under control. He is the mastermind. He is dangerous!"

Lars looked at his colleague and then turned to Ilan Bergman again.

"Is there any proof of what you just told us? I think you just cocked up a story to hide your involvement. You have been member of the right-wing group 'White Power'."

Ilan shook his head. "What? I've never been a member of that group. I have never been a member of any of those groups in my entire life."

"This is your name, isn't it?" Berger pointed to the line on the membership list that he put in front of Ilan and his lawyer.

Ilan let his fingers run over the paper. "I don't understand. This is a mistake. This must be another Ilan Bergman."

"But that is your address, isn't it?" Berger continued.

"I don't understand any of this. Check my phone. You'll see the messages and the phone calls. There are from a private number, but can't you trace that sort of thing?"

Berger calmly closed the file, while Lars handed him another document, which he had pulled from a second folder in front of him.

"We already had a look at your cell phone, Mr. Bergman. This is the list of calls and messages that were found," Berger said and put it in front of Bergman with a smooth twist.

Ilan took it and scanned it quickly. He looked a little lost when he finally said, "This can't be. There should be at least five, six of these messages, and the pictures. No, no!"

"Mr. Bergman ..."

"No, no, this isn't right," Ilan screamed and got up. He couldn't breathe. His entire world was falling apart. He wasn't the one who was going to go down for this massacre.

"Mr. Bergman, sit down!" Berger said, but it was too late.

Ilan clutched at his chest. Another panic attack. His heart was racing and as the dizziness took over, the sounds in the room faded.

CHAPTER

12

TIMO HAD DRAGGED ISA to the little café by the police station that had become his favorite spot when he needed a break. Not only because it smelled so wonderfully of freshly ground coffee beans, but because the blend of old baroque decorations with the clean modern lines of the tables, chairs and windows intrigued him. How could two clashing styles fit together so magically?

It was calm for a late afternoon, and while she'd doubted it would be a good idea to have coffee so late, she'd accepted his generous offer of a treat without hesitation.

"What did Solberg say?" she said.

He turned the cup of coffee on the saucer a few times, and then said, "He said nothing."

"What? He has no opinion?"

"If he has, he hasn't shared it with me. The one thing I'm good for is showing up to his stupid press conferences."

"He needs to be able to divert the difficult questions. And besides you look good on camera."

"Uh, what?" He looked up surprised.

"Just ignore," she said and quickly took a sip of the coffee.

He put his focus back to the cup of coffee and said, "What do you think?"

"Okay, I wish I could say Bergman's story was the most unbelievable thing I'd ever heard, but I'm afraid he's telling the truth. He was genuinely surprised about the messages on his phone that weren't there."

"I tend to agree with you. I asked Lars to get his phone records and check the bank account again. What did Bergman's wife say?"

"Not much. She said he changed after the accident, but that's all. And, Timo, ..."

"What?"

"I have to tell you she's Nick's ex," she said with a straight face.

"You want me to talk to her?"

"No, it's not that. There are no hard feelings. I just wanted you to know, since you're always so ... sensitive to those things."

"I feel like all my principles are being flushed down the drain these days," he said and then quickly glanced at her. She had an expression of confusion on her face, and he felt like he had let his guard down too much.

"Never mind," he said before she could intervene. "The question now is why? Why Ilan Bergman?"

"They need someone to take the blame. He's the perfect victim."

He sighed and looked around. The server gave him a quick smile and then attended to the customers who had just entered the café.

"Lindström, we are stuck. What if it's not about a terrorist attack? What if it's not about Global Law or Karst Engersson?"

"Then what?"

He shrugged. It wasn't their case anyway. Time to let go and let SÄPO really take over. Lay low until the internal investigation would be over. The report of the Commission on the police restructuring was going to be presented to the parliament next week.

"Nyström," Isa said suddenly, "what was this about the other day?"

"What do you mean?" he said, trying to sound as innocent and oblivious as possible, but he knew that if anyone had noticed it would be her.

"You know him."

He shook his head. "No, I think I know his brother Pauli."

"How?"

"He was a witness in an old case a long time ago. A case that has been solved. It's just a coincidence."

"Are you sure?"

"Yes, I'm sure," Timo said.

"Look, Timo, I respect you. I respect your privacy, but you're keeping something from me. The same thing goes for Breiner."

He knew he had to give her something.

"Breiner and I had a personal vendetta. Well, he had for some reason, and after a while ... well, if someone's out to get you, you get defensive, frustrated, and biased."

"Why was he out to get you?"

"I had raised his questionable investigation methods a number of times with our superiors. Unfortunately, he got the chance to get back at me, with a fairly, painful case for me personally. I can say no more."

He looked her in the eye, and for a moment, short and confusingly intense, there was a connection, more than just the fragile thread of respect.

"Your girlfriend?" she said in a voice that gave away no emotion.

"You can find out for yourself. It's no secret."

"You'll tell me when you're ready," she said calmly. "But you decided not to repay him in kind?"

"They wanted an indictment for Breiner, and I was asked to join the team because I had filed complaints against him before and I knew what he was capable of, but it had become so personal, ethically it was wrong. Besides, I was a liability. Breiner would have used my involvement to get a dismissal. So, I already told you before: I wasn't removed from the case, I resigned."

"Let's put the theory of terrorist attack aside. Breiner was murdered a year ago when he decided to betray the people he worked for. Let's assume this isn't Ormar. That gang is too disorganized to pull off something like this. They are not important enough."

"But who is?"

She put both hands on the table, and said, "The police."

He sighed. "Know very well what you're saying!"

"Who else could forge the theft report of Bergman's car?"

"That's no evidence," Timo said.

"Karst Engersson was killed because he knew, and they had to get rid of him. And hiding his murder as terrorist attack was perfect."

Timo frowned. "But it's drawing attention."

"Attention they have under control and plays very well in their cards. Now the police and government can show the public how decisive they can be. With everything that has been going on, they need that. The Sandviken killer was a factor they hadn't foreseen."

"This is taking it a bit too far. I don't think that ..."

"We need to look at Engersson. He left traces behind. Those will lead us to the people who have orchestrated this and who paid Nils Vollan to kill ten people. Take a step back, but Solberg can't know. I don't think he's involved, but he's a puppet. They need him."

"Can you trust Robin?" Timo said.

She said without hesitation, "Yes, but we'll put him in danger."

He didn't like it. He'd never consider putting a civilian in danger, but this case needed unconventional measures. Was he prepared to throw all his moral standards overboard? It had started with his personal life and now his job too. But to his own surprise he heard himself say, "Ask him to look at Engersson."

She nodded and said, "Okay."

He picked up the coffee cup, emptied it in one gulp, and then pushed the chair back. The sound of the chair legs sliding across the tile floor startled the older couple in the corner.

"Before you go, I need to ask you something," Isa started. "A favor between friends."

"Friends?" he said.

"We're not friends then?" she asked, surprised.

He changed his mind, didn't get up but leaned over, head slightly tilted looking at her face and thought about it for a few seconds before saying, "I want you to think very carefully about how you define our relationship."

"Oh, God! Timo, not that psycho stuff again! Not now!"

He ignored her outburst. "Friends, acquaintances, boss-employee, working partners, enemies, intruder-protector of the fine Gävle police department, or just people who find each other less and less irritating?"

He couldn't keep a straight face after the last words and his mouth curled into a wide smile.

Then she laughed. "I'll go for the last one then."

"What did you want to ask me?" he said.

"Can you talk to Nick?"

"Me? Why?"

"I don't know. You talked to him after the shooting, and he said that you somehow seemed to understand. He doesn't want to listen and talk to me, neither to a professional. So maybe you can try. It's bad, very bad. I can't get through to him."

He wasn't sure what to answer.

"I mean ... you're good at this psychological stuff," she said.

"I'll talk to him," he said and got up.

"Thanks. I think it's best you contact him yourself, otherwise I'm just meddling."

"Yes, but not today. I need to be somewhere."

"Mmm, a date," she said and laughed.

He frowned. "Don't forget, just people who don't get on each other's nerves! And if you must know, no ... not really."

"Not really? What does that mean?"

But he was already walking to the exit, pretending he hadn't heard her question.

* * *

"It was interesting," Ingrid said.

"What do you mean by 'interesting'? It was great fun. Admit it!"

Timo put the bottle of water in front of her. He did the same on his side, unscrewed the cap and took a quick swallow.

"Ah, at least no coffee," she called out, trying not to answer his question.

It was quiet and empty in the cafeteria of the sports hall. She should go home. It was almost 9:00 p.m. Perhaps the boys were still awake, and she could still wish them goodnight. Anton was less strict when it came to discipline and rules. But she hadn't been able to say no to Timo when he offered her a drink after her very first climbing experience.

With a mischievous look in his eyes and a smile on his face, he plopped down in the chair in front of her. She felt the gym bag, casually tossed to the floor at his side of the table, poking at her legs. How could he not look tired or sweaty at all? It had been impressive how he had almost run up that wall, in no time, while she had been puffing, sweating, and straining to pull herself up the climbing wall. More than anything else, she'd hung from the climbing rope mid-air when she had again failed to reach one of the hand or foot grips. But then she'd heard his calls of encouragement, and instead of feeling clumsy and stupid, she'd enjoyed it.

"Don't change the subject," he said.

She gave him a faint smile and poured the content of the bottle in the glass standing next to it.

"You didn't answer my question," he said and continued to stare at her. Those bright blue eyes, that handsome face, she just couldn't look at him without revealing how incredibly attractive she found him. But she still couldn't figure him out. There were clear signs he felt the same, but then at times he reverted to the same psychological crap he used on about anyone of the team, and she doubted he found her special.

"There was no question," she said.

"Okay then: did you enjoy yourself?"

"Yes," she said and looked him in the eye. For a second, she saw a flash of uncertainty, as if the confident man sitting before her was at a loss for words.

"Great," he said, bent down and grabbed something from the bag on the floor.

"You earned it." He pushed the white envelope toward her. He let his hand rest on the paper a little too long, and as she tried to take it, she felt the skin of his index finger brush against hers, subtle, unnoticeable for a bystander, but it wasn't a coincidence, it was a deliberate move. She stared at it with open mouth, and then looked up. There was confusion on his face. In an unexpected moment he had let his guard down.

He pulled his hand away, but she took it and held it for a few seconds as she let her fingers ran over the skin. She was confused; he was confused. This wasn't supposed to happen. Then she let his hand go, pulled the envelope toward her, and peeled back the flap. Although the movements seemed so well-controlled, it felt as if she could hardly keep the trembling of her body under control. He was breathing heavily, with his eyes fixed on her hands as she took out the two tickets. She didn't quite understand what she was holding. Her mind was still stuck in that moment when his finger had caressed hers, and she had responded by taking his hand.

"I hope you like it," his voice sounded softly.

"Tosca. Wow, that's ... uh, a very tragic and passionate opera. Are you sure?"

He smiled.

"You actually love this," she said.

He nodded. "Yes, I do like classical music and operas."

"When is it?" she asked and looked at the tickets.

"Next Saturday, in Uppsala."

Then the expression on his face grew serious and he sighed before saying: "Ingrid ... I think you should take Anton."

"Why?"

"I just think it's best you take your husband," he said calmly.

She understood what he wanted to say without saying it. What had happened a few moments ago couldn't happen again. He'd be tempting fate by inviting her to something like this.

"Okay, I'll ask him," she mumbled.

But she didn't ask him. She told her husband she was going to the opera with someone from work. Anton was glad it wasn't him and he didn't ask who she was going with.

Timo was more difficult to convince. There were plenty of reasons not to go. With the media storm he couldn't afford to indulge in anything non-work related. It wouldn't be appropriate. And he had to spend time decorating and working in his new house. Was there no one else she could ask?

There wasn't, and it was a shame to let one of the tickets go to waste. Reluctantly he had agreed, but that evening they met on the steps of the opera house in Uppsala, he was happy to see her and spend time with her. They could do this. They could share common interests, as friends. There was nothing strange or uncomfortable.

She looked stunning with her hair down and the simple dark-green tailored jumpsuit. He felt underdressed with the black shirt and black trousers he was wearing, thinking he had made an effort.

In that moment, he also knew it was a mistake, that he couldn't do this anymore without suffering the consequences of a broken heart or the realization that his moral values had been thrown out the window. Either way, it was the tragedy of Tosca poured over it.

* * *

"Nothing better than a bit of Puccini tragedy to brighten up the weekend," Timo said as they stepped outside.

"Well, you wanted to go," Ingrid said.

He grabbed her hand as she tried to balance on the high-heeled shoes she didn't normally wear.

"And you seemed a bit emotional," she said.

"I have a cold," he grinned.

"Sure."

"It's funny, I've seen this opera so many times that I can't count it on two hands anymore. Different places, different times, but every time … really every time I hope that the ending will be different. That somehow the bullets are blanks and that Cavaradossi survives, and they live happily ever after. His death is so disturbing. I … sorry, don't mind me."

"I get it. You almost know from the start Tosca can't save him. Love eventually succumbs to abusive power."

He nodded his head. "Yes, it's sad." Then he looked up and smiled. "So no, I'm not emotional at all."

"And now what? Shall we go for a drink?"

He sighed and then said, "I don't think that's a good idea."

"Why?" she said.

"We can't spend any more time together ... alone, just the two of us."

"Again, but why?" she said and looked at him with her beautiful green eyes. "We are just colleagues and friends. There's no harm in doing that."

"Ingrid, you don't understand. We can never be just friends ... I ..."

"We can be friends; we are friends, Timo," she said. And with every word her eyes seemed to fill with tears.

He turned his face away. "No, we can't. Not to me."

"What do you actually want to say?"

It was time to say the things he hadn't dare to say before.

"I ..."

"Ingrid, my God, it's you," a high-pitched voice sounded. Out of the corner of his eye, he saw a man and a woman walking toward them.

"Karen, Gilbert," Ingrid said in surprise.

"It's been so long," the woman cried out, took Ingrid's hand, and gave her a quick kiss on the cheek.

"Yes, it's been way too long," Ingrid said.

"Is Anton here?"

"No, I'm here ... alone ... uh, this is inspector Paikkala."

She turned to Timo who had watched the entire scene in silence.

"Nice to meet you," Karen said and shook his hand, as did her husband.

"Karen and Gilbert are childhood friends. We went to the same school. We live in the same neighborhood."

Timo said nothing and nodded politely.

"So, you are inspector," Gilbert said, "with the Gävle police?"

"Yes, I am."

"We heard about the shooting. Nasty business! Any leads on who did this?"

"I can't say much about the ongoing investigation, but we'll get them," Timo said.

"I have no doubt," Gilbert answered. "It's terrible how you guys have been beaten up by the media. People don't understand how tough it is."

Timo gave him a dim smile and then also turned to the two women. "I have to go. It was nice meeting you both."

Then he turned and walked to the train station. Their conversation had been interrupted. There was no conclusion, and he knew she wanted one. But, yet again, neither of them had been able to say what they'd been thinking and feeling for so long. And this time he was afraid it would never be said.

CHAPTER

13

"**I QUIT.**"

Isa walked across the room. She didn't know what she felt, but what she did know was that the sessions with Dr. Wikholm got her nothing. Nor had she gained insight into her own destructive behavior, nor had she been given pointers to salvage her relationship with Nick, which she already believed to be in jeopardy after just five months.

"Why? You came to me."

"The questions that answer questions drive me crazy! It's no use to me. Tell me how to change myself!"

"What were your expectations then?" Dr. Wikholm looked at her over the rim of his glasses.

She sighed and let her shoulders slump as she ran her hand along the wall. She couldn't sit down, every fiber in her body crying with rage and a restlessness she couldn't calm down.

"I don't know. Maybe a pill to moderate my bipolar behavior?"

"Are you serious?"

"No, but I just need to know why."

"Why what?"

"Why I can't hold a decent relationship. Why I tend to destroy everything that's good and sustainable. I don't think I'm afraid to commit. I just think ..."

"What?"

"That I can do better. I get attracted to men too easily. Beautiful, sexy men. I think it's my right to go after them. To fulfil my sexual desires, but that's not love."

"So, was Alex love or desire?"

She turned and looked at him, the old man still hunched over in his large leather chair. He had taken a younger woman. He had fallen in the same trap. Youth, beauty, sexual attraction.

Dr. Wikholm continued, "You call him the greatest love of your life. Why?"

"I don't know," she said. And that made her sad. Now, there was nothing left. It was all a lie. It hadn't been love at all. Alex had been mysterious, sexy, and just the most beautiful man she'd ever seen. The passion she had felt for him, had been nothing but lust. Nick was lust as well. Magnus was a challenge because he was married. And Viktor? He was her teenage sweetheart. She didn't even know what she was doing at that time. He was sweet and caring, but they hadn't been right for each other.

"Now we're getting somewhere," he said.

The tears were running down her face, but she didn't make a sound.

"You formed an idealized image of your relationship with Alex. His death made it so much harder ... no, easier to imagine it was something grander, more passionate, and more dramatic than it was. I'm not saying it wasn't love, but you need to take a step back and reevaluate it. Only then you can move forward."

She wiped the tears away. "What about Nick?"

"You have to help him, and then you also need to take a step back and think about what you really mean to each other, but be honest, be brutally honest."

"I don't think he can handle that," she said.

"I think he can. But can you? I think he needs clarity from you. Can he count on you to help him or not? Are you fully committed to this relationship, in good and bad days?"

"I am committed," she said.

"You told me you asked inspector Paikkala to talk to him. Why aren't you talking to Nick yourself?"

She sighed and said, "I tried, but he doesn't listen."

"Did you try hard enough?"

* * *

The sound of footsteps echoed down the hall. Quick steps. Someone was in a hurry and had no time to reflect and wonder about the strange looks everyone was giving him. People weren't used to seeing him in a police uniform. The black T-shirt and worn jeans had become his trademark. Even the press conferences hadn't been an incentive to worry about his wardrobe, but today was a special day.

"Boss, you look ... different," Isa said as Timo came into the office. "You've got something else in your wardrobe after all."

"Funny," he said.

"You look nervous," she said. "What's going on?"

"The interview is in two hours. I have to say I don't have a warm and confident feeling about it."

"Ah, the job interview for superintendent," she said. "I thought this was a formality?"

"There are three candidates. One of them is Finn Heimersson. He's chief inspector with the Uppsala police and a damn good detective. Tough competition."

"Yeah, I know him, but I can't say that our first encounter during the Sandviken case was an amicable one," she sighed. "I know he's your friend, but he tried really hard to get his hands on the Sandviken case, and he didn't shy away from filthy tricks to achieve his goal."

"I know," he said while he gathered the papers on his desk.

"Strange, don't you think? Why would he be interested in coming to Gävle?"

"Yeah, that bothers me too. His position in Uppsala is solid."

"Who is the third candidate?"

He hesitated before saying, "Elvin Wieland."

"Magnus' brother? Why?"

"Relax, he doesn't stand a chance. That's obvious."

"But why? Timo, you can't let this happen! This can't happen. I don't understand this."

"Wieland has no chance. Both his competence and motivation are in question, but Heimersson ... I'm worried about him."

She said, "And indeed, you have a problem."

"Why?" he said stunned.

"They usually don't like poster boys," she answered with a straight face, "they like the ugly old, close-to-retirement types. Someone like Anders. Unnoted, decent. Heimersson fits the bill better."

"Poster boy? What the hell, Lindström!"

"Oh, come on, Timo, most women in this police department have had plenty of wet dreams about you at one point or another."

"Lindström, this is quite inappropriate and since it's you I'm just going to pretend I didn't hear this," he said with a stern face and furrowed brows.

Never in his life had he felt so exposed, so openly checked out. And although she never had too many barriers that kept her from speaking her mind about things, it was the first time it got so personal.

"Sorry, bad day and bad night for that matter," she sighed.

She indeed seemed more irritated and annoying than usual.

"Nick didn't come home last night. I tried calling him so many times, but he didn't answer. At 2:00 a.m. I went to look for him. I drove around and around, and I finally found him at a bus stop a few blocks away, just staring in front of him. He didn't know why he was there and how he got there. I can't be his nanny all the time! Can you just talk to him as soon as possible, please? I am desperate."

"Okay, tonight," he said. "But can you do something for me and ask Dr. Olsson for her final report on the Jeppesen case?"

"What about you? Can't you check it with her?"

"I will be busy with the interview, I have no time for this right now," he said angrily. "I don't need to justify my actions to you. I am your boss, and I am asking."

"Timo, just speaking as a friend or someone that's not annoying you all the time, you need to get this thing with Ingrid out of your system," Isa said.

"There is nothing between Ingrid and me," he stammered.

"You mean Dr. Olsson. Yes, I've heard this thing already many times, from both of you. Well, if that's the case, don't take her out to the opera."

"The opera? How do you know?"

"Anton told me she went to the opera with someone from work. Since it wasn't me, I figured it must have been you."

"I'm not going to talk to you about this," he said indignantly, took the file and walked out the room to the forensics lab.

Two hours before the interview. He usually had enough self-control not to let the stress get the upper hand, but he wasn't too sure of his chances. It had been ages ago since he'd done a real job interview. For SÄPO no less. But recent events didn't play in his favor. Even if he wasn't responsible, the perception and opinion of the majority, easily manipulated, was always right. All he could do was try his best. He owed it to the men and women of this department. When he had started, almost six months ago, he had been an outsider, someone who still had to earn the trust of the team. The team had potential but in six months he hadn't been able to achieve anything, at least not enough to convince his superiors.

* * *

Ingrid couldn't keep her eyes of his body. He looked good in the dark-blue trousers and jacket covering the light-blue long-sleeved shirt paired with a dark-blue tie.

"Uh, what did you say?" Ingrid mumbled when for the second time in five minutes Timo didn't get an answer to his question. She was distracted. Distracted by the suit, distracted by him.

"You found particles in the flesh of the hands?"

She nodded, stared at him for a moment before saying, "Metallic particles, grease and oil."

She had to order her thoughts.

"Get it out of your system ... quickly," he said suddenly. "What is it?"

"Why are you dressed like that, and why are you here?" Ingrid said with a grim look on her face.

"I have an interview. Just so we're on the same basis, I still stick to what I said last Saturday. We are just colleagues, and we should behave like that. Now, back to business, oil and grease. This points us to where Mrs. Jeppesen was held before her death."

She could tell him she was over Saturday and how he had left her on the steps in front of the opera house. After his sudden departure, Karen and Gilbert had taken her for a drink. When she got home, it was almost midnight and she found Anton sleeping on the couch, in front of the TV. He looked so cute and handsome. She had a beautiful husband. As she sat down next to him on the couch, she wondered why he wasn't enough. He was everything she wanted and needed. A caring man, a great father despite the little insignificant annoyances. She ran her hand over his leg. He let out a moan. Then she moved up his chest and started to unbutton his shirt. He was still rubbing his eyes as she reached for his belt and slowly unbuckled it.

"What?" he had let out. She had placed her finger gently over his mouth.

Usually, he was the one who took the initiative, but before he realized it, she was lying on top of him, naked, her hands pulling down his pants, kissing his neck, licking, and nipping his chest. She was angry, but at the same time full of sexual energy she needed to get rid of, otherwise her body would explode. That evening she longed for him so badly Anton hardly had time to take in what was going on. And she didn't need Timo Paikkala. If he wanted to be colleagues and nothing else, that was what he would get.

"A warehouse, storage facility," she answered. "Not sure if we'll get anything more?"

"But that wasn't what I wanted to talk about," he said. "The last line in your report."

"The DNA analysis," she said and walked to the computer standing on the desk. She signaled him to join her.

"It's clear," she said when pulling up the report. "It's Ilan Bergman's DNA."

"His DNA showed up in the shoe where Mrs. Jeppesen's severed feet were found?"

"The cases have to be connected."

He stared at the picture of the DNA bands resulting from the electrophoresis. On the left end side, Ilan Bergman's, and on the right side the result for the unknown DNA.

"Someone is going through a lot of trouble to make us believe Ilan Bergman is guilty."

"What if he is?" Ingrid said.

"What's the connection? It seems too convenient."

"Maybe you're right," she said, "but we can't ignore the evidence."

He closed his eyes and rubbed his forehead with his hand as he let out a sigh. The light from the computer screen hurt his eyes.

"Headache," she whispered and stared at him with concern.

"Migraine," he said and let his head rest against the wall as he looked at the images on the computer. "Bergman is still in custody and now we have another case where he might be implicated. It doesn't add up."

"I can have another look at the particles that were found, and the rest of the scarecrow's clothes."

"I need to go. Keep me posted on anything you can find. Anything."

"Timo, are you going to be okay?" she asked.

He turned to her and smiled, a faint smile, before he stepped outside.

* * *

"So, what have you got for me?"

Robin looked up from his keyboard. Half an hour earlier, he had called inspector Lindström and asked her to join him in the room where he had spent the past thirty-six hours without interruption. When she had asked him for help, he had been eager and over the top to help. This was something tangible, where he could help people, where he could make a difference, but the work had been lonely. Locked in a room with computers, without sunlight for the past three days. The thirty-minute powernaps weren't doing the trick anymore. He needed a decent bed and sleep. It was his own fault. At times he could lose himself so completely in his work that he put his own health at risk.

"You need some sleep," she said as she grabbed a chair and joined him at the desk.

As if he didn't know.

"Global Law. I had a look at Vollan's finances. So, you know he received regular payments the last six months when he returned to Sweden."

"Returned?"

"Nils Vollan was in Sweden before. Three years ago, he enlisted in the army under a false name. More particularly in the marine."

"What?" she said. "How is that possible?"

"False ID, fake record. He was known as Sven Toksund. Actually, Sven Toksund existed, but died five years ago. Vollan took his identity."

"Are you kidding me?" Isa let out.

"And he spent time in Karlskrona."

"Karlskrona? That's where he probably got the floor plan. Can you find out who he socialized with? Maybe one of the other attackers was in the army too."

"No problem. What I also wanted to tell you is that he disappeared after a year. Then he showed up again a year ago, and then six months ago. And I also traced back where the payments were coming from."

"Ilan Bergman, right?" Isa said.

"Wrong. Bergman is the name on the account, but I'm sure he didn't open it."

"Who did?"

"Nils Vollan himself."

"What?"

"Look," Robin said and pointed to the screen of the computer. It showed the high-angled footage of a café's interior. The resolution was poor, but in the background, behind one of the computers, Nils Vollan was sitting.

"The account was created on-line. I was able to trace the IP address of the computer that was used to create the account and it led to an internet café near the train station in Gävle. Luckily, they kept the camera footage, and this is Vollan who created the account. There was another account he created under the name Sven Toksund, and he used the money from that account for the Bergman account. It wasn't easy, but I traced the cash flow back to an offshore account in the Bahamas. After some digging, the company that owns the account seems to be a subsidiary of a company called Brissitone, which in turn is the property of Global Law."

"What? So, the massacre at Global Law was financed by Global Law itself?"

"Or pretending to be? I need to dig a lot deeper."

Isa said, "And Timo was right. Bergman is being set up."

"Okay, come to think of it, your boss asked me to look at Karst Engersson," Robin said and closed the image on the screen and pulled up another file."

"Sorry, Robin. I know Timo gave you a list of things to do. He can be very demanding and intense at times."

"That's fine," Robin said with his eyes still locked on the screen. "Your boss is quite ... interesting. He reminds me a bit of Alex."

"He does?"

179

Robin gave her a quick glance and then continued, "Okay. This is Engersson's cell phone data for the past two years. It's a long list. The man had a busy life, both professionally and personally. He had a mistress."

"Oh, really?"

"Yes, a certain Anna Wallman."

"Anna Wallman? Where have I heard that name before?"

"She's often in the news as a spokesperson for anti-abortion groups."

"Wow. That doesn't sound right. Engersson is known to have rather central-left sympathies. He was invited by Leif Berg to speak at the Social-Democrat convention."

"And what's even more interesting: since a year ago, his phone calls to Leif Berg's office have increased in frequency ... significantly. The last weeks even daily. Another name that frequently passed by is Lauri Valkama."

"Who is that?"

"He used to work at the Finnish embassy in Stockholm, then a few years at Global Law, but now he's an administrative assistant at the Town Hall in Gävle."

"An old colleague. That's maybe not so strange."

"Calls at 2:00 a.m. in the morning of more than an hour?" Robin said.

"What exactly did this Lauri Valkama do at Global Law?"

"He was one of the accountants."

"So, he had access to the financial records," Isa said and gave the chair a spin.

"I'm not sure," Robin murmured as he closed the files on the screen.

"Dig some more in Mr. Valkama's financials."

"Okay," Robin tried to suppress a yawn. It was getting increasingly more difficult to concentrate. He could hardly find the words. More than not, his sentences were bursting with English words, his own mother tongue.

"If you can, but get some sleep first," Isa got up and gave him a kind pat on the shoulder. "You did an excellent job."

* * *

"Thank you, inspector Paikkala, for sharing your ideas and views on public safety, community engagement, teamwork, team restructuring, and digitalization. I'm sure my colleagues, like me, have plenty of questions for you."

Three men and a woman on the other side of the table. It wasn't your typical interview room. The table stood in the middle of what had been used as a ballroom in past centuries, right under a chandelier whose crystals sparkled in the light streaming in through the large, white-curtained windows. The murals depicted scenes of the Swedish independence battle from the sixteenth century. Behind the panelists there was a mirror lined with gold-leafed decorations that had distracted him several times during his speech. Timo sat in a gilded chair with an upholstered seat of worked silk and he felt less than comfortable. He wondered why the Gävle Town Hall had to be the place to have this conversation. Was it to impress or overpower him?

The people in front of him hadn't moved a muscle, hadn't said a word, or let out a sigh throughout the presentation. The expressions on their faces were neutral. Usually, he was very good at reading people but this time he had no clue. They had briefly introduced themselves at the beginning of the interview, but he knew none of them. Was this a good or a bad thing?

All he knew was that from the moment he had set foot in that room the tension had grown. He may not have known them, but they certainly knew who he was. It was a tribunal, permeated with bias and hidden agendas.

The man in the middle, sitting next to the woman, had spoken, and looked at his colleagues to start the conversation. The man on the left didn't hesitate for a moment and began to speak: "Inspector Paikkala, you have been in Gävle for six months now."

"Since April," Timo confirmed.

"Since April, right. You talk about restructuring and teamwork, but your actions over the past months haven't really given us much confidence that you can make a difference. Magnus Wieland, a brutal shooting, and a dozen of unsolved cases. Not really encouraging."

"My assignment was only temporary, and I wasn't given the mandate," Timo answered. He knew that this was coming.

"Well, that didn't stop you from doing your own investigation into the Global Law shooting, thereby obstructing SÄPO and endangering the entire operation."

"Everything we have discovered and what we have done, we have shared with SÄPO. My team has been working with them in an open and constructive way."

"That's not what inspector Solberg told me," the man said. "He described the behavior of one person in particular as quite problematic: Isabel Lindström."

"Inspector Lindström has been nothing but professional since my arrival in Gävle. In fact, she has been instrumental in solving a few high-profile cases and led us to vital clues in the Global Law shooting."

"Maybe she should be sitting here," the man grinned.

The other people at the table hadn't said a word so far and were following the conversation with increasing amazement.

"You forgot to mention she hired a consultant to do her job," the man continued in the same monotonous voice, but at the same time there was something threatening about the way he spoke.

"Consultant?" Timo said.

"Dr. Robin Gilmore. Isn't he helping your team?"

"Uh, yes, he is, but ..."

"So, we're now hiring consultants to do the job of our police officers? Efficient use of the taxpayer's money!"

"We have followed all legal procedures," Timo said. "He is an IT expert and while SÄPO wasn't able to retrieve the files, he could. He helped the case tremendously."

"I'm sure. I assume a thorough security check was done on Robin Gilmore, who is American? He is an exchange student. I wonder why he extended his internship twice in the past, but now seems to be in a hurry to go home?"

There was silence. Irritation and anger were surfacing. This wasn't fair. Or was it? Everything was true and he may have been blind to the lack of structure and guidance in the Gävle police force, but he had to believe that this team had potential and that someone like Finn Heimersson leading the department would be the wrong choice.

"I also question your emotional and psychological stability, inspector."

The others suddenly looked at him with concern. This was clearly not planned.

"Maybe the death of your fiancé hasn't been completely digested. I can imagine having to deal with such a drama is not easy, and it takes time to heal. Perhaps you should consider taking a sabbatical to reflect on your future."

Timo sighed and looked down at his hands. He could feel the headache pounding in his head and ears. Every nerve in his body was sending conflicting messages. This was becoming personal. The moment the man had mentioned 'fiancé' he had felt himself gasping for air. He hadn't been able to suppress the shocked expression on his face before finding new focus as he looked down at his hands, feeling every muscle in his body cramp up. Where did this man get the right to talk about this and pretend to understand the tragedy, he had experienced so many years ago?

"This was eight years ago. I don't see how this has anything to do with my job in Gävle. In fact, as my file will show, it has never affected my work, neither here, nor in Stockholm. I don't see how this is relevant."

"That's not entirely true as Rune Breiner would acknowledge if he were still alive. But yes, I must say you were very good at hiding your emotions, inspector. Very controlled, very closed. But like any good trauma, that emotional bomb will burst at some point. And in your position, you have to keep in mind that not only your safety, but the safety of your team and the public might be affected. I'll use Magnus Wieland as an example."

"I'm nothing like Magnus Wieland," Timo sneered. Immediately he knew that this had been the wrong response. The man only gave him an ironic grin.

"I think we should end here," the man in the middle said and gave his colleague an inquiring glance. It was clear where the gravity of power in the group lay.

"Inspector, thank you. You'll hear from us."

That was it. It hadn't gone well. He had expected the criticism of the department's performance, but not the personal attack.

"Maybe you have questions about the plans," Timo said.

"No, not really. We've heard enough."

The man, who had been questioning him the whole time, closed the folder in front of him and gave Timo his most haughty glance yet.

"But I ...," Timo stammered.

"We don't need a foreigner to tell us what to do!"

Shock rippled across the room like the sound waves of an explosion. There was a moment of silence, painful and confusing.

"What did you just say?" Timo said. In all his years with the police force, he had never been confronted with discrimination. The cultural differences had been small; his lack of depth in the Swedish language was often the only thing that had set him apart from his Swedish colleagues, although he considered himself Swedish rather than Finnish or Russian.

"Foreigner," the man at the left repeated.

"I'm a Swedish citizen, just like all of you, I assume. In addition, half a million Finnish-speaking Swedes live in this country. How can you call me a foreigner? I take it that comment was not intended as an insult nor as an expression of your prejudice against me?"

"No, you heard it right," the man said with a smile, to the shock of his colleagues at the table. "You're not Swedish, nor Finnish ... not even Russian. You're nothing."

"You know I can accuse you of discrimination," Timo said.

The man laughed and said, "Well, I'd like to see you try. If you think of having witnesses around this table, there are none. Nobody heard anything."

Timo looked at the other men and woman. None of them dared to look at him. If they could, they would crawl under the table, not to confront him. They couldn't even give him that.

This had been a formality, a mock interview. Everything was already decided. And it wouldn't be him.

He turned, opened the door, and walked out. On autopilot, he walked down the hallway toward the exit, but he didn't reach it. Halfway down the stairs the headache had gotten so bad he wanted nothing more than to run his head against the wall to make it all stop. He couldn't stop the nausea from draining his energy and in the men's room, which he was able to reach in the nick of time, he threw up. All the stress, the frustration and anger.

He had failed. Himself, the team, everyone.

CHAPTER

14

F**INN TOOK A DRAG OF THE CIGARETTE** and let the smoke come out in short puffs. He'd walked around the house a few times, hadn't said much, and looked at it again with a strange expression on his face. Timo stood a few meters away, perhaps with a little too much anticipation and pride on his face.

When the last tar-bearing smoke was blown from his nostrils and hung like tiny clouds in front of his nose, Finn said, "Paikkala, it's a hovel."

"I know there's still a lot to do, but it has charm."

"It's a dump and I don't understand why you would buy something like that," Finn said.

Timo shrugged. It was not the first time he had received such a reaction.

"If I were you, I'd move everything I have to Stockholm and buy a nice, luxurious apartment there, or even a house. With your money that wouldn't be a problem, would it?"

Timo stepped toward him through the tall grass. In the distance he heard the rumble of a motorboat and turned his head briefly to see where the sound was coming from, but the fog was still too thick and low over the lake to see anything. "So, you advise me to go back to Stockholm?"

Finn's mouth took on a sarcastic twist and after another drag of the cigarette, he said, "I knew you hadn't invited me to admire your new home."

"Why did you apply?"

"Oh, Paikkala, you are so naïve. I do what they ask me as a good little soldier. It's that simple."

"I don't understand."

"Sometimes there are things you shouldn't stick your nose in. Pride and recognition often disappear into thin air when money is involved."

Timo looked at the patch of dried grime on the kitchen window. It had caught his eye as he'd walked around the house with Finn. Only now, in the daylight, he noticed how dirty and decrepit everything seemed. He understood why George, Finn, and even Ingrid had looked at the house with some reservation.

That spot had become his focal point. Had he just heard that Finn was offered money if he'd applied for superintendent? What was it that his friend was trying to say?

"You don't get it from me," Finn said suddenly, straightening his collar. It was no longer the weather to be outside for long periods of time. "But you don't seem to understand you've pissed off people."

Timo shook his head. "No, it's more than that. Tell me what's going on."

Finn sighed, brought the cigarette to his mouth, and then changed his mind. "Okay, Timo, because we're friends. You've become a liability to someone."

"What? To whom? I'm just a simple inspector. What have I done?"

"Don't play that game! You were never a simple inspector, and you know it. Having parents like Yrjo and Valesca never made you one of us."

"My father is dead and although my mother thinks she's important, she isn't," Timo blurted. "I don't see what I've done to get people nervous."

"But you're important to someone, who doesn't like to have the spotlight on you. To that person, you've become a danger, an object for blackmail and pressure."

"Who? And how do you know that?"

"That's all I can say and know for that matter. I keep my mouth shut. I don't want to know what they think or do."

"But who are they?"

Finn gave him a glance, then looked at his feet, the polished, shiny boots that were now stained from the mud and leaves when Timo had shown him the forest, the boathouse, and the lake. Finn was right. Sometimes, he acted like a little child, overly enthusiastic and naïve, so naïve. Now his two-meter-tall friend stood before him, still trying to find the words to say what he couldn't say.

"You'll figure it out or maybe it's best not. My only advice is not to draw attention to yourself because they have the power to come after you and everyone you care about. Believe me, I know."

Finn examined the smoldering cigarette stub, tossed it to the floor and stamped it out.

"Let's see what you've done with the place inside," Finn said, walking to the front door.

Timo looked at the lake. The roar of the boat was gone, perhaps already for a while, but the feeling that something was lurking in the mist, listening, waiting had never struck him before. Was it because of Finn's story? He didn't know. He only knew talking to Finn had left him with an uncomfortable sense of threat and fear.

* * *

The smell was unbearable. It was the first thing passersby had noticed and had prompted them to call the police. Not the bloodstained white bags stashed in the back, from which strands of hair hung.

The fetid stench of rotting flesh overwhelmed the first responders so much that many had sought refuge in the bushes to throw up.

"I'm not hundred percent sure, but these are probably Kirsten Jeppesen's remains," Ingrid said.

She was glad to get her head out of the car. Even for a hardened professional like her, this was too much. The severed head, the legs, arms and torso, the skin that had split open and nearly fell off the bones, bathing in bodily fluids.

"Jesus! The Jeppesens live across the street," Berger said, looking at the house, curtains drawn. There was the occasional glimpse of Kirsten's husband and the children.

"Whatever you do, don't let them see anything," Isa said to the forensics team.

"This needs to be handled with care," Ingrid said while she removed the gloves.

"The car belongs to Ilan Bergman," Berger said.

Isa threw her arms in the air. "What the hell is going on here?"

"That explains the DNA in the shoe," Ingrid said.

Berger looked in his notebook. "The license plate matches and so does the type and color."

Isa looked at the house. "If this is Kirsten Jeppesen, the case is linked to Global Law. And Bergman was just released from custody. We need to get him back in for questioning."

* * *

"I don't understand," Ilan whispered.

Why? That word had been going through his mind ever since he'd found out. He looked at the picture in the newspaper, then at the photo he was holding in his hand. The hand that hadn't stopped shaking since everything had fallen into place. He knew how. The puzzle was complete, but he didn't know why.

The police had released him hours ago and now he was sitting on the bed in his bedroom contemplating what to do. The autumn sun was already casting its faint rays over the city, slowly disappearing for the evening to settle in. The orange glow drew a strange shape on the wall, as if he had never noticed it before. Why did everything seem so deep and sensitive now? He was aware of every single sound, smell, everything he had taken for granted all those years. It had been dark for so long. In his head, in his heart.

He listened to the noise outside. Passersby, parents with children, laughing, telling how their day had been, with so much enthusiasm it made his stomach tighten at the very idea that life just went on when his was about to fall apart.

He took the cell phone out of his pocket. Everything had been erased. Every message, every call, every link, and picture ever sent by his blackmailer. The device had been scanned inside out by the police and they still hadn't found anything. And now he knew why. This wasn't his phone. It was the same model, with all his contacts, with the entire history, except for that one crucial thing that was missing: the communication with his stalker.

But there it was, lying next to the newspaper: the real phone that was ringing now. He had expected nothing else. His stalker knew.

Ilan gave it a few more seconds and then picked up the phone.

"What are you doing, Ilan?" the metallic voice said.

"I know who you are," Ilan answered. "Stop playing games."

It stayed silent on the other end of the line.

"I'm going to the police and tell them everything," he blurted.

More silence. He froze when he heard the door squeak behind him.

"I doubt that," the voice sounded.

He couldn't breathe. His mind was unable to process the new information. He knew that voice and he had been wrong. So wrong.

"Poor Ilan, I know how you must feel, but this is the end game for you. There is no point in making you understand. You won't understand it anyway. It doesn't matter."

He turned and saw the gun pointed at him.

Yes, this was the end game.

* * *

"This is a complete disaster," Timo shouted.

"What?" Isa said.

He had that look on his face again. Irritation, out to get someone. This had been going on for days, and they had tiptoed around him. She couldn't figure out what had triggered this outburst. So untypical for the man who usually avoided letting his own emotional state heave through his work and the relationship with the people he worked with.

"We haven't progressed a single step in any of the cases. Can someone tell me what you're all doing?"

Berger, Lars, Ingrid, and Isa looked at each other.

"Boss, we're doing the best we can, but with so few people and so many cases at once ...," Berger tried.

He was brave, Isa thought, but it was better not to say anything and let the tsunami of reprimands, warnings and snarls wash over them.

But the screaming didn't come and with an icy calm Timo started saying: "Berger, find me the connection between Ilan Bergman, Nils Vollan and Kirsten Jeppesen. I'd like a report on my desk by tomorrow morning. Bergman has been released. We couldn't hold him, but we need to keep an eye on him."

"Surely, Kirsten's remains in his car is enough reason to arrest him," Ingrid said.

Timo shook his head. "I'm not sure." He then turned to Lars, "Sven Toksund was Vollan's alias. Find out everything you can about him and the people he contacted during the time when he was in Sweden. Robin already has a list. And Lindström, did Gilmore produce anything else?"

She nodded. Last time, she'd seen him, her advice was for him to get some sleep, but Robin, after barely six hours of sleep over the past three days, had put his brilliant mind to work. She had never seen such a drive, especially after mentioning Timo was not only eager to see the results but also interested to learn more about the technology he was using.

"I wanted to give it to Sivert, but Robin did it in an hour. Bergman was right. Since April, he's been receiving messages from an unknown number. Burner phones."

"So, those messages have been deleted from his phone."

"It surely wasn't Bergman who removed them. We managed to narrow the area where the signal came from, and it must be very close. Robin believes that it could even come from Global Law."

Timo said, "We thought it was Bergman, but someone else is trying to deceive us. I want to have an overview of every Global Law employee and his or her whereabouts in the past six months."

Lars sighed.

"Is there a problem?" Timo said.

The young man shook his head.

"Then why are you still here?"

"There is something else," Lars said hesitantly.

"What?"

"Bergman's father used to work at the Gävle Herald before being laid off in 2005. He died a few years later of a heart attack. But Bergman must have known about the passage."

Timo sighed. "Okay then. Let's bring Bergman in again, for the umpteenth time."

Lars jumped up, followed by the others and without a word they left the room.

"And what will you be doing?" Isa said.

He could talk to the others like that, but she wasn't going to take the crap and insults he had thrown their way. It was all too easy to blame others. Boss or not.

"If you must know, I'll contact my own network to check on Mr. Valkama, the man with the connection to Karst Engersson."

His own network? What did that mean?

* * *

That evening a deep sense of sadness and failure fell over Timo as he looked through the large windows of his living room at the water of the lake. The skies were open, and the nearly full moon spotlighted millionaire Forsberg's mansion across the lake. He wondered how the old man was feeling these days after the recent drama surrounding his family. Until six months ago, Gerard Forsberg had been the darling of the media. Now he shunned the press, as if he hid like a hermit in the spacious villa he had once built as a palace for his family. A family that no longer existed.

Fog was slowly building up. Fog, a harbinger of cold and dark weather. Dark days were coming, which would not improve his peace of mind.

He turned to the steaming cup of coffee on the living room table. In his head he could hear Ingrid say how bad it was to drink caffeine at nine o'clock in the evening. Somehow, he had to laugh about it and at the same time the thought hurt him terribly. Often in those moments just before sleep would carry him away to dreams, he couldn't control, he had imagined what it would be like if she walked around the house, not as a colleague or friend, but as the woman he loved with all his heart. The thought only made him sadder.

There was a photo next to the cup of coffee. He still didn't know why he had brought it out. When Ingrid had confronted him with it the other day, his first reaction had been to hide Caijsa's photo in a place where he would never be faced with it again. It had hurt him and disappointed him at the same time. Only then he realized how after eight years the wounds were still so open, as if the drama had just happened. He ran his fingers over the frame and then the face in the photo. She had been so beautiful, full of energy. A woman overflowing with love. He closed his eyes and felt the tears being forced out. They ran over his face. Silent tears.

He turned the picture over and sighed.

"I miss you," he whispered.

Then he reached for the pocket of his trousers and took out a crumpled piece of paper. The folds were already so worn from being carried in the pockets of his jacket and pants that he was afraid the paper would fall apart. He couldn't help but take it out and look at it every day and the last few days even more than before.

"You'll find all the answers in Gävle," he read.

What answers?

This had been the reason why he was in Gävle, the reason why he hadn't gone back to Stockholm yet. He hadn't told anyone about the letters in his mailbox, received months before he had applied for the assignment in Gävle.

A mystery. A nagging, annoying secret that sometimes kept him awake at night.

He closed the letter, put it next to the picture and looked outside again. The shimmering waves reflected the moon's light, with the dark trees in the background, like ghosts about to lash out. His stomach tightened and he sensed something was afoot. Something big, something bad. And he wouldn't be able to stop it.

* * *

"Paikkala is freaking out. Is there anything else you found?" Isa said and looked at Robin.

"Is your boss not coming?"

"No," she said surprised. "Do you miss him?"

"No, no," he said quickly, as if to explain himself. "I was just ... he wanted to know more about the AI stuff ... so I thought."

She smiled. "Unless you're up for a scolding and screaming session, I'd advise staying away from him right now. He's in a terrible mood."

"I have a whole list of potential suspects," Robin answered and pointed to the stack of papers on the desk by the door.

"For each of the cases?"

"Yep. It wasn't too bad. I let the algorithm search for Facebook, Linkedin, Instagram, Twitter and even Tinder connections. It's not perfect. You can probably rule out many of them. I've added names, date of birth, connection to the victims or possible suspects."

"How many pages are there?" she sighed and picked it up. It felt heavier than expected.

"Don't know, maybe fifty or sixty."

"Wow."

"You'd be surprised how much information any of us leave on the Net," he said.

"What about the AI algorithm you were working on?"

"Isa, seriously, I had no time. How many cases do you want me to work on? If I'm the only one, this is what it's going to be."

"What if I could get you an assistant? Like Sivert?"

"That would be great, but I think Sivert doesn't like me."

She smiled. She just had to convince Timo and that would be a difficult one. Especially now he was running around like a madman and behaving like a dictator.

She threw the papers back on the table.

"Anything I need to focus on?" she asked.

"You're the detective not me," he said and frowned.

"Well, I've got nothing better to do," Isa said, took the only remaining chair and put herself at the desk. "And maybe we can order a pizza later? It's late and I don't think you've eaten anything."

"Yeah, that would be nice." He smiled and turned back to his work.

She wasn't proud of herself. Another excuse not to go home. Or maybe she was there out of guilt, maybe to feel connected to Alex, but it was nice just to focus on work for once, away from all the drama and politics.

They had been working for nearly thirty minutes, when suddenly the ringtone of a phone interrupted the silence. It was Robin's.

He scanned the room. The phone was on the small table next to Isa's stack of papers. She wanted to hand him the mobile, but the ringing ended almost as quickly as it had started.

He reached out to take it, but she hesitated and suddenly kept looking at the display. The background photo showed a smiling Alex and Robin with his arm around his friend, but there was something about the way Robin looked at him that struck her.

By then, it had all sunk in and she knew.

"It's you," she said, seeing the anxiety on his face.

"Wha..., what?"

"You put the roses on his grave," she said without taking her eyes from him.

He stood up and took the phone from her hands. For a moment, he stared at it, with a faint smile on his face. Then the smile on his face widened, but it was melancholy and sadness.

He said: "It was one of the few times we went out together, after he got his first invited talk. He couldn't believe it. You know he was so insecure, constantly doubting his work. But that night we celebrated. I don't even remember who took the picture. Everything was so relaxed and fun, and that night, I came so close to telling him."

"That you loved him?" Isa asked.

He nodded.

"Why didn't you?"

"He would never reciprocate my feelings. Why make everything awkward and destroy our friendship over something that would never happen?"

"But it must have been hard," she said.

"It was, and I can't say that in the two years or more I've been here, I've doubted that decision so many times."

A deep sadness seized her by the throat.

He continued on the path of reminiscence: "I still remember my first day at the university as if it were yesterday. They told me I had to share an office with another PhD student. I went in and when I saw him, I didn't know what happened. It was love at first sight. This had never happened to me before. Until then, I hadn't really admitted it to anyone, not even to myself, but that first encounter with Alex changed my world."

"That's why you stayed."

"I knew he could never love me the same way, but at least I could be with him. Even when he was taking that sabbatical, he would come over now and then, and we would have these amazing conversations about ... almost everything. He was so beautiful, inside and out."

"Robin, I'm so sorry," she sighed and took his hand.

"You know, I was angry and jealous when you told me about the two of you. I know you loved him, but I felt left out. He died without knowing how I really felt about him. This was so final. I should have told him."

Talking about Alex always ended up in tears, just like in that auditorium so many weeks ago, when she came to see him with the proposal to help the police.

"You were his best friend," Isa said, "and even if he didn't know, I think he valued and loved you more than you think."

"Anyway, that's why ... for as long as I can, I'm going to his grave every week. To talk to him. It's stupid because I don't believe in God and stuff like that. But I just hope he can hear me ... somehow. And I tell him everything."

There was a long silence. And as she held his hand, she thought of her conversation with Dr. Wikholm.

Love or desire?

Alex was both.

CHAPTER

15

"**H**IS WIFE IS DOWNSTAIRS,**"** Berger said. "She found him."

"This is a mess," Isa said.

A mess. Maybe that wasn't the right word. She followed the trail of blood on the wall down to the lifeless figure sitting on the bed with his back against the metal frame. The white sheets and wallpaper were stained with gray matter and a strange paintball-like pattern, only this wasn't paint but real blood. With half of the head and face gone, she barely recognized him, but this was Ilan Bergman. As the rest of the team was walking in and out the room, she let her mind take in what she saw. The collapsed figure with the index finger still loosely hanging around the gun. She tried to imagine how his wife must have felt coming in the room and discovering the horrible scene. The image would never leave her again, burnt in her mind for the rest of her life.

"I want to talk to her," Isa said and turned to Berger.

"I'm not sure she's able to answer your questions. She's traumatized. She hasn't said a word."

"This phone was lying next to the body," Ingrid remarked.

"Maybe he left some goodbye messages," Isa said. "God knows what was going through his mind. Suicide note?"

Berger shook his head. "We didn't find any."

Dr. Olsson straightened the oversized coverall she had put over her clothes and put the kit on the floor.

"What do you think?" Isa asked.

"Classic example of suicide," Ingrid said. "Maybe a bit too classic."

"So, you feel it too?" Isa said.

Ingrid leaned over to get a closer look at the head wound and then stepped back. "The likely suspect kills himself in the end, out of remorse. Do we believe that?"

"Show me the evidence it wasn't suicide," Isa said.

Ingrid walked to the other side, took the gun, and swapped the hand for gun powder residue. Then she turned her attention to the firearm and said, "A .38. There's blood in the barrel, consistent with a shot at close range."

Isa sighed. "I need to talk to Mrs. Bergman."

Downstairs in the kitchen Eve Bergman sat motionless at the kitchen table, head buried in her hands. She didn't look up when Isa took one of the remaining chairs and placed it at the other end, facing her.

"Mrs. Bergman, I'm sorry for your loss."

Eve wiped the tears from her face and said, "Are you sure it's Ilan?"

"The body is pretty damaged, and I know you want to believe it isn't him, but ..."

Eve ran her hands through her hair and then finally looked up at the woman in front of her. "Yeah ... I know it's him."

While her face was still wet with tears, it somehow showed little sign of the emotional turmoil Isa thought she must be going through, but Mrs. Bergman had never struck her as the emotional type. She would carry the loss of her husband in her own controlled way. A bit like Irene Nordin, Alex's mother.

"But this is your doing," Eve said. "If you had left him alone, he wouldn't have killed himself. He had nothing to do with all those murders and you know it."

"I'm sorry you feel that way, Mrs. Bergman, but we need your help."

"What more do you want?"

"You came home around 9:00 p.m.?"

"Yes, I already told your colleagues that," Eve cried.

"I have to ask. Where were you this afternoon and evening?"

"I was ...," Eve started and then let her gaze wander to the woman who had just entered the room and was now standing next to Isa.

"You should see this," Ingrid said and held the phone, wrapped in a plastic bag, in front of Isa.

"What is it?" Isa said.

"The phone is unlocked. Look who he called last!"

Through the bag she pressed the buttons on the screen. "Oh, Jesus!"

"What now?" Ingrid asked.

"Let me handle it," Isa said and turned to Mrs. Bergman. "So, where were you in the afternoon?"

Eve didn't reply, almost frozen in the moment.

"Mrs. Bergman, is something wrong?"

"Uh, no ... did he call anyone? Who? He didn't call me."

Eve put her face in her hands and when she looked up, they were filled with tears again.

"We don't know what it means and in the interest of the investigation we can't reveal much," Isa said, "so ..."

"Yeah, yeah, where I was," Eve snapped. "I was working the entire afternoon, then I went to yoga around 5:00 p.m. and had a drink with a friend afterwards. When I got home, I ... I ..."

"We released Ilan today from custody. Did you know that?"

"No, I didn't," Eve said. "I was planning to call our lawyer this evening, but then ..."

"Ilan didn't call you?"

Eve shook her head and with a voice that was about to break, she said, "He didn't say goodbye."

Isa took her notebook and placed it in front of the woman who was desperately trying to control her emotions.

"Can you write down your friend's name?"

"Why do you want to know all this stuff? It's suicide. Or do you really think I did this to him?" Eve screamed, scribbled the name on the paper and threw it in front of Isa. "I loved him. This is not on me. You've put so much pressure on him. The accident. Harket's murder and now the shooting. He couldn't handle it. For the past months I saw him languish. This wasn't my Ilan anymore. You killed him!"

There was no point in arguing with Eve Bergman, and Isa turned her attention to the name on the paper. "Mila Hillborg? How do you know Mila Hillborg?"

Then she turned to Ingrid who didn't know what to say.

"Uh, I know her from yoga," Eve said. "We regularly get together for drinks. She works for the police."

"Yeah, we know," Isa said.

* * *

"How is he taking it?" Timo said.

Berger closed the door of the interrogation room and gave Isa a quick nod. She was pacing around the observation room, taking it one tic too far in Timo's opinion evidenced by the frown on his face.

Then Berger turned to Timo. "Okay. We checked and Ilan did call in the afternoon, likely just before he died, but he mentioned he never answered and only saw hours later that Bergman had tried to contact him. He has no alibi though."

"For God's sake, look at him," Isa said and pointed at the one-way glass. Nick sat slumped looking at his hands, with the same lethargic look that had hung over his face for the past weeks. She sometimes wondered if he knew where he was.

"I want to know what really happened when I was shot," Timo said.

Isa waved her arms wildly in the air. "What? Nick told you. You don't believe him?"

"They could have killed us. Why didn't they? Was it because he's one of them?"

"I could say the same about you," she said. "We don't know what you did. Why would we believe that you were shot and lost consciousness?"

The long look he had thrown her way made her stomach tighten. Eyes, ready for the kill. But as always, he poured the controlled anger in carefully chosen words that were often even more unsettling.

"Well, I have the injuries and the witness to corroborate my story. Or are we both lying? What I do know is that only Nick knows what happened after that. And if he's holding information ..."

"He's not," Isa said.

Timo let his eyes rest on her and then said without blinking. "Send him home!"

"But ...," Berger stammered.

Timo turned to him. "And then we have the matter of Mila Hillborg."

"She has nothing to do with it," Berger said.

"Didn't I just hear something similar a few minutes ago? Two of my inspectors involved with witnesses in this case. Stockholm is going to have a field day."

"It's coincidence," Berger said.

Timo sighed. "Everything is a coincidence here. Let Petrini go. And, Berger, your girlfriend needs to give a statement about her link to Eve Bergman."

With a sigh and an expression of irritation on his face, Berger went back inside.

"Thanks," Isa whispered.

"I didn't do it for you," Timo said. "There's no evidence Nick actually did anything wrong. Bergman left no message. Your man has no alibi, but as far as I know this is still classified as a suicide. But Lindström, Nick needs professional help."

"He isn't always like that," she answered.

"Isa, I'm telling you this out of concern ... for both of you."

Isa? No Lindström? This must be serious.

"Timo, I'm grateful you talked to him but ..."

"He told me he can't talk to you," Timo said.

The shock put her mind on pause. "What? Why?"

"Look, I don't want to come between you," Timo said and looked at the man on the other side of the glass, getting up and trudging to the door. "You really need to listen to him."

She wanted to yell at her boss, tell him to mind his own business, but he was right. If she'd put half of the energy she was putting now in her work, into mending her relationship and helping Nick, he wouldn't have looked like a zombie, who was now strolling to the exit, taking the bus if he could find one and put himself in front of the TV again.

But she was disappointed as well, because in her mind she had done the effort to listen to his story. Last night she had found Nick on the couch again, staring in front of him, oblivious to everything around him, so absorbed in his own world.

"Nick, please talk to me."

He shrugged and let out a deep sigh.

"Did Timo talk to you?" Isa said.

He nodded. "He did and I know you asked him. Thank you."

"Look, Nick, I don't pretend I understand, but what you're doing, isn't helping."

"I can't get that image out of my head," he said.

She took his hand.

"I am such a coward," he sobbed, "I couldn't even bring myself to attend her funeral."

"You can still make amends," she whispered.

"No, I can't. She's dead because of me. Because, stupid me, I only think about myself. She shouldn't have been there!"

Isa said calmly, "Did you force her to come in that day?"

"No, but ... she did it for me ... to help me."

"People make decisions every day, every moment," she said, "and it's never one thing; it is always a combination of different circumstances."

He shook his head and looked at her.

"I know, but it doesn't feel like that," he said and turned his head away from her. He always tried to hide his tears from her. She'd teased him about it when again he claimed to have a cold or allergy after seeing an emotionally loaded movie, but this was reality.

"She made the decision to come in that day. She made it, not you. And you didn't pull that trigger."

For the first time in weeks, he kissed her.

How she had missed his lips, his touch, just the mere breath on her skin!

She missed the sex. His charm, the way he got her into bed and the way he made love. Everything about him had been exciting. It was all rooted in his immeasurable confidence, which she admired and loved about him. But this kiss was different. There was so much sadness in it. It felt like a farewell kiss.

"Nick?"

"It's okay," he said while caressing her cheek, "thank you for listening."

"You called Eve Bergman. If she can help you, then maybe …"

Nick frowned and said, "No, no. She called me. I didn't call her."

"Uh … then I must have misunderstood. Why did she call?"

"She wanted to know how I was. You shouldn't worry. There's nothing between us anymore."

He gave her another kiss on the forehead, shuffled to the bedroom, but then stopped and said, "But there's something else … I can't put my finger on it."

"What?"

"I think I dreamt about it."

"The nightmares? About Kim?"

"I don't know," he said.

"Then what?"

He shook his head and then continued his path to the bedroom.

* * *

"Nice job," Timo said and gave Robin a pat on the shoulder. "Keep up the good work."

"Oh, uh, thanks," Robin stammered and put the laptop on the table.

Isa observed him quietly, smiled and then walked over to Robin.

"You really like him," Isa grinned as she connected the HDMI cable to the laptop. His face turned even more red than before, and he switched on the computer without giving her another glance.

An hour ago, Robin had called her with the message, "I may have something interesting for you." He had sounded more excited than usual.

This was it. Maybe a breakthrough. And she had gathered the entire team in the main conference room of the police station.

"So, tell us!" she said.

"Right," Robin said and took a seat, his fingers hovering over the keyboard. "So far, I've looked at the three cases you gave me: the Global Law attack, Daniel Nyström, and Kirsten Jeppesen. And for each of the cases we found a list of suspects, but ..."

Robin looked up and let his gaze wander over the people in the room who were staring back at him, waiting for the rest of the story.

"The cases are definitely connected," Robin finally said.

"How?" Timo asked.

"I checked terabytes of data about the cases. Social media of the victims and their families, what they posted on Twitter, Facebook, Linkedin, but also what they removed. And that's where it gets interesting. Pauli Nyström, Daniel's brother was a very active member of Facebook already in its early days. His timeline goes back to 2008. Now, in 2010 he posted several photos he recently removed, but it was easy to retrieve those."

"How recently?"

"Like a few days after the Global Law shooting."

"What's so special about them?" Berger asked.

"Let me show you," Robin said and pressed the button. The blue screen projected by the beamer turned black and then showed the picture of three teenagers, smiling, arms around each other, posing in front of a wood-slatted fence, and behind the fence the features of a house with dark painted walls and a peculiar triangle-shaped window."

"Is that Svante Engersson?" Berger said, got up and moved to the front, pointing at the man on the left.

"Svante Engersson, Pauli Nyström, and Hilko Ingberg."

"When was this photo posted?" Timo asked.

"14 April 2010. The picture was taken in Stockholm."

"They knew each other," Isa said.

"Lindström …," Timo said, but she continued by saying, "Why did the photo have to disappear?"

"Lindström, stop!"

Everyone turned to Timo.

"I can no longer lead this investigation," he said.

Isa got up and stared at him. "Why?"

"I know where the photo was taken. I know the house."

"So?"

"Case B4322-10. Then you'll know why. If you'll excuse me, I have to go." And with those words he walked out of the room, leaving the group flabbergasted, unable to say anything.

"What is B4322-10?" Isa said and turned to Robin.

Like a madman he started strumming the keyboard, until he pulled up the file everyone had been waiting for. On the screen the photo of a young woman appeared, long light-brown curly hair and green eyes with a touch of brown, a beautiful smile and all-in-all a handsome appearance.

"Oh, my God," Ingrid let out. "That's his girlfriend."

"Caijsa Jensen," Robin read.

"Did you know?" she turned to Ingrid, who was still gasping for air. The resemblance was striking. Now Isa knew why her boss was so drawn to her best friend.

"No, what happened to her?"

"She was found murdered in their home in Stockholm," Robin said. The gruesome photos of the young woman's bloodied, half-naked body left little to the imagination.

"According to the autopsy report, her throat had been cut, and she had many bruises, cuts, and broken bones. She put up a hell of a fight."

"Sexual assault?" Isa asked.

He shook his head. "There was no evidence she was raped, but …"

Then Robin looked up at Isa. "… he found her."

"I have to talk to him," Ingrid yelled.

"Ingrid, no," Isa said but it was too late. Dr. Olsson had already left the room.

"This is big," Lars let out.

Isa turned to Robin again. "Okay, let's think about this for a moment. Karst Engersson, CEO of Global Law, is Svante's father. Daniel Nyström is Pauli's brother and Kirsten Jeppesen is Hilko Ingberg's sister. They are all related to these three guys. Are we now saying the dead people weren't the targets, but it's all about their family members? The three guys on this picture?"

"We're not saying anything," Berger said. "I don't see how we should change our investigation based on one picture. Are we all forgetting terrorist attacks and so? The connection to Caijsa Jensen still seems farfetched to me."

"Two cases that are connected is maybe a coincidence," Isa said, "but not three."

"But what does that mean? Are these guys involved or the targets? And what is the connection to Timo's girlfriend?"

"Pauli Nyström was questioned as a witness in the murder case. But the murderer Thorgan Elker eventually confessed and was sentenced to life in prison."

Berger said, "Maybe Elker wasn't the murderer?"

"We need to bring them in and have a chat," Isa said.

"What do we do about Paikkala?" Lars asked.

She sighed. "Treat him like any other suspect. No exceptions."

But she knew this was going to be difficult.

* * *

Ingrid found him sitting on the floor of his office, tucked away in the corner, staring blankly ahead.

"Timo?"

He said nothing. As she approached, she saw the tears glistening on his face in the dim light streaming through the window. How could she have been so careless to throw the picture of his murdered girlfriend in front of his face the other day.

She dropped to the floor, next to him, and they sat side by side for a while. Now and then she threw him a glance. There was no point in starting a monologue. It wouldn't help him.

"I owe you an explanation," he said suddenly.

"You owe me nothing. I can't even imagine what you must have been through. I'm so sorry."

She took his hand in hers. He turned to her. She felt his grip tighten, every fiber in his body was fighting the hurricane that was coming.

He had come so close. For years, he had tried to replace that horrible last image of Caijsa with happier memories. His inner soul had found rest. At least he thought so. But the nightmare was back, and all the progress was gone with just one picture. Gone. Eight years and back to square one. He hadn't realized how fragile his emotional stability was, how he had balanced despair and hope. His newfound inner sanity had never been put to the test until now. This time there was no safety net, no family to fall back on. George, his mother and even his brother. But was he alone? He felt the soft skin of her fingers slide over his hand.

"Thank you," he said.

"Of course. I couldn't just leave you like that, Timo. Just tell me what you need."

"I need time to let this sink in. I don't understand what this has to do with Caijsa."

"We'll find out," she said softly. He gave her a faint smile and nodded.

* * *

"Nick, please, please, pick up the phone."

Isa walked restlessly across the room. She had promised him to come home earlier after the interview and continue their nightly conversation. Ten calls and no answer. Had he done something stupid? The annoying feeling of danger had haunted her since he had disappeared through the exit after Berger had questioned him about Ilan Bergman. It had faded for a moment when Robin had made the big reveal, but now it was back, and she needed to know he was okay. Worst-case scenarios were going through her head. He had hanged himself, he had taken pills, he had walked to the station and thrown himself in front of a passing train. Why had she let him go like that and why did everything feel so much sharper, deeper, like imminent danger about to strike?

"Yes," it sounded suddenly through the speaker.

"Nick, finally," she sighed, unable to hold back the tears. They were tears of relief and happiness. She'd heard enough sadness that morning.

"I was resting," he murmured.

"I was worried," she let out. "Are you okay? Berger wasn't too harsh, was he?"

Silence.

"Nick?"

"No, everything is okay. You don't have to worry. I know what you're thinking. I'm not going to kill myself or so. Just, don't worry."

"Look, something has come up and I'll probably be home late," she said. "Are you going to be okay?"

"I'll be okay. Don't worry."

When she broke the connection, the sense of fear hadn't passed. She closed her eyes. There was chaos in her head, and she had to be focused, now Timo wasn't there anymore.

Timo. The hardest part was still to come.

CHAPTER

16

AS TIMO WALKED DOWN the hallway, people looked at him with concern, like the policeman at the front desk had done when he had put the badge and the gun on the counter, the two things that defined him as a police officer. He couldn't quite figure out if it was pity or outrage, or maybe suspicion all together.

He'd had enough pity for the past eight years. That was one of the reasons he had left Stockholm. After all these years, he was still the fiancé of the poor woman who had been murdered. There was always a lingering urge to make things easy for him, as if he couldn't bear harsh remarks or hard truths.

Maybe he hadn't been able to cope the first years, but he thought he had grown stronger. Step by step, but even that had been an illusion. He'd needed Ingrid to get him out of that safe corner in his office. Courage was what he needed to survive the next days, and the pointers from his former psychologist to keep his sanity.

And suspicion and outrage, yes, he'd had his share of that too. It was always the husband or the boyfriend, until proven otherwise. And in the minds of many, he was still the ruthless killer who had taken the life of his girlfriend.

"I'm so sorry," Isa said as Timo pulled the chair and sat on the other side of the table in the interrogation room. A room he had been in many times, but now he was the one being interviewed.

"Don't apologize, do your job," he said.

Isa took a deep breath, straightened up and gave him a quick nod.

"3:15 p.m., interview started with Timo Paikkala," Berger said, turning on the recorder.

"Caijsa Jensen, born in Stockholm on 18 October 1980, was your girlfriend at the time of her death on 15 April 2010?"

"We were engaged," Timo said. "I proposed to her a month before her death."

"On that day, 15 April, you found her murdered in your home," Isa said. "Tell us what happened."

"That morning, we had an argument." As always, he only realized afterwards this was the last thing he'd said to her. It hadn't been a huge fight, just a quarrel. A stupid quarrel.

"About what?"

"She had decided to go back to work. I thought it was too early."

Isa frowned. "Explain."

Timo swallowed a few times and then said, "She'd had a miscarriage a week earlier, and I thought she wasn't physically nor mentally ready yet. And I didn't think it was safe."

"Why?"

"Thorgan Elker."

Berger said, "The man convicted of murdering her?"

"Caijsa was a clinical psychologist at the Karolinska University hospital in Stockholm, and he was one of her patients until he became obsessed with her. In the months before the murder, he'd been stalking her, had broken into our house and we suspected he was the one who had left dead animals in the garden, but we couldn't prove anything. I wanted to move, but she refused to let him control her life."

"Did you report this?"

"Yes, of course, but as you and I know, if there's no evidence, there isn't much the police can do. I wanted to install an alarm system, but by then it was already too late."

"What happened to make him so obsessed?"

"I don't know, and I don't think she did either. As far as I know, he had mental issues, but was never considered dangerous."

"So, you didn't want her to go," Isa said.

"But she was determined, and I thought it wasn't worth the argument, so I said nothing and let her go. She went for a run first, and I went to work. But she never made it to the hospital."

"You were with the Stockholm police at that time?"

"I just started as inspector," Timo added. "And I was assigned my first big case."

"You were twenty-eight. Quite young to be an inspector."

He raised his shoulders. What was he supposed to say? Was he too young? He never really had thought about it, and there was no crime in being ambitious and taking the opportunities that were given.

"And you were at work the entire day?"

"I tried to call her twice to make sure she was okay, but she didn't answer," he said.

"And you weren't worried?"

"I thought she was busy at the hospital. I didn't know something could have happened to her. Besides it was very busy at work. Kristina and I were investigating a serial rapist, and it was a crucial moment in the investigation."

"That's Dr. Kristina Rapp?" Berger said.

"Yes," Timo said. "She's a criminologist working with the Stockholm police."

"You are friends?"

Timo sighed. "Not that again! There's nothing romantic between us, not then, not now. I didn't kill Caijsa because I had a so-called affair with Kristina. We are just friends."

Although for Kristina it had been a different story. Years after Caijsa's murder, she had told him she was in love with him, but he hadn't been able to reciprocate her feelings.

Isa flipped through the file.

Each time it amazed him how the file had grown thicker over the years, but it was deceptive. The case was closed eight years ago.

"Rune Breiner didn't think so. He was one of the investigating officers. Even after Elker was convicted, Breiner was very persistent, given the many addenda in the file where he accuses you of killing Caijsa."

"Many of my colleagues at that time testified I was at work the entire day," Timo added. "I don't know why, but Breiner was on a witch hunt."

"You could have killed her in the morning and gone to work that day. The coroner was unable to determine the exact time of death."

"I could have, but I didn't," Timo said with a straight face.

"So, you came home that night," Berger said.

"I came home," Timo repeated. "I came home, and on the doorstep, I already had a feeling something wasn't right."

He gasped a few times. He couldn't fall apart now. He was supposed to be the confident man, who had an answer and an opinion about everything, but talking about the most devastating moment in his

217

life, again, after so many years, was as crippling as the day he had found her.

"Why?"

"There was a red stain. At first, I thought it was paint, but then why would there be red paint. The door was open and when I entered ..."

His voice broke. He remembered being unable to enter the house for months after the murder, afraid of what he would find. He had sold the house. He had bought a new one half a year after her death, but now and then he had stopped by on his way to work, because with the old house, all the sweet memories of her had disappeared. Her smell, the way the heels of her shoes had clamored across the rooms, the way she had sung in the shower, just big enough for the two of them. The way she, after a difficult day at work, had snuggled next to him on the old couch she'd inherited from her late grandmother. Thorgan Elker had taken that away from him.

"I saw her in the doorway between the hall and the living room in a pile of blood."

"And then?" Berger said.

"And then ... I don't know," Timo said.

"What do you exactly mean, you don't know?"

"I really don't know. People told me afterwards they found me on the street screaming for help, but I can't remember. I was covered in blood. They told me I had tried to resuscitate her and had already called an ambulance. But I don't remember any of it. Three days later, I woke up in the hospital. Everything before that is a blur. I only found out later she had been tortured, and her throat was cut. There was nothing I could have done to save her."

"Timo, I ...," Isa said and reached out to take his hand.

"No," he said, pulled his hands away and let them rest on his lap.

He could do this.

"By then it was over. Thorgan Elker had confessed to the murder. His clothes with her blood on them were found in his house, along with the knife he had used to kill her. He was found guilty and sentenced to life in prison."

"He never gave a valid reason for the murder, and the brutality of the way he had killed her," Berger added.

"And you never talked to him?" Isa said.

"No," Timo said. "To this day, I still wouldn't. I would have killed him without hesitation. That's why I never went to the sentence hearing."

"But Caijsa's parents did."

"They have never had to deal with the image of her dead body. I hope no one ever has to go through something like that."

Isa stared at him for a moment.

And then he recalled she had. In the ambulance with Alex. Unable to save him.

Berger said, "Thorgan Elker died in prison in 2015."

"He committed suicide," Timo whispered.

Never again would he have the chance to confront Thorgan, to ask him what had gone through his mind when he had attacked and killed her. Timo thought he had time and that one day he'd have the courage to ask Elker all those questions. What had she ever done to him? Coward. Big coward! Elker had chosen the easy way out.

"You told me you knew Pauli Nyström," Isa said.

"I don't know him. I never met him or spoke to him. I only read his name and saw his picture in the file. He was the witness who testified that he saw a man looking like Thorgan Elker near our house the morning she died."

"He came forward when the police made a public appeal to the media," Isa explained. "Pauli Nyström was visiting relatives in Stockholm together with his mother and stepfather, and that morning he had gone for a run when he saw the man hanging around your house. His testimony led to the arrest of Thorgan Elker."

"I know," Timo said annoyed. "Is there a question?"

"Did you know Svante Engersson and Hilko Ingberg before you came here?"

"No."

"These are all local guys. Six months ago, you suddenly show up in Gävle. Coincidence, isn't it? Why did you come to Gävle? We know you specifically requested this assignment as superintendent."

It was time to tell them. He reached for the pocket of his trousers, took out the letter and placed it on the table in front of them.

"What is this?" Isa asked.

"A few months before I got the assignment, I received three letters. No sender. Just ... well, read it."

"You'll find all the answers in Gävle," Isa read and then looked up. "What does that mean?"

"I don't know," Timo said. "But I have to admit this triggered my interest and that's why I asked the commissioner for the job."

Isa turned the letter around and put it closer to her face.

"Don't bother. I had it checked for fingerprints. Nothing."

She leaned back and gave him an inquiring look. "Where were you on the morning of 19 June when Daniel Nyström disappeared?"

He shook his head and said, "I don't know anymore."

"And what about 20 September? The day Kirsten Jeppesen disappeared."

He shook his head again and then said, "Probably here, at work."

"Kirsten Jeppesen was kidnapped in the morning. You could have taken her before coming in, and then killed her later that day."

But he knew very well what he had done and where he had been that night. Something stupid. Feeling gloomy, with another migraine lingering in his head—he had plenty of them these days— he had gone to the pub and had two beers. Two women had tried to strike up a conversation with him, but he had declined, politely but firmly. The combination of the alcohol and medication had rendered him dizzy and before he knew it, he was standing in front of Ingrid and Anton's house like a stalker. He so desperately wanted to ring the doorbell and tell her he was in love with her, that he wanted her to leave her husband and be with him. But he had backed off, had stood there at least another half hour, weighing it all in his head, and then had gone back to the police station and taken a taxi to his house. That night everything had gone through his mind: Ingrid, Caijsa, his family, his career. For the first time in a long time, he thought of his dead father. How he had been a disappointment to him. He had chosen a different path than his privileged family had wanted. He had been proud of his independence and stubbornness, but that night he felt like a failure. He wasn't independent at all. He still relied on the money and security of the family fortune. Such a farce. He had built nothing of value. He couldn't even tell the woman he loved about his feelings. When Isa had picked him up in the morning, he had only slept for an hour.

"So, you have no solid alibis for when Daniel Nyström and Kirsten Jeppesen were abducted?"

"Obviously not. Look, I don't have a car. How could I have done all that? You must realize I had nothing to do with the Global Law shooting and any of the murders."

"You still had a car when Daniel disappeared, and it's not that hard to rent one. As for the shooting, I wonder why they didn't kill you when you were gunned down," Isa remarked. "Was this because you were part of the conspiracy? You could have planned it all, while your accomplices carried it out."

"Why? Why would I kill all those people? Except for Pauli Nyström none of them have anything to do with Caijsa or myself."

"Maybe there is more to Caijsa's case than we know."

"As far as I know Thorgan Elker is the killer. He was convicted and he died in prison. Case closed."

"Case not entirely closed," Isa intervened.

He looked up surprised.

"Do you know that a few months before his death, Mr. Elker had asked for a lawyer and had told him he was innocent? That he had been under the influence of drugs, medication, and that after so many years he was finally lucid and that he knew what had happened. He demanded a revision of his trial."

No one had ever told him that.

"No, I didn't. Then how come all that evidence was found in his house? The blood on his clothes? The knife?"

"His request was denied because there was no new evidence to support a retrial," Isa added, "but it sheds a different light on the matter."

There was silence. What was he supposed to say? He didn't believe it. Why had Elker confessed? Why after so many years?

"Didn't you ever want to know what and why this had happened to her?" she finally asked.

"Do I need to know every detail of the horror she went through before her death?"

"Maybe that's better than letting the imagination take over?"

"No, it isn't." He stopped, looked down at his clenched hands, "because reality is always worse than you can imagine."

He sighed and then continued, "I didn't kill all those people, but the connections are clear. We ... you just have to find out why someone is targeting the family of these people, and why exactly these people."

"Thank you, inspector Paikkala, for the advice. We will take it into consideration. For now, we have no further questions."

Berger turned off the recorder and organized the papers scattered across the table. Isa stood up, looking at Timo.

He was emotionally drained, his body hanging like a puppet over the chair, staring in front of him. She gave him a gentle pat on the shoulder. When he didn't react, she leaned over and asked, "Are you okay?"

He nodded and then said with a soft voice, "Yes, just give me a moment."

Berger and Isa stepped out, leaving him alone in the interview room. He ran his hands through his hair as he tried to take in everything that had happened since the morning. The revelation, the interview. Everything had hit him like a truck crashing down the slope at high speed. Why? Why was someone targeting all these people? Pauli Nyström had just been a witness. But the others had been there too. And why target the families? Were there more? Maybe it wasn't over.

CHAPTER

17

MARCEL HAD TO BLINK A FEW TIMES, but then he recognized the man standing outside his door.

"Timo," he yelled and without hesitation he threw his arms around him, pulled him inside, and for a few minutes they stood there, wrapped in the warmest embrace they both had experienced in a long while.

Timo hadn't seen him since Paulina's funeral. In the past eight years, not a week had gone by that Timo hadn't visited Caijsa's father. But the journey from Gävle down to Stockholm took the inspector almost two hours one way, and it was getting harder to do every week. So, he had stopped going, but today he had. He needed to talk to him about his daughter and the surprising events of the past days. A part of the drama was still so vague. The months after Caijsa's murder he had lived in his own world, not really present in the moment. Marcel and Paulina had taken care of him while dealing with their daughter's murder. His mother and George had been there too, but in the end, it was Marcel and Paulina who had pulled him out of that bed and helped him to get back on his feet. Shared grief. He owed them so much.

"How are you?" Timo started the conversation as he poured the coffee into the two mugs on the kitchen table.

"Well, my eyesight is getting worse. They want to do more tests to adjust the meds. Blood glucose levels were too high again."

Marcel had never been thin and athletic, but he seemed to have gained even more weight since Timo had last seen him. Marcel's way of coping was to drink and eat. His refusal to follow his doctor's advice had only made things worse. They'd all had their death wish at some point. Paulina's had been the pancreatic cancer. For Timo the racing and rock climbing. For Marcel the diabetes.

"Quit alcohol and moderate your sugar intake, and actually do what the doctors tell you to do," Timo said.

He put the cup in front of the old man, and continued, "You need someone to take care of you."

Marcel sighed and took a first sip of the black coffee.

"Mmm, you haven't lost your magic touch," Marcel said. "I don't understand how you do it. Same ingredients, same machine, but when I make coffee, something different comes out."

Timo smiled. He remembered sitting in the same living room and while Caijsa, bored and unable to hear yet another coffee story, had walked away, Marcel had listened patiently to his stories. Even when Timo had told him about his kopi luwak experience, a coffee made from semi-digested coffee cherries that had passed through the digestive system of an Asian palm civet.

"Why did you never remarry after your divorce?" Timo said.

A muffled smile appeared on Marcel's face. The divorce had happened a long time ago, but Timo knew the old man still felt sorrow and heartbreak when he looked back on it. Marcel had once told him about their marriage. Paulina had been a restless soul. The first years of their marriage had been exciting and full of love. After Caijsa's birth, grind and frustration had taken over, and soon Paulina had fallen into a state of unhappiness and resentment. And then she met Nelvin, a young, attractive salesman who swept her off her feet. The affair lasted for more than a year before she finally filed for divorce and moved out. Caijsa had been ten. Paulina married him a year later and that was it. But not for Marcel.

"Because I thought she would eventually come back to me. Paulina was the love of my life. I couldn't see myself being married to anybody else."

"Marcel," Timo said, taking his hand in sympathy.

"And you, my dear boy, what about you? Do you have anyone else?"

"No," Timo said.

Marcel watched him for a moment. "Maybe a few more wrinkles, here and there, and a few gray hairs, but otherwise you're still a very handsome man, Timo."

"Oh, thanks," Timo said.

"When Caijsa introduced you to me ... us, you were still a boy. You weren't a couple then, but you were so polite and lovely and even then, you filled a room with your presence. I knew you were the man who could make my daughter happy. She glowed when she looked at you. You were so perfect together. So much chemistry. Anyway, that's all gone now. So, you should practice what you preach, dear Timo. I've made my choice, but that doesn't mean you have to do the same. It's been eight years. It's time to move on. You're still young, and I know you want a family, but you won't stay young forever."

"I'll keep that in mind," Timo smiled and let go of his hand.

"By the way, I saw your mother a few weeks ago," Marcel said.

"My mother? Here?"

"Yes, it was really a coincidence. I was just coming out of the store, when she entered together with your brother and his family."

Timo nearly knocked over the coffee mug on the table, then said, "She didn't tell me she was in Sweden."

He stirred the spoon into the coffee, then put it back on the table.

Marcel observed him a moment, before saying, "Still fighting over ...?"

"We're not fighting," Timo said quickly. "The conversation always gets heated when that one topic is brought up."

And that was his father. His real father.

Timo sighed. "I just wish for once she was interested in my life."

Marcel took his hand. "She is. I know she is, but maybe you can reach out to her. I don't want you, when you get to my age, to suddenly realize your entire family has abandoned you. Exactly what happened to Nelvin."

"Nelvin? Are you hanging out with him?"

"Look, Timo, it might be hard to understand, but we've both lost people and okay, he took the love of my life away from me, but when you get older and you find yourself all alone, sometimes these are the only people left."

Marcel took a deep breath and then blurted, "We've decided to share this house. He'll be moving in two weeks."

"Are you sure that's wise? I remember you were at each other's throats the whole time, and now you're talking about living with that man. I really don't want to get a call one day that one of you killed the other."

"Come on, Timo, it's not that bad. I'm old and I just need someone, even if we bicker all the time."

"You're not old and remember Nelvin isn't alone. He has two more children."

"Ah, Lyn and Cal, yes ... but they don't talk to their father anymore."

Lyn and Cal, the twins, Caijsa's siblings. Caijsa had always been so protective of them. Their mental instability had put a lot of strain on the family. Cal had spent most of his childhood in and out of mental hospitals, and Lyn had been diagnosed with Asperger's at a young age. Timo had always wondered if they had been the reason Caijsa had taken up psychology.

"I didn't see them at Paulina's funeral, but maybe I just didn't recognize them. It's been more than eight years, and they were still so young when Caijsa died."

"They were there and they're doing quite well. I think they are both married. Cal has two children of his own. But they hold Nelvin responsible for their mother's death."

"Why?"

"Paulina had made her decision. She didn't want the chemo. There was only 5% chance of survival anyway and she was so tired of fighting. But they wanted her to get the treatment she needed, and when Nelvin backed his wife's decision, the twins were disappointed and angry. So, you see, Nelvin is alone too."

There was little Timo could say. Marcel Jensen was a stubborn man. The old man pushed the chair back and tried to get up, but he fell backwards, panting, and red in the face.

"Are you okay?" Timo asked, trying to help him up.

Marcel turned to him, smiled, and then took Timo's head in his hands and kissed his forehead like a father would.

"I'm fine, Timo, I'm fine."

Marcel shuffled into the living room, supported by Timo, and dropped onto the couch.

"Marcel, I'm not just here on a social visit," Timo said.

"Oh, what is it?"

Timo told everything that had happened the last days and Marcel listened to it open-mouthed.

"And you're a suspect?" Marcel finally asked.

"Not officially. But the police need to be thorough. I would have done the same."

He bowed his head and when he looked up again, he saw Marcel still staring at him with a confused look on his face.

"Did you know Thorgan Elker claimed to be innocent?" Timo said.

Marcel casted his eyes down. "We visited him in prison in early 2015," he admitted suddenly.

"Why didn't you tell me?"

"Timo, you were ... we thought you wouldn't understand. You were still so ... how shall I put it ... angry."

"But you could have told me anyway."

"Paulina wanted to talk to him. She had to face him and ask him why he killed our daughter. Not me. Like you, I wasn't ready to sit across the table and have a civilized conversation with that man. But I went anyway. Paulina needed me."

So typical Marcel. Paulina could have taken Nelvin, but he had been willing to sacrifice his own sanity to help her. Love of his life, indeed.

"And what happened?"

"He looked so ... less evil than I imagined. He spoke eloquently. I started to have doubts."

"That he had done it?" Timo asked.

"Yes. Paulina had so many questions, and he couldn't answer any of them."

"Maybe he didn't want to talk about it," Timo said.

"No, he got so many things mixed up. He couldn't give details. Have you ever read the police report?"

Yes, he had. Not the forensics report, but the interview and the confession. Years ago.

Marcel said: "He claims he killed her in a fit of anger, and that he was under the influence of his medication, antidepressants. Yet, he was found to be culpable. You can question the way this investigation was conducted."

"What are you saying? That the police investigation was rigged? That he was innocent? I can tell you he wasn't the only one on the radar."

"I know, my dear boy. You've had your share of trouble as well."

Timo couldn't believe it. His own judgment had been clouded and perhaps it still was. The mere thought of Thorgan's innocence turned his stomach, but it took more than the suspicions of an old man, who grew melancholic and weak at the sight of his loneliness. There was no real evidence.

Marcel gave him a smile and then said, "But keep in mind that this case may be more complicated than we all thought."

"That's what I'm afraid of."

Timo emptied the cup and stared at it for a while.

"Do you ever talk to her?" Timo said.

"Who?"

"Caijsa."

"Yes, I do," Marcel answered. "I think about her every day."

"Do you go and visit her?"

"In the columbarium, you mean?"

Timo nodded.

"No. Do you?" Marcel said.

"Yes, when I'm in Stockholm."

"Strange, I never saw you as a spiritual person."

Timo sighed. It wasn't easy for him to admit it. "I know I'm talking to a box and there's only ashes in it. I don't believe in an afterlife, but there's something cathartic about it. Saying things out loud, even if it's the greatest nonsense or the most banal fact. After a day full of frustration or excitement, we used to tell each other everything when she was alive. Now that's gone and I miss it."

He wiped a tear away. "I miss it so much."

"I know, my dear boy," Marcel whispered and took his hand.

* * *

"Where's Timo?" Ingrid said, peeking through the door of Timo's office.

"Not here," Isa said, looking up from the computer. She had taken the liberty to claim his office now that Timo was gone.

"He's suspended" Isa continued, "so you won't find him here."

Maybe she should know where he was. After all, he was now a suspect. She looked at her friend for a moment. They had been friends for so long. For years, Isa had felt the bad one, the one who needed guidance, who had to be reprimanded. She just couldn't play by the rules like the decent, morally elevated, and dull Ingrid, with her great looking and successful husband and two beautiful boys. This time the roles were reversed, and she had to be there for Ingrid, but she just didn't know how.

Ingrid sighed. "I just ... it's horrible that story with his fiancé. I was wondering if there's anything I can do. Or maybe you?"

"Me? Why?"

"You both have lost loved ones in such a dramatic way. I don't know how I can help him. I don't even know how to help you. I just don't know what to say."

"Ingrid let's face it, he's been mourning Caijsa for eight years, while I already had a new man in my bed, three months after Alex's death. I don't think I'm the role model here. I think whatever your advice is, it's still better than mine."

"I know you're quite different in dealing with pain, but you've experienced it. You know what it is."

"Maybe you're right," Isa said and closed the laptop. "But still ... I think he'll listen to you. I don't really know what to think of it."

"You think he has something to do with the murders?"

Isa shook her head and then looked at the window. It was raining. Big, heavy raindrops, pounding against the glass of the window.

"I don't know," Isa had to admit. "Eight years is a lot of time to think about revenge. I'm starting to believe Elker didn't kill her. Maybe Timo knew that."

Ingrid shook her head and said, "No, he's not like that."

"You asked for my advice. Maybe that deep sorrow Timo took with him all those years turned into long-festering hate. Elker died and then suddenly it turned out he was innocent. Or maybe not? I don't know."

Ingrid walked up to her. "And how are you holding up?"

"I'm okay," Isa said.

But she wasn't. Nick, Timo, Magnus, Sandviken. Those last two cases hung over her like a sword of Damocles. It was official now. Serial killer Mats Norman was going for a reopening of his case, and there was a good chance he would get it, now the Commission of Inquiry had ruled that serious mistakes had been made. The lead investigators in his case were both compromised. One faced a disciplinary committee to investigate her relationship with one of the victims, and the other was tried as a murderer. Every move, every decision they both had made in the investigation was now under scrutiny.

And Magnus himself pleaded not guilty by reason of mental insanity. His confession, witnessed by his family and a handful of police officers, was up for debate and could be dismissed.

Why did Magnus have to make everything so difficult and painful? For his own family, for Alex's family, for herself. It was easy to blame her, given her reputation and the disciplinary complaint.

She needed Ingrid. Their friendship had gone through rough times the last months. Because of Timo? She had to admit she was jealous.

She needed human affection, and for her, it usually meant sex. Nick hadn't touched her in weeks. Except for that one kiss, he trembled every time she approached him. She wanted to tell herself she had become a better person and she could rise above her own needs and think about others, but she hadn't. It was very clear from the sessions with Dr. Wikholm.

That evening she drove around and ended up in the same nightclub where she had met Nick so many months ago. She didn't know what she wanted. She should support her man at home and help him through the most difficult period in his life. But it was like an addiction. Each time she told herself she would change. It had been the same with Magnus. A year into the relationship, she had sex with other men. She had loved him, but sex usually had nothing to do with love. Not for her. Magnus knew, even though she didn't realize it until after the breakup. And he could handle it if he knew it wasn't love. Until Alex. Alex was love, no matter how hard she tried to deny it at first. But she wondered if she could have stayed faithful to him. Damaged Alex wouldn't have been able to cope. It would have pushed him over the edge.

Nick. She had never considered that relationship as something serious. He was too much like her. Casual flirts, one-night stands. Sex and passion. They would have split up after a while anyway. She hated she was now in a situation where he was dependent on her. The guilt, the moral obligation to help him was holding her hostage in a relationship she wanted to give up. She had told Dr. Wikholm. He had nodded, scribbled a few words in his notebook and had given her nothing useful.

And then Timo. Could she at least admit she found him attractive? But that man was not one to play with. He saw through her. He had a way of getting under her skin most of the time, while on the other hand, he was her biggest supporter. He saw her potential as a detective but disapproved of her messy personal life. She would never stand a chance with him. And why was she even considering that possibility?

It wasn't busy for a Friday night. There was a small crowd of youngsters on the dancefloor, a little tipsy and making a fool of themselves, but they didn't seem to care. Two older men sitting at the bar, but none really her type. She had lied to Nick, told him she wanted to work late, now that she was alone, with Timo suspended.

She recognized the bartender. It was the same young man who had served her the night she had met Nick. He looked good. In fact, he had been her target before the lawyer with Italian roots had seduced her.

He smiled as he approached her. "You're back."

"You remember me," she said, surprised.

"How can I not," he said and leaned over to look her in the eye.

He was hot and just what she needed right now.

"Thanks." She smiled back and twisted a lock of hair around her finger.

"What do you want?"

"A dry martini would be good," she said, unable to take her eyes of his perfectly shaped body. The simple black T-shirt and jeans reminded her of Timo. It was almost her boss' trademark.

"You know ... I'll be off in half an hour," he said softly as he pushed the cocktail glass toward her.

They even didn't reach her car. He pulled her into a pantry. She heard him panting heavily as he unfastened the belt from her pants and pulled them down along her legs. Then he went for her thong, while she let her hands ran over his chest feeling every muscle underneath his shirt. He started to kiss her neck and moved down to her chest. The white blouse she was wearing was nearly torn apart as he went for her breasts. She couldn't stand it anymore. The craving, it felt like she was about to explode, but then something strange happened. A voice of reason, telling her she couldn't do this to Nick. He deserved better and if she didn't come to her senses now, she would never become the woman she wanted to be.

"Stop," she said and pushed him away.

He gave her a confused look.

"I'm sorry. I should never ..."

She pulled up her pants and thong, and closed the blouse over her breasts, and gave him a quick look. He seemed rightfully disappointed.

"I'm sorry, so sorry," she said as she closed the door.

It was time to change.

CHAPTER

18

"**SO, CAIJSA JENSEN IS THE CONNECTION?**"

"Likely," Isa said.

The man in front of her had gotten on her nerves, insulted and questioned her work, but now neither of them knew what to make of the recent events.

She said, "Bergman was murdered. He was sedated before the gun was put in his mouth. Dr. Olsson found a puncture mark in his neck. I think Bergman knew who his stalker was."

"Paikkala?"

She sighed and looked up at the ceiling. "So, let's assume Elker didn't kill Caijsa, but those three guys or their families have something to do with her death. They know who the real killer is."

"They were witnesses," Kristoffer said.

"And they needed to die. But why now? Why not eight years ago?"

"Our murderer only found out recently he was seen."

"Could be, or ..." She looked at the window again. When would it stop raining? They had an almost steady flow of rain the last days. So depressing!

"I don't think inspector Paikkala has anything to do with it," she said hesitantly.

"Let's hope so. We don't want another Wieland."

"Paikkala is not Magnus Wieland," she said determined.

He gave her an ironic grin. "Yes, like your intuition is that impeccable? You didn't even realize what your partner had done."

He was right, but she didn't need to be reminded of her mistakes.

"By the way, they shut down Forsmark One yesterday," Kristoffer said with a straight face. "It hasn't been announced to the public yet."

"What happened?" she said.

He leaned against the wall. "The unit was shut down after an electrical failure, but the worst thing of all was that the safety system was overruled. Luckily, an observant engineer took action, and he was able to prevent worse. The incident is being investigated, but it's clearly ..."

"Sabotage. But I thought security measures were increased?"

"They were, but obviously not enough. It's an inside job. The saboteur knew exactly what he was doing. I wish I could say this is all connected, but I can't. Continue to investigate the Jensen angle. I won't stand in your way. Not this time. SÄPO will take care of the rest."

She nodded. This time he managed to fold his mouth in a soft smile before he disappeared.

She turned to the file on the desk.

The paper in front of her had been there for at least an hour before Kristoffer Solberg had walked into her office unannounced. Isa had read the lines over and over, but it didn't quite sink in. Her mind wasn't exactly on the case. She sighed and bowed her head again. Start from the top!

The forensic report on Thorgan Elker's death. The man was found hanging from the window bars with the bed sheets.

She flipped through the pages describing the scene, pictures of the evidence and the body, and then stopped at the page where the coroner had described the condition of the body and had noted on the facial sheets the presence of bruises and injuries.

My God, this man has been used as a punching bag!

This couldn't be right. In the following pages, she read that Thorgan was regularly beaten in prison. For years, the management had tried to protect him, isolating him from the rest of the inmates, but it wasn't that successful.

There was discoloration of the skin on the back of the neck that had caught the coroner's attention. It was fresh, probably sustained before the hanging. Had he tried something else before committing suicide or was it the result of a blow that had knocked him unconscious? A beating that had gotten out of hand?

"Inspector Lindström?"

In front of her stood an older man in police uniform. She jumped up and said, "Commander Eriksson, what brings you here?"

"Sit down," the gray-haired man said.

There was something irritating about his voice. She couldn't pinpoint exactly what it was. Something in the frequency spectrum made her hair stand on end. It was as if thunder was rolling across the room. She'd only met the man once, a few years ago, at a fundraising event. She couldn't recall anymore what it was about. He'd given a speech, and even then, she'd barely been able to sit through the entire presentation.

He grabbed a chair and sat across the table.

"Let me get straight to the point," he said. "We have concerns about inspector Paikkala."

"Why?"

"I read your report of the interview. The man has no alibi."

"Well, he does for Global Law. He couldn't have killed all those people. Why would he? There is no reason. We still are in the dark about what happened. According to ..."

"You're not here to jump to conclusions based on hunches. Just because he doesn't have a clear motive doesn't mean there isn't one. Dig a little deeper. Until then, inspector Paikkala is suspended."

Why was he here? What was so important he had to come to Gävle to make this point?

"I hope to see a full report on inspector Paikkala by tomorrow."

She couldn't say anything, and just nodded.

"And let me remind you that a lot will depend on this report," he said and stood up, "your former colleague Magnus Wieland has said some nasty things about you ... time to think about your own career."

And with those words, he disappeared, and she could almost hear him running down the hall. She shook her head and dropped onto the chair.

Was this a threat? Why did they want to get Timo?

She turned to the pages and started reading again. None of this made sense. Was Thorgan Elker murdered? But why? The only people to gain anything from his death were Caijsa's family. Revenge. And then things didn't look too great for Timo. But would death really be what they wanted? Wouldn't life in prison be so much more tormenting than a quick death? And how would they have killed him? It meant that a fellow inmate or a guard was involved. She had to talk to the guard who found him. There was a note about him in the report. Anskar Ramvall. He lived in Vallentuna, north of Stockholm. She could make the trip tomorrow or the day after, together with Berger, if he wasn't too busy entertaining his girlfriend, Mila. Maybe she should give Lars a chance to show what he was worth. He seemed to be down these days. Lars and Berger were friends and competitors at the same time. They had known each other since high school, went to the police academy together and started working as police officers in Gävle about five years ago. They were ambitious, trying to outsmart each other, both at work and in their private lives. Perhaps Lars felt left out, now his friend had found a new purpose in life. He certainly didn't like Mila. After trying to talk to Isa about his concern with Mila, he had kept his mouth shut, but it was clear he still didn't trust her. Perhaps Lars also struggled with fits of jealousy that clouded his mind. There was nothing in the young woman's behavior that was out of the ordinary, except that she knew Eve Bergman. She had admitted it and had explained to them, but she hadn't known Eve was the wife of a suspect. Mila had met Eve at yoga class, and the police hadn't found anything suspicious. So, what was it that had aroused Lars' suspicion?

*　*　*

"Why do you want to talk to me?" Timo said. He was standing outside the interrogation room, looking a little lost when he ran into Isa in the hallway. She had called him the day before to come in.

"This isn't an interrogation," Isa said quickly and pushed him into the room.

"What's wrong?" he said.

"Why are they out to get you?"

"Uh?" he let out.

"Why does the chief of police come to Gävle to say … no, to threaten me that if I don't draw the right conclusion in my report about your involvement, it could have serious consequences for my career?"

"And what is the right conclusion?" he said with a straight face.

"You tell me," she growled.

"Look, I can understand they don't trust me, and they just wanted to make sure you take this case seriously."

"Don't make excuses for them," she said.

Why couldn't he be angrier? She had been in the same situation a few times and it had been a frustrating experience. Why was he the calm, rational and trying-to-look-at-it-from-all-sides boss? He had to boil inside.

"And I'm sorry to tell you, but you aren't that important," she added.

"I don't know why they would be after me," he sighed. He closed his eyes for a moment, and then took a deep breath.

"How have you been?" she said.

"Bored."

"Don't you have lots of stuff to do in the house?"

He gave her a look of disappointment.

"That's a hobby. God, I wouldn't even call it that. Those are chores. I don't want to spend my days fixing floors, breaking down walls, painting, and redecorating rooms."

"Hang in there," she said, "this will be over soon."

"Will it? I'm not so sure. Have you talked to Pauli and his friends?"

"Not yet. We will, but we're having trouble finding Pauli Nyström."

"Why? Did he disappear too?"

"He's supposedly on a camping trip with his work buddies, but no one can reach him, and nobody knows where they are."

"Or is he hiding?" Timo said.

"Could be. But what would he be hiding from? I'm worried he might be our next victim."

He sighed.

"The link between all these people is Caijsa," Isa said.

He stopped and stared at the wall. "Actually, that's not true. They are all family of Pauli's friends. Maybe we have to see Global Law as a separate incident."

"And the link with Engersson is a coincidence?" she said.

He shrugged. "God, I don't know anymore."

"Another witness was mentioned in Caijsa's file."

She stopped and looked at him. Every time she mentioned Caijsa's name he crumpled.

"Mrs. Ylva Heimer," she continued.

He shook his head. "Never heard of her. Why was she mentioned?"

"She was walking in the park near the house and heard a woman scream. I wonder if she saw more."

"You want to talk to her?"

She nodded.

"Well, I am not your boss anymore. The call is yours."

* * *

Mrs. Heimer's daughter received the inspectors at her home in Hudiksvall. Her mother had died two years ago in a strange car accident that until this day still puzzled the family. One evening, coming home from work, her husband had found her mother squeezed between the car and the gate of the house.

"I am sorry for your loss, Mrs. Bodil."

She shook her head in appreciation but said, "It's been two years."

"We're here because we wanted to talk to you about an old case involving your mother," Isa continued.

The young woman looked up in surprise. Meanwhile her husband joined them in the living room.

"What old case?" the husband said.

"Just hear them out," his wife said in a low voice.

"Your mother testified in a murder case about eight years ago. Caijsa Jensen."

"The young woman who was found dead in her house," Mrs. Bodil said.

"Yes," Isa answered.

"Can you tell us a little more about your mother's involvement," Lars continued.

"My family is from Stockholm. My parents lived there all their lives until my father died, and my mother came to live here in Hudiksvall. My husband ..."

And she looked at him. "My husband is from the area, and we met at university. Anyway, eight years ago she was a witness in that murder case. However, her testimony got disregarded."

"Why?"

"My mother had ... problems. Mental health problems, which got exacerbated by the medication she was taking for her epilepsy. She testified she had seen that poor woman in the park before, crying. And later, she had seen two youngsters running away. She was questioned about that, but she got confused about the timeline and she couldn't give any details. So, her testimony was refuted. And honestly, I can't blame them."

"She saw Caijsa Jensen in the park?"

"Yes, she was adamant."

"And she never identified the young men?"

"No, the police accused her of giving a false testimony," Mrs. Bodil said.

"And what do you think?" Isa said, taking a closer look at her. There was hesitation in her voice, and she looked unsettled.

"I'm not sure. Mother could be very confused and drowsy at times, but she had her clear moments. I think she truly saw something."

"Did she talk about it later?"

"Now and then, yes ... but after a while she stopped talking about it ... until."

"Until?"

"About two years ago or so, just before her death ... she had just moved in with us. We went to visit relatives in Gävle, and in the grocery shop, she got all excited. She had recognized one of the men."

"After so many years?" Isa asked.

"She said he had a distinctive tattoo on his lower arm. A snake."

Lars turned to Isa. "Pauli Nyström has a snake tattoo."

"Which grocery store was that?" Isa said.

Mrs. Bodil looked down at her hands and then shook her head. "I really can't remember but he worked there."

"And a bit later, your mother died in that strange accident?" Lars said.

"Yes ... I still blame myself. I wasn't home that day. A friend had picked me up to go to work. The car was in the driveway, and there is a little slope, but I swear the handbrake was on. I still don't know what she was doing there. She wasn't well. I thought she would stay in bed."

"Neighbors said they saw a car parked outside the gate that day," Lars said. "Maybe she had visitors?"

"She hardly knew anyone. I read it in the police report, but they never found the owner of the car."

"And in the months or weeks before your mother's death, did you see anything strange?"

She shook her head, but this time her husband intervened, "Actually yes."

"Hans?" Mrs. Bodil said as she gave him a surprised look.

"A few weeks before the accident," he started, "I just got home and there was a black car parked in the street and Ylva was talking to the driver, but as I stepped out of my car and I wanted to see who it was, the car drove off. I later asked her who it was, but she said she didn't know the person. She hadn't even gotten a good look at him. He seemed to be a foreigner who asked for directions."

"You never told me," his wife said and gave him a sharp look. "And neither did you tell the police."

"I didn't think it was important," he stammered. "It isn't, is it?"

Isa ignored his request for reassurance, and said, "What was the brand of the car?"

"Uh, a Volkswagen station car," Hans said.

"Same description as mentioned in the police file. It could be the same car that was parked in front of the house when your wife's mother died."

Hans dropped in the chair, eyes fixed on the wall in front of him.

"One last question," Isa said, "did your mother ever mention Thorgan Elker?"

"No, who is that?"

"Never mind," inspector Lindström said.

When Lars closed the front door behind him, he said, "She was murdered."

"Yes, but why?"

"Daniel Nyström worked in a grocery shop," Lars said. "Daniel and Pauli were very similar in appearance."

"But not the tattoo. I think she saw Pauli. He now and then worked there as well. But we already know that Pauli was a witness in Caijsa's case. That's in the report."

"That brings us to: who was the second man?" Lars said.

"Or men."

"Men?"

"I think they were all there. Question is, why would they want to hide it?"

Isa took the key from her pocket and opened the door of her 15-year-old Volkswagen. She ran her eyes over the garage and the gently sloped driveway for a moment. "And I wonder how Mrs. Heimer died without anyone seeing."

245

"The gate shields a large part of the house from the street. What happens behind it is hidden from passersby."

"Someone must have heard something. A scream, an argument, something. And she must have let her killer in. Why? Did she know him?"

Lars shrugged and got into the car.

"And there's no way that car could accidentally drive backwards."

"It could have been a malfunction in the parking brake system," Lars said, "although it was never detected."

"Can someone with enough knowledge of cars make the sabotage look like an accident?"

"Someone like Timo? He knows a lot about cars."

She sighed and pushed the key into the ignition. "Timo is not a murderer."

* * *

The next day Lars and Isa traveled nearly two hours to Vallentuna. Lars, always up for a good and long story in which he could demonstrate his storytelling skills, was silent. They'd been driving for half an hour, and he hadn't said a word except a few grunts and sighs.

"You are particularly cheerful today," she said, giving him a quick glance, then turning her attention to the road again.

"Is there something on your mind?" she asked when he didn't answer and just kept staring outside. It was unusually warm for the time of the year. Temperatures should hover around zero degrees Celsius, but it had been an enjoyable ten degrees outside, and the heavy rain had subsided.

The car drove south, past open fields and wooded areas where the fog slowly began to lift.

"You know ... I don't understand it. Berger, of all people ... the guy who can't even buy a TV without basically checking off twenty things.

The man has doubts about everything and now he just moves in with her, after knowing her for how long? Two, maybe three months."

"Well, he's careful when it comes to some things," she admitted, "but not when it comes to his career, for example."

He turned toward her and said, "Mmm, maybe you're right."

"When people are passionate about something and they know it's right, they're willing to do anything. Just my two cents."

"And he's passionate about Mila," he mumbled.

"Why are you so against Mila anyway?"

"I don't have anything against her ... it's just there's something about her I don't really trust," he said, leaning to the right to scan the area outside.

"So, you have something against her," she remarked.

"Just leave it," he snapped, resting his head in his hand, but then suddenly turned to her. "Are you sure she has nothing to do with Bergman? She knows Eve Bergman. Maybe ..."

"No. We checked and other witnesses from the yoga class confirmed that Eve and Mila met recently. It's really a coincidence. And could it be that you're a little jealous?"

Jealous of Berger over Mila? She wasn't his type. Jealous that Berger had met someone to share his life with? Maybe. He felt lonely these days. No one would admit it, but the recent events, the attack on Global Law, had impacted everyone. It was one of those moments when you were suddenly confronted with how fragile life was and how easy it was to take everything for granted. He longed for someone to share his dreams and life with. Sometimes, he felt desperate. Why hadn't he met the right girl yet? Was he too picky? Maybe there was no one out there for him. Everyone seemed to be in a relationship, and he was left behind.

"Just focus on the road," he said, ending the conversation on the topic.

* * *

Anskar Ramvall lived alone in a small house near the center of Vallentuna. A small but stately old house, beautiful in the summer when the roses bloomed, but in the winter dark and desolate, surrounded by trees with empty branches. He had been on sick leave since the beginning of the year. Colon cancer. He was diagnosed shortly after his wife's death at the age of fifty-seven. It wasn't the greatest moment of his life. He had reconnected with his estranged son, but the relationship remained difficult. He didn't need all this commotion in his life, and when inspector Lindström had contacted him about Thorgan Elker he had hesitated about her request for an interview, but he had finally given in.

"Thorgan Elker. Yes, I remember him."

The man sitting at the table was pale, looked tired and almost emaciated. Isa thought it might have been a mistake to drag him through such a tiresome interview as this, even though they had driven nearly two hours.

Anskar had to stop a few times to catch his breath or organize his thoughts. He told them every little thing wore him out these days. He had no pain today, but some days the pain was almost unbearable. Little by little, the chemotherapy was poisoning the remaining healthy cells in his body. The verdict hadn't come yet, but he knew his body was giving up, and in a sense, he had made peace with it.

"Take your time," Isa said softly.

"Thorgan Elker," he repeated, "he got beaten up a lot by the other inmates or clients—that's how they call them these days—even though he tried to keep a low profile. They always found him."

"He had mental problems," Lars remarked. "Still, he ended up in prison. This man belonged in a psychiatric hospital."

"I dunno, but he's never seen a doctor during his stay there," the old man said.

"I read in the report there were doubts about his suicide," Isa mentioned.

"Yes ... two days before it happened, he'd been in a fight with an inmate—dunno his name anymore—and injured his arm. Wasn't broken or so, but he could hardly use it. He was in a lot of pain, but he didn't want to see a doctor. So, how could he have made a noose of bed sheets?"

"He could have made it before, and if he was determined to end his life then painful arm or not, he would have managed to do it," Lars remarked.

"But that's it," Anskar said, almost breathless. "He wasn't depressed. Sure, the assaults were tough, but he had filed a request to revise his court case, and his lawyer told him he had a good chance to reopen it."

"Why was he targeted by the other inmates?" Isa said.

"Dunno. It started almost from the beginning. The moment he arrived."

"Did he have any friends?"

"Friends? No one has friends in prison."

"People he hung out with then," Lars corrected.

"There was one guy, young guy, convicted for his part in the murder of a policeman ... Mikael Dahlberg, I believe."

"Mikael Dahlberg? Elin Dahlberg's brother, one of the serial killer victims?"

Anskar shrugged. "I don't know her, but I knew Mikael as a polite and helpful young man. I know he had bad friends, and he had stolen cars, and dealt drugs, but I couldn't believe he was involved in that policeman's death."

"But he was convicted," Isa said. "The police officer pulled him and his so-called friends over for speeding. The car was full of drugs and weapons. He may not have fired the fatal shot, but he was an accomplice."

"Why was Elker socializing with Mikael Dahlberg?" Lars interrupted.

"I really don't know why," Anskar said.

"Going back to the suicide, who found him?" Isa asked.

"I did," Anskar said. "I ... uh, ... I know it's a job and it wasn't the first time in my thirty-year career as a prison guard, I found an inmate dead, but I ... it got to me. I didn't understand. Why would he take his own life five years after the murder? There had been the hope of a new trial."

"A new trial that would never happen," Lars said.

Anskar looked at him stunned. "I didn't know."

"Was the door locked?"

"No, it wasn't but I guess the cameras in the corridor would have picked up all the people who entered his cell."

Isa remembered this wasn't mentioned in the reports.

"Did Thorgan ever talk about Caijsa's family?"

"He spoke to the parents once. It left an impression on him, and he was very quiet afterwards. Almost humble and respectful. And I know he had sent letters to her fiancé the last years before his death."

"He did?"

"Never got a reply," Anskar said. "He was very disappointed."

"Do you believe he was innocent?"

He waited for a moment.

"I thought about it for a long time," he reminisced, "but yes, I do think he was innocent, and I have to ..."

"What, Mr. Ramvall?"

He licked his lips, opened his mouth, and then closed it again. There was doubt. But about what, she couldn't quite figure out. A moment later, he frowned and looked down at his feet.

"Never mind," he said, and with those words he closed the conversation.

CHAPTER

19

HILKO INGBERG WAS A PALE YOUNG MAN, skin and bones, not looking too bright, a scruffy appearance with his old tattered and stained T-shirt and holes in the pants he was wearing. It was hard to imagine he was Kirsten Jeppesen's brother.

"Mr. Ingberg, thank you for coming," Lars said.

"Do you know more about my sister's murder?" he sniffed. He was edgy, running his hand over his arm, scratching it now and then, and constantly looking around.

"We're looking at several leads," Lars continued, "but we want to talk to you about your friend Pauli Nyström."

"Pauli? What does Pauli have to do with this?"

He almost jumped up, his eyes blinking, moving quickly from one side to the other.

"Tell me about him," Isa said calmly.

"But ... I don't know ... he is just a friend. We hang out together, but not that often."

"You've been friends since high school?"

He nodded. "Yeah ... since seventh grade."

"What is he like?" Isa asked.

"Just a good mate ... that's ol. Nothing special."

"What do you do together?"

"We usually go to pubs."

"I see," Isa tried to keep his gaze, but he lowered his eyes and kept looking at his hands.

"Eight years ago, Pauli was a witness in a murder case."

"Yeah, I remember ... nasty business."

"You were there as well, just like Svante."

He raised his shoulders.

"Your old teacher said you were very close. Best friends. You did everything together. So, I wonder where you were that morning when Caijsa Jensen was murdered."

"Look, I have nothing to do with that. Pauli went for a jog that morning and saw them arguing. That's it."

"Arguing? He claims he saw Thorgan Elker hanging around the house. He never mentioned seeing the woman."

"Uh ... then I must be wrong," Hilko stammered.

"Where were you?"

"I don't remember. Probably in bed. Yes, that was it."

"So, you admit being in Stockholm?"

Shock was written all over his face. "Uh ... yeah."

"And where were you staying?'

"The hostel Pauli's mother had booked."

253

Isa tore a piece of paper from her notebook and slid it towards him along with a pen. "Write the name down."

"I'm sure Pauli must have told you."

"Write it down," Isa said, leaning back nonchalantly to let her eyes run over the man who was growing increasingly nervous.

"I don't know. It's been eight years."

"If something like this happened, so close to where you were staying, it would definitely leave an impression," Lars commented.

"I wasn't there," Hilko sneered.

"Do you know Ilja Klust?"

"Who's that?" the young man said.

"He owns a grocery shop in the center of Gävle," Lars said. "Still doesn't ring any bell?"

"Maybe," Hilko said. "I think he's the guy Pauli's brother worked for."

"Ilja Klust is well known to the police for dealing drugs. We picked him up and he admitted he and Daniel had a lucrative business. That's why Daniel had so much money, and I think that's how Pauli got his drugs. Daniel was his drugs supplier, wasn't he? And maybe even yours?"

"I don't do drugs," he yelled.

Isa folded her mouth in an ironic grin. "Hilko, come on. The trembling hands, the eyes, the way you shuffle in your chair. You are a drug addict."

"When did it start?" Lars said.

"I told you, I'm not an addict," Hilko said and clenched his fists.

"When did it start?" Isa insisted.

He shook his head, then let out a deep sigh. "In the tenth grade. For all of us, but it started with Pauli, and only soft drugs in the beginning. The hard drugs came years later."

"And Ilja and Daniel were the dealers?"

He nodded.

"How did you get the money for the drugs?"

"Ilja gave us chores to do. Delivering packages, stealing stuff to pay for it."

"And is that what you were doing on the trip to Stockholm? Doing chores for Ilja Klust and Daniel Nyström. That was convenient, wasn't it? Pauli's family was visiting relatives and he decided to invite his friends to come along."

"What? No!"

"Or were you planning to do something else?"

"Like what," he went into defense mode.

"Maybe Pauli had taken drugs and decided it was time for a party. He saw Caijsa Jensen in the park and decided to have some fun with her, but it got out of hand."

"No, no, we ... Pauli had nothing to do with her death!"

Isa watched him as she slowly turned the pages of the file. He was almost jumping up and down in his chair.

She said, "In 2015 Pauli got arrested for dealing himself and went to jail. In Stockholm."

Hilko calmed down and nodded. "Yep ... he was released in 2016. Then his daughter was born, and he found a job in construction, and I haven't heard much about him since."

"Well, he went to prison again in 2017 and was released beginning of this year. And guess who was there to pick him up?"

Hilko shook his head wildly. "That was just a small favor. I haven't seen him since."

The scratching irritated Isa. The repetitive motion, the rocking, the sniffing and little coughs. There was nothing about this man that deserved her pity. He was hiding a lot, about his friend Pauli, about their involvement in the murder of Caijsa Jensen, about the murders of their relatives.

"Hilko, if you know where Pauli is, you'd better tell us," Lars said.

"Ask his girlfriend."

"Ex-girlfriend. She hasn't seen him in weeks. He hasn't come to visit his daughter. I think your buddy has reverted to his old habits."

"Try his new girlfriend."

"So, you do know what your friend is up to these days," Isa said.

"Okay, okay. I've seen him a few weeks ago. He was all upset about his brother's disappearance. He was scared, really scared."

"Why?"

"I don't know, but he had been receiving letters."

"What letters?" Isa said. "Threatening letters?"

"No, weird stuff. A page with one word 'YOU', and then a few more with 'You know why'."

Isa suddenly remembered the letter Timo had put on the table in front of them. He had received letters too. What was going on?

"Look, can I go ... I need to go," Hilko pleaded.

"And you?" Isa asked.

"What about me?" he said.

"Did you get any letters?"

"Uh ... no."

He quickly looked at his hands again, which were now in his lap. He had them under control, but not the rest of his body. Isa knew full well he was lying.

"Some final questions. Then you can go."

He shuffled back and forth in his chair.

"How was your relationship with your sister Kirsten?"

"Normal, okay. Nothing special."

"When was the last time you saw her?"

He sighed and said, "Six months ago."

"Six months ago? Apparently, you weren't that close after all."

"Her husband didn't approve of my ... lifestyle," Hilko answered.

"Where did you get the money for the drugs?" Isa asked.

"Maybe you stole from her," Lars added, "she caught you and you killed her."

"Jeezes, man, what do you think of me? I told you where I get the money. Ilja Klust. I didn't need to steal from her."

"That's not what her husband told us," Isa said. "I think your family didn't want to have anything to do with you."

* * *

"Anton, what is this?"

"What do you mean?" The blond man looked up from his laptop as his wife entered the study to confront him.

Each time, the grandeur of the room impressed Ingrid. The dark wooden desk in the middle of the room and behind it the large windows overlooking the garden. The small salon with glass table and leather seats next to it. Everything radiated luxury, the way Anton wanted it, but it wasn't her thing. She wouldn't have minded something more toned down.

"You signed the consent form for Benno's weekend trip?" she said.

Her husband looked at her confused. Benno's trip, with his friends from Scouterna. Their oldest son had been looking forward to it for a while.

"I thought we decided not to let him go this time until his grades got better?"

"He's doing his best. One weekend trip with his friends shouldn't matter that much. Let the boy have some fun."

"Jesus! Anton, can't you just back me up for once?" Ingrid cried in frustration. "Why am I always the bad one here?"

"You're not," he said and closed the laptop.

"Yes, I am. Every decision I take, everything I say, is overruled by you. The boys don't take me seriously. How can I ...?"

The volume of her voice had gradually increased as she expressed her frustrations until she was nearly out of breath.

"What are you so angry about? Ingrid, ever since we got back from vacation, for months now, you've been so tense. You are constantly in a bad mood. The slightest thing I do or say, is torpedoed as if I've done the worst thing ever. Have I done something wrong? What? Tell me what to do!"

Had she? Yes, he irritated her. From the morning to the evening, from the moment she woke up until she laid her head down at night. And that irritation had only grown.

"It's just ... I feel like a maid ... I'm just here to clean up, iron, make dinner, make sure the kids get to school. We had agreed Benno should concentrate on his studies."

"No, you've decided," he said with a straight face. "You've got it wrong. Everything has to be done your way. You're not giving me the chance to be involved. I feel left out, out of my own family."

She could see where the frustration was coming from, but it was the result of trying to cope with the pressure of running a household and a full-time job. She knew he understood that or at least in his mind he thought he understood, but perhaps he didn't really grasp what it meant.

"Anton, you're barely here! How can you expect me to involve you?"

"And when I'm here, you ignore me," he said. "I'm here now."

"Well," she said as she walked over to the desk and put the paper in front of him. "Here's your chance to be involved. I'm out of here."

She turned around and headed for the door.

"Where are you going this late? Ingrid?"

"Don't know ... work, somewhere else," she said. "I need to clear my head."

Minutes later Anton heard a car drive away. She had never done this before. He tried to call her, but she didn't answer. Now he was getting nervous. She probably needed 'me-time'. Perhaps he had simply underestimated the pressure she was under. The events of the past months had everyone on edge. She was drowning in work. On top of that, her new assistant Mila needed a lot of guidance, and she just couldn't handle it.

But neither could he. Even if he hadn't seen the horror of the attack, the fact that he'd lost colleagues, that something like this could happen to ordinary people like them, had impressed him more than he wanted to admit. He had talked little about it. He didn't want to put more stress on her, but he felt left out. He should have told her. They needed to talk more.

She would be back. She just needed some breathing room, time to reflect.

He went upstairs to his children's bedrooms. Benno would still be awake.

Ingrid was sometimes so naïve to believe an eleven-year-old would quietly go to bed at 9:00 p.m. His son would be tapping on his computer until midnight, chatting with his friends most of the time.

"Benno," he said as he opened the door. Benno jumped up, tried to hide the computer but knew it was too late.

His wife was right. Benno wasn't doing great in school. He needed structure and focus.

"We need to talk about the trip," Anton said and sat down on the edge of the bed.

* * *

Timo lay on the floor in his living room. It was just something he did every now and then. He found it relaxing to stare at an imperfectly done wooden ceiling, to the extent he would sometimes wake up in the middle of the night and realize he had fallen asleep on the floor. And then, with pain all over his body, grasping he wasn't twenty anymore, he crawled to his bed.

It would be so much better with a ceiling fan. Then he could follow the mesmerizing movement of the blades spinning endlessly. Yes, he needed a fan. Mediterranean style. Probably it wasn't so common in Sweden, and his mother would disapprove of the clash in style.

It brought back memories of his childhood. Good and bad. Like that time, when on a trade mission to Kenya, he was bedridden with high fever. He remembered his mother's face so vividly. So much fear and despair. But somehow the monotonous movement of the fan brought peace. He stared at it as he tried to think about his friends, school, and how he could go back exploring. Years later, she'd told him the terrors she'd endured, not knowing that it wasn't malaria or yellow fever, but just the common flu. He often thought about it when he was at odds with her again and thought she didn't love him. His mother at his bedside, thinking she would lose him, while he followed the blades of the fan between the fever flares and dreamed of wild voyages of discovery with the mechanical sound of the ventilation fan in the background. How stupid and ignorant he sometimes was.

He ran his hands over his face. Most of the time he did his best thinking in complete silence, alone, trying to focus his mind by not overloading it with anything else.

When would he start thinking like a police officer again? Everything was so emotionally charged now; he could hardly get the buzz out of his head. Thorgan Elker, the man he'd been trying so hard to get out of his life, had stormed back in again. What if he was innocent? What if the killer was still out there? He needed to get justice, for Caijsa, for Marcel and Paulina, and himself.

He jumped up. What was this? It sounded like a soft knock on the door. The doorbell didn't work. He hadn't gotten around to fixing it yet.

He waited. Maybe it was the wind or the rain. The bad weather was back, and it had been stormy for most of the day. There was a second knock. No, someone was at the door. But who? He hadn't expected anyone that late. He didn't expect anyone at all, and it was too late to pretend he wasn't home. The light from the living room was shining through the windows for everyone to see. He got up and walked to the door. Through the small window next to the door, he recognized the person.

"Ingrid? What are you doing here?" he said when he opened the door.

She took a deep breath and then said, "Look, hear me out! Don't interrupt me. I have to tell you this, or it will never be said. I love being around you. The intense looks, the flirtatious conversations, the tension between us, ... the unspoken desires. But it's not enough anymore. It's simply not enough. I want more."

Without another word, she took his head in her hands and pressed her lips to his. For a second, the passionate kiss was met with surprise and hesitation but then he took her in his arms and continued to kiss her, each touch intensifying the desire for more. This was what they had longed for, for so long. All barriers had been knocked down, shattered under the burden of so much maddening passion.

CHAPTER

20

TIMO WAS STARING AT THE CEILING again, but this time he wasn't alone. He held her hand so tightly, as if he never wanted to let her go.

"You were right to stop me," she whispered and looked up to see his face, which had turned into a smile. He looked relaxed and happy. So beautiful, and only she was allowed to see it. She had come to him that evening for more than just a kiss. She wanted him, all of him, but he had been the smarter one, the more reasonable of the two. As much as he wanted it, this was not the premise he'd wanted to start their relationship with. Now, lying on the couch in his living room, in his arms, she knew it had been the right decision. She'd been annoyed and angry with Anton, and these were never the best reasons to start something she couldn't turn back. But they had crossed a line, and she might not call it adultery, she had kissed him, she had wanted to sleep with this man. In her mind, she'd done it dozens of times. She was cheating on her husband, and she didn't regret it, none of it. And if she were to do it all over again, she wouldn't have waited or doubted endlessly whether this was what she wanted.

"I already regret it," he laughed and gently pulled the lock of hair from her cheek to kiss her again. His touch ignited every neuron in her body.

"I want you to be sure," he said. "Absolutely sure, because this is all so complicated: Anton, Caijsa."

"I look like her," she said.

He quickly turned his head and said, "You are nothing like her."

He had said it in such an angry tone that it shocked her.

"I didn't ...," she said and lifted her head.

He sighed, looked up at the ceiling and took a deep breath as if to make a confession. "I need to tell you something."

She sat up to look at him and then let her hand ran over his face.

"I never told anyone, but I wanted to leave her," he said.

She didn't say anything, but somehow it didn't come as a surprise. There had been the pain of loss, but so much shame and guilt, more than anything else.

"I loved her so much. I miss her, but ... she could be mean, and the months, even the years before her death, I don't know what had happened, she had become insufferable, vindictive, extremely jealous. I didn't understand. I didn't think I had given her a reason to be like that. She made me feel insecure, while I was always so confident. I started to doubt myself."

"But you wanted to marry her?"

"That conversation should have been another one. I had prepared it so carefully in my head, all those weeks. I kept telling myself it would get better, like those first years. We were so head over heels in love in the beginning. But it got worse. We were fighting, not talking and it felt like we were just dancing around the difficult issues. I was scared. And that evening I wanted to tell her I needed space, but then I found the test and she admitted she was pregnant and I ..."

"You couldn't do anything than the most decent thing and you proposed to her," Ingrid said.

"And then she died, and I felt so ...," his voice broke.

"Timo, I feel your pain, the guilt, but it's time to let go. Caijsa is dead and you can't keep on punishing yourself. Let the guilt finally become grief and move on."

He nodded, unable to say anything. The tears sparkled in his eyes.

"Ingrid," he said then with the softest voice, "your husband and children ..."

"I love them," she said quickly, "but you ... I've never felt anything like it in my entire life. I can't describe it, but you possess me, every inch of me, every part of me. Timo, I'm so crazy in love with you."

She continued: "I wanted to tell you so many times, but I know my marriage was standing between us. I can't fight this any longer."

She bent over to kiss him. He answered it with more passion than she could handle. A world just for them, and she wished it would never end. She wanted to stay in his arms forever.

"I have to fix this first," he stammered, caressing her cheeks. "My life is a mess right now."

"What are you going to do?" she asked.

"Honestly, I don't know, but I need to do something. I'm going crazy here. I should be out there, investigating the case."

"So why aren't you?"

"I can't. I'm suspended."

"Nobody believes you had anything to do with these murders," she said.

"I know, but it doesn't have to be true to destroy someone's reputation."

"But Timo, everyone respects you and when you officially become superintendent ..."

"I won't be superintendent," he said.

"What do you mean? You are the perfect candidate for the job."

He came closer and took her face in his hands. She felt his warm breath on her neck and cheeks. Those beautiful blue eyes.

"I might not ...," he said.

The ringing of her cell phone sounded across the room.

"It's Anton," she said and stared at it. The ringing kept going. She didn't know what to do. She put the phone down.

"Answer it," Timo said. "He's worried about you."

The ringing stopped.

She knew he was right, but she kept looking at the device on the couch. "I don't think I can pretend."

Two men. Both so different. Which one did she love more? The new, handsome, and sexy one, whom she'd fantasized about for months with an almost raw animal lust, or her husband, caring, sweet, but who took her for granted.

"What do you want?" he said softly. She felt his hand slide down her spine.

She couldn't stay with him. She had to go home. How did people, who had an affair, deal with this?

"I have to go home," she finally said.

He gave her a forced smile and nodded.

* * *

Timo escorted her to the car parked in front of the house. The wind had died, and the rain had stopped. It felt like he would never see her again.

They had spent hours in each other's arms. It felt good, but it wasn't real. And reality was she belonged to someone else and that for once he was the bad guy, the one who broke up a family. Panic rushed in. He had to let her go to be with another man. Where there had been guilt before, there was jealousy now. A feeling he hated, but like everyone else, he wasn't immune to it. From now on, he wanted to call her his.

She was about to open the door of her car when he pulled her closer and then stopped, wanting to take in the beauty of her face, lit by the dim light of the outside lantern. For a moment, he wanted to pour all the feelings and thoughts of the past months in a long romantic speech, for which he couldn't find the words. Instead, he let his lips touch hers. It was different from the hot and passionate kiss with which she had invited herself in. This one was drunk with love and made him feel like it was just the two of them in the whole world. But what had they done? His life would become so much more complicated. Would she take him as a lover? He didn't want to be second. He shouldn't be in second place.

She sighed. "I want to stay with you, but ..."

"You need to go," he said.

He knew the drive home would be a long one. When he finally saw her drove off, there was a nagging feeling that from now on everything would be different. He could never forget the kiss, the hours she had spent in his arms.

But someone was watching them from behind the dense wood. The car was parked just a few meters away, on the small road by the house, hidden from view. Every detail immersed in darkness. The dark, hooded stranger had been watching the entire scene. With every smile, every touch and every kiss, the fingers had dug deeper and deeper into the leather of the steering wheel. The rage was unstoppable.

* * *

"Listen to me for a second," he said.

Isa shook her head and said, "No, Timo, I can't let you in on the case."

She closed the door. Several times curious passersby had nearly poked their heads through the doorway to see where the commotion came from. That morning Timo had woken up and decided his vacation was over. He had to take his life in his own hands, and although he trusted Isa, things weren't moving fast enough. Caijsa's shadow was hanging over everything he did, and more than ever he felt he couldn't move on. He couldn't ask Ingrid to give up her family if he didn't even know how to properly close this chapter of his life. And there was doubt he maybe unconsciously projecting his longing for Caijsa—the young Caijsa, the woman he had fallen in love with almost twenty years ago— onto Ingrid. She looked like her, but he refused to admit that was the reason why he loved her.

He said, "I know more about this case than anyone. Let me help you."

"But you're biased and even if I wanted to," she sighed, "I just can't."

"You need help. Sitting at home and doing nothing drives me crazy. And it doesn't matter anyway."

"It doesn't matter?' she said surprised.

"If someone is out to get me, it doesn't matter what I do. At least I should be able to help."

"But it does matter to me, and it impacts the team," she said.

She was right, but for once he had to think about himself. If this could help him move on, he should grab the opportunity. Eight years was a long time to put his life on hold. Maybe unconsciously he knew Caijsa's murder wasn't really solved and that a piece of the puzzle was still missing.

"I need closure," he said and looked at the floor. He didn't want to see her glances of pity. And there was pity. A lot.

"I understand, but what would you do if you were in my situation?" she continued.

"Oh, I'd suspend you and refuse to let you work on the case," he said without blinking.

"Timo, can't you just lie for once? Why do you have to be so honest all the time?"

He smiled and said, "But did it work?"

She sighed. "If I do this, we need to be discrete."

"Okay, okay," he said. "Thank you."

She threw herself in the chair and shook her head, contemplating about what she had just done.

"Lindström, I really appreciate this, and the last thing I want to do is to put you on the spot and get you into more trouble."

"It's too late anyway. Eriksson won't like my report."

"What did you write?"

"The truth. And the truth is there's no indication you're in any way involved ... so far."

"I know, but what did you find out?"

"There is doubt about Thorgan Elker's involvement in Caijsa's murder."

She quickly glanced at him. He knew she expected a reaction, but he had everything under control.

"Anskar Ramvall told us Thorgan had sent letters," she said.

"What letters?"

"Letters to you," she said and looked him straight in the eye. This time there was shock written on his face.

"Yes. He wrote me letters. I never read them. They are still lying in the bottom of a box, under layers of useless stuff."

"Why keep them if you'd never going to read them?" Isa said.

"Because one day I might," he said. "The day I can finally look at Caijsa's death with some distance and maybe accept Elker's explanation."

"Thorgan Elker didn't kill her. Maybe that's in the letters too."

"So, you think he's innocent? They locked up an innocent man?"

"Maybe. And we need to investigate his death. He was probably murdered."

"Do you have proof?"

"No, but I want to talk to one more person."

"Who?" he asked.

"Mikael Dahlberg."

He frowned and gave her an inquiring glance.

"Cell mate of Thorgan Elker. He's still in Stockholm."

"The name sounds familiar," he said.

"He's the brother of Elin Dahlberg, one of the girls who were captured and killed by serial killer Mats Norman. I don't know if or how this has anything to do with this case. Anyway, I'm planning to go to Stockholm today. Are you coming with me? Otherwise, I'll take Lars or Berger."

"I'm going with you. But there's something I have to do first."

But Ingrid hadn't been there. Mila told him Dr. Olsson had received a request that morning to inspect a crime scene and she would probably be back later that day.

He was disappointed. With that surprising evening still in his mind, he had to see her. The confrontation with her husband. How had it gone? Calling her right now seemed so intrusive. He didn't want to put her in an awkward position, but he hadn't slept all night, thinking about her, his mind swinging between guilt, passion, and hope.

* * *

He got into the car with Isa. It took about thirty minutes before Timo asked her to pull over and he took over the driving. How she could be such a bad and irresponsible driver, he still didn't know? Another half an hour for her to get over the humiliation and the subsequent sulking. She'd driven him around for the past month and had put up with the constant remarks about her driving style, but she had enough. He should buy his own car as soon as possible. She wasn't a free chauffeur.

She changed subject. "And how is the house?"

"Oh, coming together nicely," he said, "still lots of stuff to do."

When he thought about it, there was a lot to do. It would probably take him years to finish it. And then the cycle would start all over again repairing things that weren't right or were already broken.

"Do you like living in Gävle?"

"Sure, it's nice and quiet."

"I guess it must be very different from Stockholm?"

He turned his head to her and said, "Is this going to be some sort of interrogation about the case?"

Her reaction was a bit fiercer than he'd expected when she suddenly yelled, "No, no, not at all!"

He knew she just wanted to have a chat with him, get to know him a little better. He knew everything about her, and she didn't know anything about him. Even with the case that had come so close to his personal life, he still couldn't let his guard down. There should be a separation between private life and work. A barrier he had always considered sacred. When personal life got intertwined with work, things got complicated. But hadn't he just done the opposite by letting Ingrid in?

"I just wanted to keep the ...," she stammered.

He smiled. "... the conversation going."

"To be honest," he started, "I don't know where my home is, maybe it was Stockholm at some point with Caijsa. But that is all so tainted by what happened."

"So why did you stay eight years?"

"I don't really know. I guess mostly because of work and Caijsa's parents. I didn't want to leave them. I owe them. When I came back from the hospital Marcel took care of me."

"Caijsa's father?"

"Yes. And then George and my mother. They sold the house and ... I just ... I was in such a bad place that all this has passed me by without realizing it."

"I'm sorry," she whispered. "George seems to be a good friend. Ingrid told me about him."

"Old friend of the family," he said.

George was a great friend, were it not for that one important detail about who his real father was. Maybe it was all in his mind, but there had been those little details. Children usually pick it up, sense it. Small dishonesties, differences in treatment between his brother and him. The dramatic events in France. And George had always been there. Even when he was still married, he hung around his mother all the time. Whatever she said or wanted, he did. When she was on the phone again, crying and sobbing about the latest fight with her husband, George was there in no time to comfort her. His mother had been a passionate woman, she still was. Yrjo, his father, had been quite the opposite, calculated, ambitious and distant, and to this day Timo didn't really understand what had connected them, why they had fallen in love when they had so little in common.

Married women and affairs. He was part of the same club now.

"You have a brother?"

"Yep, older brother ... we don't get along," he said.

He hadn't seen him in a year. They didn't call or talk. They had learnt that it was best to avoid each other.

"I'm sorry to hear that."

"And what about you? Sister? Brother? Are your parents still alive?"

"I'm an only child, and yes, my parents are still alive. Almost retired. They live in Gävle."

"So, you're a Gävle native," he smiled.

She nodded. "You could say that."

The conversation fell silent for a while as they drove down the road south to Stockholm.

"Do you miss her?"

He had to get over the shock of the question first before he could say anything. Why would she ask something like this? Had Ingrid told her about their conversation? It couldn't be.

"Of course, I do," he stammered.

"If you ever want to talk," she continued, "I'm here for you."

"Thanks," was all he could say. But she wasn't the one he was thinking of. Ingrid would be his sounding board if she let him.

* * *

"You knew Thorgan Elker," Isa began.

The man sitting on the other side, looked very different from the photographs in his criminal record. Mikael Dahlberg was not even thirty, but the wrinkles on his face, the thinning hair that fell messy over his forehead, and the stubble made him look a lot older. Prison life had done that to him.

When he started talking, the low, crackling voice betrayed he had been a nicotine addict since his teens. It was the only addiction left. The desire for heroine had died out years ago. An achievement of which he had been proud, although the temptation hadn't completely disappeared.

"Yes, I knew him," he said. "He's dead."

"We are re-examining his case."

"Why?" Mikael asked.

"You were here when he died," Isa continued ignoring his question.

"He committed suicide."

"Where were you exactly when they found him?"

"Don't know," he said and looked at his hands.

"According to the police report you were in the kitchen, where you've been working since 2012."

"So, I must have been there," he said.

"The statement was made by your good friend Anskar Ramvall," she continued.

"My good ... what?" he said. If his eyes could shoot fire, he would have burnt the room down.

"He wasn't my friend."

"Why would he claim he was? He spent a lot of time with you and Thorgan at that time."

"Look, I was in the kitchen. You can check the cameras."

"So everyone says, but the truth is none of the camera images were useful because there were simply none. At that time, the cameras weren't even working. Very convenient."

He shrugged. "I know nothing about that. Thorgan was my neighbor all those years. There's nothing more to say."

"Do you know Pauli Nyström?" Isa said.

He began to shuffle nervously in his seat.

"Yes. He was only here a year."

"At one point, Thorgan, Pauli, and yourself were neighbors."

"For a little while," he said.

"Did Thorgan and Pauli socialize?"

"Not that I know of," he said.

He sighed, cleared his throat, and said, "Look, Pauli was a real asshole. When he came in here, he started a lucrative drug business, with the support of Anskar."

"Anskar Ramvall?"

Mikael gave them a faint smile. "You do know he got fired a few years ago?"

"Was he?" Isa asked. "He told us he was on sick leave."

They hadn't done a background check on Ramvall. It didn't seem necessary. That was a mistake.

"For his involvement in dealing drugs. He was transporting drugs in and out of prison for some inmates. I heard he finally got a mild punishment. I don't know what anymore—community service or something—because they didn't want to give too much buzz about what had been going on."

"So, Anskar was part of Pauli's network?"

"Yeah. Pauli threatened inmates and guards, picked fights, all with the help and protection of Anskar. They were experts at intercepting official complaints from other inmates. Usually, these people ended up in hospitals or their families were threatened. I tried to stay away from them as much as possible. When Pauli was released, Anskar kept running the show until he was caught."

"Could Pauli have killed Thorgan?"

He lowered his eyes, glanced at the white table, and ran his hand over it. Then he looked Timo straight in the eye and said, "Anything is possible. With Anskar's help, the man was capable of anything."

* * *

"Is there anyone?"

Her voice echoed across the room. It felt like an open space and the smell overpowering her olfactory system was a mixture of rusty nails and mouse skitter.

She couldn't see much. A dim light shone through the small windows, high in the warehouse walls. It resembled the artificial light from the lampposts outside. Ingrid didn't know how long she'd been unconscious, but it couldn't be long. What did she remember? The phone call about a corpse had led her to a deserted area of Gävle. To her surprise, there were no police, no one, and after looking around for a while, she'd tried to call the station, but concluding it was useless as there was no signal, she had gone back to her car. After opening the door, she couldn't remember anything, until she ended up here, sitting on a hard, unstable chair, not knowing where she was, hands tied behind her back, with the wood of the chair in between. The slats of the backrest were poking and scratching her spine.

And she was so thirsty.

She took deep breaths. Panic was not allowed. A clear mind was what she needed now. She'd seen Timo do it when Magnus, with the gun pointed straight at his forehead, had threatened to kill him. The control that man had shown had been unbelievable, and he had later explained to her that whatever situation she was in, no matter how helpless and precarious it seemed, she should never give up and she had to fight for her life. There would come a time when distress would take over, but she shouldn't give in. Her children, Anton, Timo. She should focus on them, just them.

"Is anyone there?" she yelled again.

The sound of her voice bounced off the dusty walls.

But no one came.

CHAPTER 21

THERE WASN'T MUCH TO SEE. The prison cell was now occupied by another inmate and probably looked different from three years ago. Bars on the window, and blank walls in an ugly gray color where the paint was starting to flake. On one wall, pictures and letters were attached with a glue dot. There was a steel door and a separate room with a toilet and sink where you had hardly any room to maneuver. But the cell was clean and orderly.

"Elker was found hanging from those bars," Isa said and pointed at the window.

Timo couldn't believe he was standing in the cell where Thorgan Elker had died. He wished it wouldn't impact him that much, but it did.

"Seems feasible," Timo said, while studying the window and the bed. The window was high enough to get traction.

"I still don't understand why he would kill himself after five years in prison," she said.

"Something must have triggered it," Timo replied.

"Mmm, maybe."

"When are the cell doors closed?" Isa turned to the guard standing outside, watching them, struggling to suppress a yawn of boredom. The excitement of police inspectors visiting the prison today should have put him on edge, but these days there wasn't a lot that got him excited anymore.

"Only at night. And we do daily rounds at 11:00 p.m. and 7:00 a.m."

"So, during daytime anyone can go in and out?"

"In principle, but there are cameras in the hallway. These days they are working. If someone were to enter or leave, they would be taped."

"But not in 2015," Isa remarked.

The guard gave her an indifferent look.

"Who is in the neighboring cells?" Timo asked.

"To the left, no one right now. The new prisoner will arrive later tonight. To the right Mikael Dahlberg."

"Can we see Dahlberg's cell?" Timo asked.

Without saying a word, the guard led them to the next cell. It was empty. After the interview, Mikael Dahlberg had gone back to the kitchen.

Another austere room that was mirrored in layout compared to the cell they had seen before. Timo wasn't quite sure what he thought to find there when he walked in and saw the bed on the left and the table and chair against the window, almost covering the entire width of the wall, with horizontal bars running from one end to the other. On the right wall, a white board with dozens of pictures.

"The man is popular," Isa mused.

Timo walked aimlessly around the room and stopped in front of the wall of pictures.

Photos with comrades, party photos, a sea of snapshots of people and places that bore a significance in Mikael Dahlberg's life. Mikael had enjoyed life before he had ended up here. Letters from friends, girlfriends, decorated with hearts, and behind one of them Timo found a half-hidden picture.

Mikael Dahlberg and a young woman. Timo took the photo and studied it, almost mesmerized. This was important, but his brain was too slow to give him the information he needed. There was something about the woman. She had her arm around him and smiled. There was something familiar about her. Was it his sister Elin? She was too old for that.

"She looks familiar," he said and showed the picture to Isa.

Isa turned around. "Eve Bergman? That's Eve Bergman. How ..."

He froze. "No, that's Lyn Hjort, Caijsa's half-sister. She looks different now, but it's her."

"So, Eve Bergman and Lyn Hjort are one and the same," Isa said.

"We need to talk to Dahlberg again," Timo said.

* * *

Mikael stared at the picture in front of him.

"Who is this woman?" Isa said.

Silence.

"This isn't going to help your case at all," Isa said.

"My case, my case ... it doesn't matter at all. It's too late anyway. I did what I had to do."

"What have you done?"

He looked at the photo again and a soft smile appeared on his lips. "I met Lyn years ago. I don't remember exactly when, but I do know where:

in the youth center. We were both still teenagers. She was weird, and she didn't have it easy, but I found her interesting, and we spent a lot of time with each other."

He ran his fingers over the photo a few times as he talked about Lyn.

"You were in love with her," Timo said.

"Yeah," he said and sighed. "But she wasn't in love with me. I would have done anything for her, but she was only interested in some guy who didn't even know she existed. And then she married that loser."

"Ilan Bergman," Isa said.

"Yeah. Anyway, I'm here, she's out there. I can't blame her."

Isa leaned backward, calmly looked at the man and then turned to Timo who had quietly observed everything. "But I think you helped her."

"Helped her?" Mikael blurted.

"There he was: the man who killed your friend's sister, in the cell next to you. You couldn't let that pass."

"I didn't lay a finger on him," Mikael yelled. "Maybe you should ask Pauli and Anskar what they were doing in Elker's cell just before the suicide."

"You saw them?"

He nodded.

"Why didn't you say anything?" Isa asked.

"Pauli Nyström? Really? That man is dangerous. He murdered ..."

"He murdered Caijsa Jensen."

Mikael looked at her with big eyes.

"When Thorgan Elker saw Pauli in prison, everything came back. He remembered. That's why he wanted to have a retrial, that's why he had to die. Pauli beat you to it. I guess you and Lyn planned to kill Elker, but it didn't quite turn out the way you thought."

He bit his lip and said, "You can't prove a thing."

"And then you told Lyn about Pauli and his friends, the real killers. And she took it from there, didn't she?"

"I have nothing to say," Mikael said, gave them a last sarcastic grin and leaned back with a deep sigh. The interview was over.

* * *

With the phone pressed to her ear, Isa headed for the exit. She didn't realize that Timo was trying to keep up with her. He couldn't quite put his head around it. Thorgan was innocent. All those years he had put so much energy in hating that man, and now it was all in vain. Tears, sleepless nights, the anger, he had given everything until there was nothing left anymore, for the wrong man. He felt so tired, drained of everything. The previous night had been short. Another of those nights and he would be a wreck by the end of the week. He saw Isa in front of him stepping outside with determined pace, the phone still in her hand. He quickly checked the messages on his phone before stepping in the car for the more than two-hour drive. No message from Ingrid.

"Ah, Lars," he heard Isa say. "We need to pick up ... what?"

Then he saw her forehead curl into a deep wrinkle as she listened to the voice, mouth open.

"What's wrong?" Timo said after she got in the car.

"This is bad. Ingrid is missing."

The next moment he wanted to press the gas pedal and drive off as fast as he could. This was Lyn's doing. He knew it.

* * *

"She was supposed to pick up the children, but she never did," Anton stammered. "What happened to her? An accident?"

Around 6:00 p.m. he got a call from the school. No one had come to pick them up. He'd tried to call Ingrid a dozen times, but her cell went straight to voicemail. His parents had been happy to look after the children while he drove around looking for his wife, but soon he had ended up at the police station.

"Something is wrong," he continued, "this is so unlike her."

"I have to ask," Isa said and gave him a quick glance. "Did you have a fight? Did she take some time to reflect?"

"We had a fight the other day, but we talked it through and it's all good now. Besides, Ingrid would never leave her children. Isa, something is terribly wrong. You should look for her."

Anton was right. Ingrid was a devoted mother. Her children always came first.

"Anton," Isa said, taking his hand as a sign of comfort, "we'll find her, I promise."

She got up and gestured one of the police officers to take care of the devastated husband.

Timo had stood silently in the corner of the room, watching the entire conversation. Like the man at the table, he felt powerless. Was it his fault? Was it because she had come to his house that night?

"You're back in," Isa said as she passed him by, and handed him the badge and gun. "I need you."

He took it without saying anything.

"Lars called the hospitals, but no one was brought in who matched her description, so we can rule out an accident for now," Berger said as he entered the room.

"Mila said Ingrid got a phone call about a new case," Timo remarked.

"When was this?" Isa asked.

"Just before we left for Stockholm, around noon. I don't know how long she's been gone."

"We didn't get any notification about a new case," Isa said.

"This is Lyn's doing," Timo whispered.

281

Isa gave him an inquiring glance. "But why? Why would Lyn take Ingrid? She has nothing to do with Caijsa's murder."

"Isa, I ..."

Then she suddenly turned to Berger. "Check with your girlfriend when Ingrid got the call and if she mentioned where she was going."

"The signal of her cell phone dropped near Sälgsjön," Lars said.

"What's in Sälgsjön?" Timo asked.

"Not much. A stone quarry and forest, and that's about it."

"That doesn't mean she was there. Somewhere in the neighborhood."

"But why would someone kidnap her?" Lars said.

"Let's not make too many assumptions here," Isa warned them, "maybe there was an accident, and we just don't know it yet. Send out an official APB. Check any traffic cameras along that route for her car."

"Isa, can we talk?" Timo said.

* * *

"So, tell me," Isa said.

For once, the roles were reversed. How many times had she not been summoned and lectured about her reckless conduct? Now it was her turn.

"Last night Ingrid came to my house," he said.

There was no point in hiding it from her. Ingrid was in trouble and if this could save her, he should do everything in his power to help.

"Why?" she snapped.

"She wanted to talk ... that's all."

"Really?"

"Nothing happened," he said quickly.

"Does Anton know?"

"I don't think so. I don't know. I haven't spoken to Ingrid today. I know as much as you do. But Isa ... I don't think this is just about Caijsa. I think it's about me."

"What do you suggest we do?" she said calmly.

"We need to find Lyn Hjort or ... Eve Bergman. If what we think is true, she murdered all those people."

Ten minutes later they reached the Bergman house. The entire street was shrouded in darkness. Not a sound. The people in their houses were oblivious of the activity around the simple attached house in their neighborhood. The blissful stillness and comfort of dreams was all that kept them away from the commotion that was about to start. With a thunderous sound they broke down the front door when they got no reaction after ringing the bell a few times, and a handful officers made their way to the living room, the kitchen and garden in the back, and up the stairs to the first-floor rooms. But there was no one.

"Put an APB on her car. Berger has the license plate number."

"She's not here, Isa," Lars said.

"I've noticed," Isa said angrily and went upstairs. A few moments before, she'd seen Timo climb the stairs. In the bedroom, she saw him sitting on the floor, an opened box of photographs lying next to him. He let the photographs go through his hands.

"Caijsa and Lyn," he said. "I found the box on the bed. The closet is empty, apart from a few shirts and men's trousers. No money or jewelry. Nothing. She took it all with her. Except these pictures."

He looked at the bed with the big bloodstain and the spatters on the wall, still marking the place where her husband had so-called killed himself.

Then he turned back to the pictures. The young girl, barely looking in the camera, smiling and her older sister with her arms around her. So protective. Caijsa had been her hero. But the next pictures in the pile were more surprising.

"That's you," Isa said bending over to see what he had in his hands.

"You haven't changed a bit," she said.

And another picture of him. He didn't even know that these had been taken. At parties, with Caijsa. Had Lyn been there? He couldn't even remember.

"There's a cell phone in the box," Isa said and took it out.

The device wasn't locked.

"Timo," she said and showed the picture on the cell phone.

"This is my house, here in Gävle," he said and shook his head.

As he swiped through the rest of the pictures. Not just pictures outside his home, but inside, taken through the window, outside the police station, together with Isa, Berger, and Lars. And a copy of the letter she had send him: "You will find all the answers in Gävle."

"You've got a stalker on your hands, Timo. You were right. This is not about Caijsa. It's about you."

"She left the pictures for us to find," he said.

Obsession, a dangerous game. He had never paid attention to Lyn. She was Caijsa's sister. He'd been friendly and had maybe talked to her a few times, but he'd never given her any reason to believe he was interested in her. Maybe she thought he was responsible for her sister's death.

"And now she has Ingrid," Timo said. "Isa, she's going to kill her."

"Timo, think! Are there any other places where she could be? Her brother? Her father?"

"I'll call them," he said.

She got up and went downstairs.

"Lars, Berger, Pauli and his friends are yours. If our theory is right, they are responsible for Caijsa's death."

* * *

It took them a while to get hold of the people they needed. Through Marcel, Timo got Nelvin's phone number, and it was almost 5:00 a.m. in the morning when he called the old man. The conversation was difficult, not because they were on bad terms, but because the man's hearing had deteriorated rapidly over the past years. Maybe it wasn't such a bad idea for Marcel and Nelvin to live together. They were both in a bad shape, maybe they could help each other.

"Lyn? Why do you want to talk to Lyn?"

"Look, Nelvin, I can't say much, but I need to talk to her about Caijsa. Any idea where she might be?"

"She hasn't talked to me in a year or so," he said, then stopped and started coughing, a nasty morning gurgle. "The last time I saw her was at her mother's funeral. She came late, left early, and didn't say a word to me or her brother. People told me afterwards she was looking for you."

"Uh, okay ... she lives in Gävle, with her husband," Timo said.

"Husband? She's not married."

Had Lyn led a double life?

"Could she be with Cal?"

"I don't think so, but I'll give you his number. What's the urgency?"

Another deep cough, before he dictated the phone number.

"And could she be anywhere else? Family, friends?"

"No, my dear boy. I just hope that one day she'll forgive me."

Silence. A needed silence to wipe away the emotion that was surfacing.

"I hope you find her," he said and cut the line.

Timo sighed. "This is hopeless."

Out of the corner of his eye, he saw Anton sitting on the wooden bench in the reception area, staring in front of him. He knew it was best to avoid him, but how could he? It was his fault his wife went missing.

"Anton, are you okay?"

Timo got up and walked over to the man who was slumped on the bench. Anton was distraught too, with a track of tears down his face. Every time someone would pass by he'd jump up, full of hope his missing wife had been found, and then dropping back onto the bench when there was no news.

"Why don't you go home?"

It was funny how everyone tended to give the same advice when no one really believed it. Going home was the worst thing to do. Sitting there, somehow having the illusion that you could do something useful was so much more comforting.

"I don't understand it," Anton whispered. "Why would anyone want to harm her? We are just an ordinary family. Could it have something to do with her job? But she just works in the background. She has no enemies. She's just Ingrid."

Anton let out a deep sigh, then put his head in his hands and said, "I love her; I don't want to lose her."

Timo didn't say anything and just looked at him. It was his fault this man's wife was in danger. He didn't deserve her. That evening in his house had been heaven, all he'd wanted, but now that he saw Anton, worried, and devastated, Timo knew he wasn't important. Her family was. They needed her, so much more than he did, and he had no right to come between them.

"Anton, I promise I'll find her," Timo said, placing his hand on Anton's shoulder. The man looked up and gave him a distant smile.

"Thank you," Anton whispered.

At that moment Timo's telephone rang. He looked at it for a moment. An unknown number. He let his finger hang over the accept button but answered anyway.

"Hello, Timo."

He didn't recognize the voice right away.

"I believe you are looking for me."

"Lyn?"

"Indeed. It's been a while since we spoke. I was so sorry you weren't there after Ilan's death. I had expected to see you. But now you can make it up to me."

"What do you want?"

"You."

"I'll do as you ask, but let Ingrid go."

"Not yet ... maybe I won't let her go at all."

He walked down the hall to an abandoned conference room.

"Don't harm her," he said. "Please."

"Then you do what I tell you. You get in your car and drive south, direction Sälgsjön. I'll call you again in ten minutes. But Timo, don't tell anyone. Otherwise, Ingrid is dead."

CHAPTER

22

"**I NEED YOUR CAR,**" Timo said as he entered Isa's office.

"Why?"

"I have something urgent to do."

She looked at him in disbelief at first, then reached into her purse and took the key out. "But I'm going with you."

"Isa ..."

"It's Lyn, isn't it?"

He sighed and averted his eyes.

"I won't just let you go alone," Isa said sternly.

"But Ingrid's life is at stake."

"And yours."

"She won't kill me," Timo said.

"This is the end game for her. She's been stalking you, she killed people. There is no way out for her anymore. You know as well as I do that this will escalate. What do you need to do?"

"She asked me to drive south. She'll contact me again when I'm in the car. I need to move fast."

"Then let's drive south. I'll warn the others."

"Isa, no."

"This is not up for debate. She won't see them coming."

He gave up. She was right. He couldn't do this alone. There was too much at stake, but either way people would get hurt.

This time Timo let Isa drive. The fatigue started to weigh on him. He quickly checked his phone and then closed his eyes for a while as she pressed the pedal and drove direction Sälgsjön. Kilometers behind them, a series of police cars followed. Isa had ordered them to keep distance. As soon as they'd hear from Lyn, she would send them the location.

He woke up with a shock. What if they were too late? He would never forgive himself. Just like Caijsa, he could have prevented this. If he had stayed with her that morning, she would still be alive. If he had stayed away from Ingrid, she wouldn't have disappeared, and Anton and her children wouldn't have to endure the anguish of not knowing where she was and what had happened to her.

"It's all my fault," he said.

"Timo, it's not. There is no time for misplaced guilt. We should just concentrate on finding her."

"She kissed me," he blurted. He didn't know why he had said it, but it was as if he needed to get it off his chest.

"And you?" was the only thing she said.

"I kissed her," he said.

He couldn't forget the moment Ingrid had pressed her lips on his and he had surrendered to temptation. It had been such a long time he'd felt this way. He wanted more, he wanted Ingrid, and he didn't care he lusted after a woman that wasn't his.

"And what are you going to do about it?"

He turned his head away from her to look outside. What did he want? He wanted Ingrid to leave her husband, choose him and only him.

"I don't know," he whispered.

"You want my advice?" she said, looking straight ahead, her hands firmly on the steering wheel, but since he'd confessed, she'd held the wheel even tighter than before.

"What would you do?" he asked.

"I've already done it," she answered, "and look how it turned out."

"Magnus?"

She sighed and then—as if she needed to get it off her chest as well—said, "I received a letter about his hearing."

"But you and Magnus, that's not exactly an example of a normal situation," he said.

"Affairs are never normal situations. They are, by definition, messy, and emotional."

"I don't want an affair," he said.

She gave him a quick glance. "Cute but naïve."

He shrugged. Maybe.

Outside, the first dawn appeared on the horizon. Hesitant at first but then, within seconds, the red glow of the rising sun spread over the entire field of view and gave the environment something magical. The dark outlines of the trees silhouetted against the glow of the sun, about to shed its rays on the newly awaking world. In the distance, the sand hills of the pit appeared. Already at that time of day, early in the morning, there was a bustling activity around the gaping depths with machines coming and going and the excavators digging their way through the mounds of sand and gravel.

The car continued driving deeper into the forest on the unpaved and damaged road. A cloud of dust whirled up and settled on the car windows dampened by the morning dew.

He looked at his cell phone.

"Why hasn't she called yet? It's been more than fifteen minutes."

The road was getting narrower and bumpier, and Isa stopped the car.

"This can't be right," she said. "She's leading us on."

At that moment the phone rang. He put his finger over his lips to tell Isa to be quiet and turned on the loudspeaker.

"Yes?"

"What have I told you?! You haven't listened. This has consequences."

"No! Lyn ..."

The connection was cut.

He looked at Isa with an expression full of horror.

The next moment it felt like the car hung in the air and he jerked forward, restrained by the seat belt, and then fell backward against the back of the chair as the side of his head hit the window. Seconds before he lost consciousness, he saw the window on Isa's side shatter. The car pulled sideways, and her body rocked back and forth like a doll until her face disappeared into the inflated airbag.

When he woke up, his vision was blurry, and his head was pounding.

"Get up!"

It took a moment before he realized the door of the car was open and the person standing next to him was pointing a gun at him.

"Lyn?"

"Get out. Now!"

His head was spinning.

"Don't bother looking for your gun. I have it."

"Isa," he whispered, and turned to face her. She lay unconscious beside him, blood dripping from the cut on her forehead.

"She's hurt," he said.

"You should have thought about that before you decided to ignore my demands. Get out now or I'll shoot her."

And Lyn pointed the gun at Isa.

"Okay, okay," he said, pushed himself up, staggered when he saw the open sky, as Lyn pointed the gun at him again. Everything went in slow motion. She motioned for him to walk to the other side.

The pickup stood a few meters away, only slightly damaged at the bumper, while the driver's side of Isa's car was completely crushed. He feared for Isa's life.

"She needs help. You can't leave her."

"I can and I will," Lyn said firmly. "You and I will take a short walk. That way!"

She pointed to the muddy forest road leading them away from the car and deeper into the woods.

He started to walk. "What are you going to do? Where are we going?"

She gave him a sarcastic smile. "My dear late husband's family have an old sawmill there. His mom told me. God, that woman is annoying, but she was a wealth of information, and she didn't even realize it."

"You killed Ilan."

"I had to. He found out ... well, that isn't exactly true. I made sure he found the pictures."

"What pictures?"

"The pictures of the accident, his stolen car ... your pictures. I wanted him to know how he fitted in the bigger scheme of things, and that his death had purpose. But the idiot wasn't too bright. He thought it was you. That you changed his phone and rigged the evidence. And then, for some strange reason he tried to call Nick."

"You've been stalking me," Timo said and stopped.

The headache was getting too much for him, and he had to gasp for air to numb the pain and lessen the nausea.

She grinned and pushed the gun against his back. The cue to shut up and keep walking. They walked in silence for a while until the building appeared in the distance, its green roof partially covered by the trees.

Lyn motioned for him to enter through the half-open rusted metal doors. It was freezing cold inside. He felt the draft coming from everywhere. The hall was larger than he had expected. Judging by the oil spills, now almost burnt into the soil, he could tell trucks had been kept there in the past. Ruptured tires lay on the floor, next to broken glass and rusted remnants of what used to be the exhaust of a vehicle. Through the broken windows, the faint rays of sun drew a thin line on the dirty floor. At the back was a green door. In the corner before entering the next room, he noticed a chair, the wooden back, partly discolored by large stains. Was this blood? Was this Ingrid's blood? A puddle on the floor. He couldn't tell if it was blood or the result of the heavy rainfall over the past days, seeping through a leak in the roof. The trickling sound of water hitting the surface surrounded him.

"Move on," Lyn's voice echoed throughout the room.

So many scenarios went through his head. This wasn't good. Timo stood now in front of the door and took a deep breath. He had to be prepared for what lay behind the green-painted door with the metal hook, which was used as a lock. He put his hand on the door and pushed it open. With a high-pitched creaking sound, the door swung open, and he walked through the doorway into the room.

"Timo?"

CHAPTER

23

INGRID OPENED HER EYES and looked up when she heard the door bounce against the wall. She was still sitting in the chair in the middle of the hall, with the light streaming in through the windows, almost like a spotlight drawing the viewer's attention to the spectacle that was about to unfold.

"Timo," she whispered again.

How he would have loved to run up to her and take her in his arms.

"Are you okay?" he said.

Ingrid nodded but could barely hold the tears.

"Everything will be okay," he said.

"Are you sure?" Lyn's voice rang out as she approached the woman in the chair. "You two lovebirds don't seem to understand the gravity of the situation."

She grabbed Ingrid's hair and pulled the head back, looked at the woman for a moment, then said, "I don't think I need her anymore; she served her purpose." Then she let go of the hair, stepped back, and aimed the gun at the back of Ingrid's head.

"No! Timo!" Ingrid screamed. In an ultimate attempt to save herself, Ingrid tried to pry her hands free. The chair slid wildly back and forth with the sudden movements.

His heart sank into his shoes. Just a second, but then he walked over to them with his hands up, as if he was trying to calm a child. "No, wait! Let's talk about this. I'm here. Talk to me!"

"Stay where you are!" Lyn yelled, the gun wildly waving in front of her.

He saw the tears streaming down Ingrid's cheeks.

"Okay, okay. What do you want?" he said.

Lyn gave him a bewildered look and then shouted, "What do I want? How can you ask that? You, of course. I've always wanted you, since the day Caijsa brought you home to us, more than what ... fifteen years ago. You know what I am. It's difficult for me to trust people. Mom, Caijsa, were the only ones. No one else understood me, not even Cal. All the boys in my class were mean and not interested in me. They found me scary. Of course, I was always on a higher level in thinking and understanding things. No one can follow me. But then there was you. The most beautiful man I'd ever seen in my life. God, I didn't know how to behave around you. I think we barely said a word that first time. But you were my first and only crush."

"I ... didn't know," Timo said flabbergasted.

"Of course, you didn't. You were too busy with Caijsa. I was a nobody."

"No, Lyn ..."

"I know. You did talk to me, you listened to me. You were the only one who was really interested in what I had to say. I am in love with you. But ... Caijsa was there, and I could never hurt my sister. Such a dilemma."

"What about Mikael and Ilan? They loved you."

"I met Mikael at the youth center. We started to hang out. He wasn't my lover or boyfriend. We were just good friends, but I know he wanted more. And then I met Thorgan Elker."

"What?"

"I loved Caijsa, but to be honest, I don't think she loved me that much; I was a subject of study for her," Lyn said and looked at Ingrid again. The woman was staring at the floor in front of her, shaking, her face flushed with tears, and eyes widened in terror as if everything could be over any moment.

"Caijsa loved you," Timo said.

A sarcastic smirk appeared on Lyn's face. "If you say so. Anyway, one day I was sitting in the waiting room of the hospital, Caijsa's practice, and I saw him. We started talking. It didn't take long for me to understand how I could use him. He was vulnerable and easy to manipulate. And then I started feeding his delusions a bit, and ... Caijsa's insecurities."

"Jesus! But why?"

"I never wanted Caijsa to die. I just wanted to put some pressure on your relationship."

He shook his head. All that time, he thought he had done something wrong. He had felt so bad about his failed relationship with Caijsa, and now he found out Lyn had manipulated it all.

"For years I thought, like anyone else, Elker had killed her, and I truly felt guilty about my sister's death. In the end, I never achieved what I wanted. You were grieving so much, it pulled you even further away from me. I had to make it right, so you could move on. Thorgan was responsible and he had to die. It was such an unbelievable coincidence he ended up in the cell next to Mikael."

"And then he died," Timo said.

He held his breath. Behind Lyn, on the other side of the room, he saw a shadow move from side to side.

"Not because of me. Nyström."

"And then you realized Elker didn't kill Caijsa."

Now he recognized the silhouette. Isa. Thank God, she was alright.

Lyn laughed, then turned back to Timo. "Yeah, we were all that stupid!"

"Why kill all those people? Why kill the families?"

"They had to feel what you and I have been through all these years. Killing them was too easy. They needed to know what horrible things had been done to their loved ones! I only regret Engersson died that easily. He should have suffered the most. But it was a compromise I had to take."

He felt sick. "Now what?"

Lyn smiled and then said, "We all know I won't survive this."

"Lyn, you can still stop this. I'll help you whenever I can."

She stepped over to him, stood in front of him, still holding the gun, then let her hand ran along his face.

"Oh, Timo, so naïve. Of course, you're coming with me."

"No!" Ingrid screamed.

Without giving Ingrid another look, she continued, "I understand why you chose her. A Caijsa lookalike. I was confused myself when I saw her in my living room after Ilan's death. It was as if Caijsa had come back to life. But I immediately realized you couldn't resist the temptation. Well, she'll watch you die. And then we'll be together ... forever."

"Stop, police!" Isa yelled and stepped into the light.

In that moment of confusion, Timo took Lyn's hand and squeezed so hard she couldn't keep hold of the gun. As it fell to the ground, Isa ran over to him. Timo felt how Lyn's body relaxed and gave up. She lifted her head, and for a moment, he felt sorry for her. She had wanted to kill him, and as a police officer he had to condemn what she had done, but as Caijsa's boyfriend, he understood why.

"Don't forget about me," Lyn whispered before Isa handcuffed her.

* * *

"How do you feel?" Isa said as she removed Ingrid's restraints.

Ingrid didn't know what to feel. Her mind was empty. Like a zombie she stared straight ahead, as if everything had been miles away. She heard everything her friend was saying, but she couldn't quite grasp it.

"Stay here, I'll get someone," Isa said, got up and left.

Timo was just staring at her, as if he didn't know what to do either. This was all so confusing. She could have died. If he hadn't been there, if Isa and Timo hadn't stopped Lyn, her children might not have a mother anymore. She would never see Anton again ... and Timo.

Then he knelt beside her and took her hand. It felt good. She needed him and he needed her. And then suddenly the tears came. Out of nowhere. And once they came there was no stopping them. Her body started to tremble, and she had never heard the sounds, she was making, before. She felt how he wrapped his arms around her, trying to dampen the shocks of the crying, and she put her head on his shoulder.

"Everything will be fine," he said.

Only then she saw the blood on his face and the bruises.

"You're hurt," she said and touched his face.

"That's nothing," he said, took the cell phone from his jacket and gave it to her.

"Call Anton. He's worried."

She nodded, took the phone and with trembling hands began to pin the number, now and then stopping to think whether the number sequence was correct.

Timo looked at her patiently as she nearly broke down when she heard her husband's voice and Anton, overwhelmed with joy, tried to calm her down.

"And are you okay?" Timo turned to Isa, who had witnessed the entire scene. "You need to do something about that nasty cut on your forehead."

When she saw the bloodstains on her fingers after running her hand across her forehead, she sighed. "Probably a concussion. I feel okay. But my car is a total mess."

"Time to buy a new one then," he said.

"I don't know. It was my grandmother's."

"Then maybe it's time to let go. The memories will stay, Lindström. You don't need a car for that."

* * *

"Svante, so here we are again. Let me get straight to the point. We've got your friend Hilko in the room next door and it's only a matter of time before he'll talk. Whoever talks first, wins the prize."

"Talk about what?" he jumped up, his eyes darting nervously between Isa and Berger.

"Caijsa Jensen."

The young man could hardly contain the anxiety that took over every fiber in his body.

"I don't know any Caijsa Jensen. And Hilko is not my friend."

Isa put the picture in front of him. "That's you, Pauli Nyström, and Hilko Ingberg."

"So?"

"In Stockholm on 14 April 2010. The day after, a young woman named Caijsa Jensen was found murdered in her home. The same home you see in the background of this picture."

"That's coincidence," Svante snapped.

"Your friend Pauli ..."

"Pauli is also no friend of mine," he said quickly.

"So why were you in Stockholm eight years ago? We were able to pull a lot of pictures from Pauli's Facebook account. Pictures taken over the last ten years ... at parties, trips. You and Pauli. You, Pauli, and Hilko."

"We talked to your mother," Berger said. "She confirmed that, much to the dismay of your father, Pauli was almost family."

Svante shrugged and continued to stare at the picture.

"Strange that these pictures were deleted from his account weeks ago. Why?"

"You should ask him," Svante said.

Isa dropped into the chair, leaned back, and grinned. "We would love to, but it's going to be a bit difficult. Pauli Nyström is dead. He was found yesterday, lying at the bottom of a cliff near Höghällsvägen. He's probably been there for over a week. Neighbors told us a man, very much looking like you, picked him up from his apartment last week. A camping trip with the work buddies. Right."

"It can't be me. I was in Uppsala the entire week and weekend ... with a woman."

Isa leaned forward, looked him straight in the eye, and then said, "It was you who killed Caijsa Jensen, wasn't it?"

"I don't know what you're talking about," Svante said calmly.

"Hilko is talking, a lot, Svante. And it looks like he's portraying you as the mastermind."

Svante looked at the man sitting next to him, his lawyer. "Jesus, man, what a useless idiot you are," Svante yelled. "Just say something!"

The man looked over his glasses at the young man, then turned his attention to the file on the table in front of him.

Isa smiled. "We have a witness."

"Witness," Svante jumped up. "What fucking witness?!"

"Pauli was sent to prison for drug possession three years ago. Lucky for him, he ended up in the same cell block as Thorgan Elker and Mikael Dahlberg. Nyström was a narcissist and couldn't keep quiet. One night he told everything to Mikael Dahlberg, knowing very well no one would even dare to report him to the police. But Thorgan Elker recognized him, probably overheard the conversation, and started a procedure to revisit his case. Pauli got scared and he killed Elker, but he didn't know that Mikael Dahlberg told his friend Lyn Hjort, Caijsa Jensen's half-sister, everything. The world is small, Svante. And Sweden even smaller."

Svante kept looking at her, with the same arrogant grin when he had entered the room. He turned to the one-way glass. He knew who was standing behind it. The boyfriend of the woman they had killed.

Isa said, "Let me tell you what I think ... no, what I know happened. That morning you and Pauli decided to go for a walk. You'd noticed her the day before, in the garden of the house, and Pauli, all high and agitated, had a plan. His drug addiction had been getting worse and this time, you decided to join him."

"I don't do drugs," Svante said.

"Of course, you use drugs. I can see it in your eyes, the way you behave. You are a drug addict. You all are."

"What happened that morning?" Berger said.

Svante sighed and looked at his hands. "Okay, we were high. Hilko was still in the youth hostel. It started with ... well, Pauli wanted to go for a walk in the park close to where we were staying. Little did I know he had already set his sights on the woman. We saw her in the park. She was walking home, after jogging or something, when Elker attacked her."

"Attacked her?" Isa said.

"They had an argument, and it was escalating. I thought he would hit her, and then Pauli intervened. Elker backed down, and we accompanied her to her house, but when we got to the house, Pauli had other plans."

"What plans?"

"I didn't know I swear. She opened the door and before I knew it, he pushed her inside and hit her. As she lay unconscious on the floor, he tried ..."

"To rape her?" Isa said.

He nodded. "But she woke up and defended herself, fiercely, kicking and hitting. There was a huge struggle. He was kicking her, tried to strangle her, but every time she managed to fend him off. Then Pauli took out a knife and stabbed her."

"He had a knife with him?"

Svante nodded.

"And where were you?" Isa asked.

"I froze ... I didn't know what to do."

"And you did nothing to save her?"

He looked at his hands. "She wasn't dead, but Pauli was freaking out, shouting she would recognize us and that he couldn't go to jail. Then he cut her throat. It was a mess. Blood everywhere and we needed to clean up, but ..."

"Elker?"

"Yeah, he was still hanging around the house and when Pauli looked up, he saw Elker staring through the window. But he looked confused, like before. I'm not sure he really understood the situation."

"Elker was psychotic. When did you decide to put the blame on him?"

"When we saw him looking through the window, there was no doubt. He was the perfect scapegoat. It wasn't difficult to follow Elker. When we knew where he lived, we planted the knife and stained his clothes with her blood."

"And Mrs. Heimer?"

"Who?" Svante shook his head.

"The woman who saw you running away from the house."

"I don't know her," Svante said.

Isa jumped up, paced across the room, and stopped at the one-way screen.

"That was a nice little story, Mr. Engersson, but I think the story gets closer to the truth when I replace Pauli's name with yours. It was your idea. You killed Caijsa Jensen."

Svante gave her a look of a thousand deaths.

"You went back to the youth hostel. How did Hilko get involved?"

Silence.

"I think Pauli couldn't keep his mouth shut and told him," Isa said. "And you all decided to keep quiet."

"And then daddy got involved, didn't he?" Berger said.

Svante bowed his head.

"Pauli came forward as a witness. You needed to put the suspicion on Elker as soon as possible. But Karst suspected from the start something wasn't quite right. You had to tell him."

"Are you claiming that Karst Engersson, one of the most renowned lawyers in the entire country, was involved in covering up a murder?" Svante's lawyer said.

"That's exactly what I'm saying," Isa let out.

"There's no proof," Svante laughed.

"The police officer, originally assigned to the case, was removed after a day, and replaced by Rune Breiner, on specific request of commissioner Martinsson who was a close friend of Engersson. Martinsson was later charged with taking bribes and stepped down."

The lawyer looked at the young man sitting next to him, now in total control of his emotions.

Isa continued, "And what did Breiner have to do? Well, make sure that, no matter what, suspicion was diverted from Karst Engersson's son and his friends."

"My father had nothing to do with this," Svante said.

"Oh, but he did, and if the Elker lead didn't work out, there was always the boyfriend. That's why Rune Breiner was so adamant about proving inspector Paikkala's involvement in his fiancé's death. Especially after inspector Paikkala accused Breiner of being a dirty cop."

The lawyer jumped up and tried to intervene, Svante started to say, "Just prove it. I won't say anything anymore."

"Okay then, Svante Engersson, you are under arrest for the murder of Caijsa Jensen and Pauli Nyström. Anything you say can be used ..."

CHAPTER

24

HER FIRST RESPONSE, WHEN SHE HEARD THE boyish high-pitched voice that had said the name in the most perfect English followed by 'Hello, who am I talking to?' was to end the phone call immediately. It was quiet on both sides of the line. Isa didn't know what to do. Instead of getting her ex-husband on the phone, her eight-year-old son waited for an answer. How could she tell him she was the mother who had abandoned them when she had felt that life and marriage were closing in on her, suffocating her, obscuring her creativity and dreams? Two kids in less than two years. Getting stuck in a world and a life she didn't want. And she had run, as far and as fast as she could. As she thought about what to do, she ran her fingers over the letter. She had made up her mind, or maybe she hadn't. Hearing her son again after all these years had stirred up so much more than she had expected.

"Uh, can I talk to Viktor Clausen?"

Silence.

"Mom?"

The phone nearly slipped out of her hand. How did he know? He was only three when she last saw him. Three years old. A beautiful blond little boy with bright green eyes. Shy and scared, clinging to his father's legs as if his life depended on it. Her daughter standing next to him, confused and angry. Isa had knelt beside them and told them everything was going to be alright, that they had to go away for a while and that she would visit them whenever she could. She had visited them once and then never again. It had proven to be too difficult. She couldn't be the woman and mother they expected her to be.

How could they even remember anything about her? They were so young when she had left them.

"I ...," was all she could say.

"Isa?"

Viktor?

Then she turned around and saw Nick, standing a few meters away from her, watching her. It was the first time in weeks he looked so relaxed, so sane. It was as if he was finally at peace with his inner demons.

She pressed the red button and put the phone on the table.

"Why did you hang up?" Nick said.

"We need to talk," she said.

Any excuse would do not to talk to the man she'd abandoned so many years ago. Her first love. They had been so different in many ways but, as always, love had blinded them to the incompatibilities that had made married life so devastatingly difficult. At least they'd had the courage to end it before it had left its mark or so they thought, but it had scarred them and with them the children they had so foolishly and recklessly brought into this world.

"I think this conversation is more important," Isa said.

She followed him as he walked into the living room and settled in one of the comfortable chairs that had been his safe haven for the past weeks after the horrific Global Law shooting. He had come a long way in a short time, but it was just the beginning. He had to get rid of the baggage that would hold him from achieving the new goals he had set for himself.

"You shouldn't hang up on them," Nick whispered, bowed his head, and took a deep breath. "Isa, I ..."

"I know what you're going to say," she said quietly.

It was strange. For once, she didn't know what she felt. Sadness? Relief? Was she glad or not?

"Isa, when we met, it felt so good," Nick began, "but this drama got me thinking."

He turned to her and took her hand.

"I've tried to go back to the man I was before, but it takes so much energy. The flashbacks, the anger, the guilt take their toll and I don't know if I want to be that man again," he said softly. "Looking back at myself, that man, who went through life almost without any sense of morality, he seems so shallow and self-centered, and I need to change that."

She stared at her feet for a while. No, she didn't want to lose him. But was she in love with the new Nick, the man he aspired to be, or with the old one?

"And I'm part of the package you'd like to forget," she said.

"No, no, I don't want to forget you," he said, "but I just need some time to myself, to figure out what I want, what kind of man I want to be. Kim ... I need to give this somehow a place. And Eve. How could I not have seen this?"

"I think you did. Unconsciously, you knew it was her pointing that gun at you. Your mind just wasn't able to process it and connect the dots."

"And that scares me. What else is wrong with me?"

"Nothing is wrong with you. Like you said, it just needs time."

She took his head in her hands and kissed him. This was so brave. She could never do what he intended to do. The soul searching could be quite confronting.

"What are you going to do?"

"I've taken a sabbatical," was his reply. "I'm not sure if Global Law is where I want to be. There are many associations that give free legal advice to the poor, and I want to be part of that until I know what I want to do in the future."

"Nick, just know that you're a great lawyer. Don't throw that talent away."

He nodded. "I'm moving as soon as I found a place to stay."

"Take the time you need," she said. "I'll be here if you need me."

She didn't know how this would turn out. Would she ever see him again? He'd move on and she'd still be the good old Isa she'd always been. Erratic and restless. Looking for love, but in fact settling for sex.

She didn't feel for Nick the way she had felt for Alex. No one could live up to Alex.

And in two hours, she would face the man who had taken Alex from her. Did she really want to see Magnus? What a mess this all was. Alex, Magnus, Viktor, and Nick. Four men. She had loved each one of them, but in the end she was alone.

* * *

The final hearing to establish Magnus Wieland's accountability for the murder of his rival Alexander Nordin took place in the courthouse close to the police station.

Isa was late and took a seat in the back. Magnus stood in front, next to his lawyer.

"... taking into account the psychiatric tests, the testimonies of the ..."

She no longer heard the judge's words. Magnus looked so different from the proud and handsome man she'd known. He looked old. She'd never noticed it before, but most of his hair was gray now and he had lost weight. He just stared straight ahead. A few rows ahead of her sat Sophie and Anna, his wife and daughter.

"... not guilty by reason of insanity. However, the court orders that Magnus Wieland be admitted to a psychiatric hospital for an indefinite period ..."

Not guilty? How could this be?

She was about to jump up and shout how unfair and rigged the entire judicial system was when she heard someone come in and take a seat behind her.

She turned and faced the woman she hadn't seen since their last confrontation months ago where Irene Nordin, Alex's mother, had confessed to being an accomplice in the murder of Annette Norman, the wife of serial killer Mats Norman.

The old woman gave her a friendly nod. Strange. This was the same woman who had blacklisted her since the secret relationship with her son, who had died at the hands of the man who stood in front, listening to the court's verdict. It should be easy for Irene to blame the unethical policewoman who had seduced the poor young man and driven the love rival to the point where he saw no other option but to kill his competitor.

"Irene," she whispered.

"Inspector Lindström. We need to talk."

"About what?"

"About him," Irene said and pointed at the man, head down, trying to take in what the Swedish community had decided as an appropriate punishment for killing a man.

When Isa turned her head to look at him again, their eyes met, but there was nothing positive about it. Hate. Was it hate she felt? She only saw shock in his eyes.

"What about him?" Isa said.

"Do you think he got the punishment he deserved?" Irene said.

The old woman had said it in the calmest and most controlled voice Isa had ever heard anyone talk about their son's murderer. But as the words billowed through the air between them, she saw the clenched fists and the growing tension in the woman's face. This woman was out for revenge.

"What do you want?"

Irene put a forced smile on her face and said, "I know you understand. Think about it and if you want to talk, let me know."

Irene got up and left the room before Isa could say another word. She didn't like the woman, but her words had planted a seed, a dangerous seed.

* * *

Robin put the rose on the grave. The last rose, the final red rose. In the photo those beautiful eyes were staring back at him. Two years. A PhD, so many nice, wonderful people he'd met. Sweden had been kind to him. But it was time to say goodbye, and he didn't want to go. The past days he had shown a brave face to the world he didn't want to leave. He had said goodbye to Isa and the rest of the police team. They had thrown him a little party, which was more than he had ever hoped for. He had told them he was happy to go home, start a new career and be with his family again, but he felt lost and alone. It felt like he would start all over again, leaving behind that part of himself that had truly loved and lived for the first time. He preferred to stay here, with the crushed heart that would never mend. He needed the pain. He needed the weekly trip to the cemetery. It was the only thing he looked forward to. How sad!

How could he ever let go? Let Alex go. He touched the marble stone of the tomb, then looked at the suitcase next to him. There wasn't much he wanted to take with him. His whole life in 0.05 cubic meters. A pair of sneakers, the ones he wore the day, more than a year ago, when Alex and he had decided to do something about their fitness and went for a jog. After two tries and many embarrassing moments, panting and sweating like crazy, they'd given up. But it had been a moment to cherish forever. The blue T-shirt he'd been wearing the day Alex had told him he was coming back to the university to finish his PhD. And the gray sweater he'd worn the day Alex died. The day he couldn't stop the love of his life from running to his death. Had he only known.

"Farewell, my sweet love," he whispered, touched his lips, and then bent over and placed the tips of his fingers on the picture. "I love you ... forever."

Big, deep breaths to keep the tears from flowing. He got up, picked up the suitcase and took one last look at the tombstone.

* * *

"Look who we have there," said Isa.

Kristoffer leaned against the wall as he quickly wiped his glasses and gave her a smile. She was sitting in one of the small conference rooms, going through a file, when he had knocked softly on the door.

"I came to say goodbye," he said.

"Mission accomplished?"

"Not quite ... far from it actually. In Gävle, yes, but we still face a huge threat."

"Oh, Forsmark?"

"There's too much activity within the far-right groups these days, but we're also getting a lot of conflicting messages. I really don't know what's going on."

"If we can help," she said.

"Thanks, but this is really something for SÄPO."

"You look tired."

"Well, a third little one doesn't help much either," he laughed.

"Ah, the bliss of sleepless nights! Congratulations. Boy or girl?"

"Another girl. Lissa."

She smiled, and then there was an awkward silence. A passerby gave him an inquiring look, and then he said, "Look, I want to apologize. I totally misjudged you. You're a good detective."

"Apologies accepted," she said.

"I've heard about the Disciplinary Committee. If I can help you, let me know. I'll put in a good word for you."

"It'll be all right. How bad can it be?"

He thought about it for a moment and then closed the door. She looked at him in surprise.

Then he pulled out a document from under his coat.

"Isa, watch out. This is the Breiner file. You didn't get it from me," he said, placing it on the table in front of her.

She took it in her hands and said, "This is almost nothing ... how can that be?"

"Exactly. Parts have been left out. Interviews are missing. You will see that a large part of the text has been crossed out. This file has been manipulated."

"By whom?"

"Someone inside the police," he said and sighed. It was as if he had spoken the greatest blasphemy.

She opened the file and started flipping through it.

"Keep it to yourself. I could get in trouble for this and so could you."

But she hadn't heard him anymore. She looked at the list of calls Breiner had made over the years and two names had immediately caught her attention.

"Nelvin and Paulina Hjort," she said softly.

He frowned and shook his head. "What?"

"Why did Breiner call Nelvin and Paulina Hjort?" she said.

"Probably as part of the investigation into Caijsa's murder?"

"In 2015? And the years after. And they called him regularly. Why?"

He was standing next to her now, running his finger over the lines on the sheet.

"Elker was murdered in 2015," Isa said.

He looked at her. He didn't like where this was going. "Do you think they had something to do with his murder? It was Pauli Nyström, no?"

"But Pauli is dead, and his so-called accomplice Ramvall denies everything." Then she sighed. "I don't know, but Breiner was a police officer. One who could fix things, get things done. Even murder."

He plopped into the chair next to her. "What do we do with this?"

She closed the file and looked at him, "Nothing. There's nothing we can do. Maybe I'm wrong and this is something very innocent. And ... I think it's time to put the Caijsa Jensen case to rest."

* * *

Timo put the cardboard box on the table and put the books in one by one.

At least, it wouldn't take too long. He didn't have much stuff anyway. Somehow, he'd known he wouldn't be in this office long.

"What are you doing?"

He turned around. Ingrid stood at the door watching him. For a few seconds, he stared at the woman in the doorway as if he needed time to process who she was and why she had been standing there.

"How long have you been there?" Timo said.

She smiled. "A while."

He turned his attention back to the box. "How are you?"

"I'm okay. Timo, I want to thank you again for saving me. I owe you my life."

"It's my job," he whispered.

"But you're dodging my question. Why are you packing?"

"The new superintendent is coming in two weeks."

"The new superintendent? But I thought ...? Why? Who?"

"It's official," he said. "Finn Heimersson will be the new boss. He's a good guy."

She closed the door and walked over to him. "Heimersson? That makes no sense. He has a good position in Uppsala."

He stared at the floor. What more could he say?

"What are you going to do?" Ingrid asked.

"I don't know. Go back to Stockholm maybe. Jakobsson has been asking when I'll be back."

"You can't go," she whispered and took his head in her hands. He put his hand on hers and sighed.

"You've been avoiding me," he said.

He could fool himself and say she had wanted space and time to recover from the ordeal she'd been through, but truthfully, he was afraid to face her, to hear what she had to say. His feelings hadn't changed. They had even become stronger. But she? There was something about her behavior that worried him. She seemed nervous. Suddenly the air felt so cold, as if someone had opened a window in the middle of a snowstorm.

"I know," she said in the softest voice. Then she looked up, took his face in her hands, and kissed him. He felt the passion boil in him again, but at the same time a deep sadness took hold of him.

"I wanted to talk about what happened at your place that night," she said.

He couldn't say a word. Numb, unable to articulate the fear of what was to come. A 'dear John' moment. Of course. He should have known he was just a distraction. He had been warned. Married women think they need something else, but in reality, they don't.

"You have to understand," she said. "Kjell, my youngest, has these nightmares about my kidnapping. I have to be there for him. I can't ..."

His voice almost broke. "You can't be with me."

A single tear ran down her cheek. She kissed him again, walked to the door and gave him a final glance before disappearing into the hallway. He heard only the metallic sound of her shoes hitting the floor and slowly dying away.

He put the notebook in the box. His fingers had dug deeper and deeper into the leather cover when she had said it, until he couldn't ignore the pain anymore. Stupid, so stupid. What did he expect? That she would give up everything to be with him. But somehow, he was relieved. Was it really Ingrid he loved or just the image of Caijsa?

Caijsa. Would there ever be closure? Tomorrow he would talk to Lyn. There were so many questions unanswered, and he desperately needed answers. He still didn't feel like he could move on. Not really.

CHAPTER

25

"**You look like crap!**"

Isa threw herself in the chair on the other side of the table where Timo was sitting.

"It's not exactly a fun day," he sighed.

"What happened?"

He shrugged and stood up. The lingering headache was growing in intensity.

"Finn Heimersson," he said.

"Ingrid told me. How on earth did he get the position?"

"It doesn't matter. He will be the new superintendent, and you have to give him a chance."

"You're my boss, Timo, and no one else."

"Just don't make it harder than it already is," he said.

He walked to the window. He felt so small. So much he still wanted to do, so many plans. He couldn't complete or start any of them. He had let them down. Simply because Eriksson didn't like him, because they were out to get him, because they didn't want a foreigner to lead Gävle's impressive police force. God only knew why. Nothing made sense.

"It is what it is," he said.

"What will you do?"

"He offered me Magnus' job," he said calmly.

"You should take it."

"Look, Lindström. I don't know what I'm going to do. I'm not sure if I'll stay."

"Why?" she said and joined him on the other side of the room.

Before she knew it, she was running her hand over his arm. After realizing what she'd done she pulled her hand away, but not before noticing the blue in his eyes becoming more intense than usual. He stared at her with widened eyes and a raised brow, as he backed away from her.

"I'm sorry," she stammered.

He walked to the desk. Distance. He needed distance.

"Timo, you should take it. Look, we may not have welcomed you with open arms and you are ... weird sometimes, but you brought us together. You made us work as a team. You did that. You belong here. We need you."

Did he really belong here? If he couldn't be superintendent, being an inspector in Gävle was a step back in his career, and then he needed another reason to stay. Ingrid would have been the only other reason to stay, but she'd made up her mind. Stockholm was a better choice. He could keep the house in Gävle as a weekend residence. When it would be fully refurbished, he would be able to sell it. Plenty of options.

"I haven't done anything special."

"Think about it," she said, walked to the door and gave him one last glance before leaving.

"Thanks," he said.

She closed the door and there he was, all alone again, with his doubts and self-pity.

He took the laptop from the cardboard box that had been sitting on his desk for days. Finn and Ingrid weren't the only reasons his mood had plummeted. Talking to Lyn had been a mistake. She was a master manipulator. And although he knew she took pleasure in getting people upset and planting ideas and doubts in people's heads, he couldn't forget what she had told him.

He took a deep breath and then opened the file on the computer. Caijsa's autopsy report. He read the first lines and already found himself trembling at the thought of having to read more. The headache turned into a full-blown migraine. He scrolled down and stopped at the section about the internal examination.

"... the lesion in the womb is consistent with a spontaneous or surgical abortion ..."

He stared at it and read it repeatedly until the letters on the screen started to dance before his eyes, and the nausea had become so bad he had to run to the restroom to throw up.

He thought about Lyn and the smile on her face as she had implied that the love of his life had held secrets from him. Devastating secrets, that had put his entire belief to shaky ground.

* * *

A day earlier, Timo had seen Lyn in the closed psychiatric ward of the Gävle hospital, awaiting a full evaluation. He had asked Nelvin to go with him, but the old man couldn't. After the loss of Caijsa and Paulina, Nelvin couldn't face the fact his daughter was on trial for the death of fourteen people. A mass murderer. How did it get this far?

"They say I have autistic psychopathy," she began.

"How do you feel about that?"

"How do I feel? I don't know. How should I feel? I think they're right. I'm probably a danger to society, and to you in particular. So why did you come to see me?"

"I need answers," he said.

"To what?"

"Fourteen people. Why?"

"I only killed five," she said.

"Then, who killed the others?"

"I already told your guys I don't know. I don't know any of those people who were involved in the Global Law shooting, except for Nils Vollan and the guy who shot you. I made sure he'd never make a mistake like that again."

"They found his body in Sälgsjön."

"Yeah. Nils had the nasty habit to surround himself with idiots ... who didn't listen. You know ... Nils and I had made a deal. I wanted Engersson. He wanted ... someone else."

"Who?"

She smiled, and for the first time since he had stepped in that room, he felt a certain uneasiness.

"Someone who wasn't there and was supposed to be there."

"You know," he said.

"It's not difficult. Who was Engersson supposed to meet that day? Who could be so important?"

"Berg? Leif Berg? This is big."

"If I were you, I'd be very careful. Behind the scenes, things are moving fast."

"How did you get involved?"

"I needed a distraction until I had run down my list of people to kill. I needed to complete my task. After that, I didn't care what happened to me. Everyone thought it was a terror attack. No one would suspect it was about a few people specifically, except for you and your team, but you didn't connect the dots. At least not fast enough, which gave me some time. And it had something nicely dramatic about it. Killing Daniel was somehow disappointing. It was my first kill. I hesitated too much. I didn't feel it was right. But Engersson had to be special. It was his son's idea to attack Caijsa. All the others were accomplices, cowards. I wanted Svante Engersson to experience what it is like to lose someone who has protected and guided you all your life. I wanted to take away his guardian angel. But when I shot Karst, it was also disappointing. He didn't suffer long enough."

"How did you meet Nils Vollan?"

She gave him a grin. "Online. You'd be surprised how easy it is to find people who want to give up their soul for money. He had a mission: assemble a group to take out Berg and create chaos and fear. I paid him more to take me along."

He looked at her for a while and then said, "No, the idea came from you. You've been orchestrating this since the day Mikael told you about Pauli Nyström. And why did you drag Ilan into this?"

She shook her head and then said, "Oh, Ilan ... I don't think I loved him, but I never wanted to use or hurt him."

"Then why did you?" Timo said.

"It was supposed to be Nick."

"Nick Petrini?"

"Yes, he was so easy to seduce. Of course, he thought he was seducing me. How stupid men are? I had it all worked out, but I wasn't sure if I could keep him under control. I needed something to blackmail him. And then came the evening ... when that woman died. I was following Nick. There was this Global Law party and when I saw them both, Nick and Ilan, leave the building, I ... I still don't know why, but I felt I had to follow Ilan rather than Nick. And it paid off."

"You saw him with Marie Lång?"

"He hit the girl with the car. I knew right away this was a fantastic opportunity. I didn't need Nick, but I needed Ilan. I knew it was risky. You could have recognized me, but that would have been a coincidence. Who would have suspected the poor wife?"

"And you started to stalk him, blackmail him?"

"Nils Vollan murdered Frank Harket and took the car. Ilan was such an idiot. I sent him a picture of the car in the warehouse of his own family, and he didn't even recognize it."

"How did you manage to change the report of the car theft?"

"Vollan," she said, "he had enough connections within the police force."

"Jeezes! And the card had to lead us to Ilan?"

She nodded. "At least for a while, until everyone was dead. After that, I didn't care anymore. I was hoping you'd arrest me. But it took too long. You released Ilan, and you were on the right track. I needed something dramatic."

"Ilan had to die," Timo said.

"Yes, unfortunately. I sedated him, put the gun in his hand and then in his mouth and fired. And having Mila as a witness was genius, don't you think? She's not very observant. I killed Ilan in the afternoon, just after work, and then I went for yoga. I came in late, but she didn't realize it."

"The others ... how did you abduct them?"

She threw herself against the back of the chair and then ran her hands through her dyed black hair.

"A broken-down car, a sick child and a desperate mother, that's all it takes to get people to open the door and walk to your car, only to find out that the baby in the back is a doll, before feeling the needle in their neck to sedate them."

"Is that also the case with Mrs. Heimer? You forgot to mention her."

She frowned and gave him an angry look.

"Six, not five people," he said, while he kept his eyes fixed on her.

"Mrs. Heimer was different. I just wanted to talk to her. Mikael had told me about Pauli, and I wanted to check my suspicions, but her son-in-law intervened the first time. The second time, she was confused. She invited me in, oddly enough. There was no plan, until she started talking about Caijsa's murder. The scream she had heard, Svante and Pauli. And she had done nothing. Nothing."

"She tried. She went to the police, but they didn't believe her."

"She should have been more persistent," Lyn snapped.

"So, what happened?"

"I was so ... angry. She was so oblivious about everything. When we went outside, I saw the car keys on the table in the hallway. The car was in the driveway. By the time, we were outside, she was so out of this world, she didn't even realize I was there. I opened the car, put down the handbrake and pushed it. She was standing at the gate. The car hit her and pinned her in the corner."

"How did you get out?"

"Climbed over the fence in the back. No one saw me."

"Why, Lyn? Why didn't you go to the police?"

"Sure, with Rune Breiner leading the investigation again. He was paid by Engersson to manipulate the case. He couldn't ignore the evidence against Elker, but he was out to get you."

"I could have handled Rune Breiner," Timo said.

"No, Timo, I don't think you realize the power these guys have. I've seen it. The Engersson family has money, connections. Don't think this is the end, and don't ... trust anyone. I'm your only friend. I defended you!"

"What are you telling me?"

"Nothing ... leave it," she said and turned her face away from him.

"No, Lyn. You ..."

"I love you," she blurted. "I would do anything for you. I wanted to protect you, give you the justice you and Caijsa deserved."

He was taken off guard. "I ... never knew ..."

"Do you remember a conversation at our house a few months after Caijsa announced the two of you were a couple? It was about something stupid. I think we were deciding which movie to see as a family."

"No, I don't."

"Well, I do. As always, everyone had an opinion, a different opinion. Cal and Caijsa screamed the loudest, and everyone ignored me ... as always. Until you ... you gave me the chance to voice what I wanted and since then, you've always been so nice to me."

"That's not love."

"It's love, to me. You saw me when everyone thought I didn't matter. But I feel, I do have emotions, Timo, maybe not like most of you. And Caijsa's death was terrible. I didn't want that to happen."

"You found it terrible because of what it meant to you," he added, "not because she died a horrible death."

"For me ... yes."

"And you," she continued, "I studied you for a long time."

He felt uneasy, being reminded again he'd been the subject of stalking. That someone, even if he hadn't realized it, had poked into his private life, had analyzed everything to the bone, and then had used that information to manipulate him.

"You're easy to figure out," she said, giving him an artificial smile.

"Probably I am," he said and looked down at his hands.

"But Caijsa even more."

"What did you do?" he said surprised.

"I was Caijsa's study object. I know it was never her intention, but she couldn't resist it."

"No, Lyn, she loved you. She wanted to help you."

"I doubt that. Anyway, we had these sessions where we talked about my progress, how I could improve my social skills and how I could relate to my environment. What she didn't know is that I was putting ideas and thoughts into her head. It was so easy to drive a wedge between the two of you. Have you never wondered why she had these episodes of jealousy and mistrust?"

He had always wondered how a strong woman like Caijsa could be so insecure. He had given her no reason to worry about his devotion to her, but she had moments when she began to question his actions. Where he'd been, who he had talked to and if there had been other women. Young, beautiful women and whether he knew them. He couldn't figure it out. It had brought him to the point where he had considered leaving her.

"After a while she understood what I was doing. And I think she understood why. But I had a new victim. Thorgan Elker. I used him to put pressure on your relationship."

"You put her in danger," he said.

"Yes, I realize that now," she admitted. "But ultimately it wasn't him who killed her, and the relationship between the two of you was already bad. I had nothing to do with that. She wanted to leave you anyway."

"Leave me?" he said. "No, we were getting married. She was looking forward to starting a family with me."

"Ah, yes, the baby. Very unfortunate about the miscarriage."

Her face showed no sign of the sarcasm she had put in those last words.

"She lost the baby," Timo said.

She remained almost motionless, folded her hands, and then looked him in the eye.

"Yes, of course she lost the baby ... supposedly."

"What do you mean?" he said and started to shuffle nervously in his chair.

"If I were you, I'd check her medical records," she said.

"Caijsa was your sister," was the only thing he could reply. "Why would you spread these lies about her?"

"No, Timo," she shook her head. "I want you to know what she was capable of. I know you doubted your relationship, but she had been doubting it much earlier. Ask yourself where she was all these hours of late working, the workshops, and the conferences she went to."

He could hardly breathe. Caijsa, the woman he had put on a pedestal, had kept secrets.

"Who? Who was she having an affair with?"

She gave him an ironic grin, and then said, "You look down and concerned, Timo, but you shouldn't be. I will always be here for you, no matter what. That's more than Caijsa or anyone else you're interested in can ever say."

She looked intently at the bewildered expression on his face. Inspector Paikkala, respected by many for his strong vision and insight, was speechless.

"No," he screamed, "no, don't do this to me. I need closure."

"Oh, poor little Timo. Why do you think you are entitled to having closure? Why do any of us? There's only going to be closure when you finally realize how she really was. She was a treacherous bitch, and she didn't deserve you. And neither does that pathetic woman who calls herself a doctor."

"Honestly, I was surprised and disappointed," she continued, "I thought you would have gone for the tall, handsome one and not the plain married one. That just shows how human you are, and that you are just like everyone else, not better, not more decent. But I think I understand. She's Caijsa. You don't love Dr. Olsson; you love the image of Caijsa. How she was, how she made you feel. But reality check, my dear Timo, she's gone, and I'm the only one who really cares about you. For Dr. Olsson you're only a digression, a means of revenge. I guess she must be frustrated with Anton's exploits. I understand her. If I had a husband who slept around like he does, I'd do the same."

Timo could hardly utter a word.

"Oh, yes, I know Anton. He was another name on my list. But in the end, I think I made the right choice to take Ilan."

She looked out the window into the hallway. On the other side, one of the orderlies, who had been watching them, saw her sign to come in.

"I have to go now, but I know you'll be back."

She stood up and then looked at him. "But, Timo, be careful! This isn't over yet. A storm is coming and there is nothing to stop it. The wheels are already set in motion."

THE END

Printed in Great Britain
by Amazon